CONAN

Look for all these Conan books from Tor

CONAN
THE WARLORD
BY
LEONARD CARPENTER

A TOM DOHERTY ASSOCIATES BOOK

CONAN THE WARLORD

Copyright © 1988 by Conan Properties, Inc.

First printing: March 1988

A TOR Book

Published by Tom Doherty Associates, Inc.
49 West 24th Street
New York, NY 10010

Cover art by Ken Kelly

ISBN: 0-812-54268-1
Can. No.: 0-812-54269-X

Printed in the United States of America

0 9 8 7 6 5 4 3 2 1

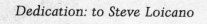

Dedication: to Steve Loicano

CONTENTS

CONAN

Prologue: The Skeleton Troop

The Varakiel marshes were a desolate, legend-haunted place for a child to grow up in. From eastern Nemedia they stretch in uncounted leagues of isle and fen toward the sun's birthplace in the Brythunian steppe. Impassable alike to foot, hoof and boat, the great swamp has ever been a stagnant backwater of history, its miry expanse fabled as a death-snare for armies and a last refuge of hunted men.

For a boy of only eleven summers, life on the edge of such a vast, unexplored tract could be tantalizing in its sense of brooding mystery. The forlorn squeak of the marsh birds and the fluting of wind across nodding reeds permeated the soul, especially if the child was a dreamer, without brothers and sisters, and given to wandering away from familiar fields against his parents' warnings.

Lar had left his log raft far behind in the excitement

of exploring the new land he had discovered—land that his father, strangely, had never spoken of. Doubtless the harsh old man knew of it, for he knew more of the Varakiel than anyone, and he reverenced its secrets.

Perhaps, then, this part was secret. Whether the cryptic expanse of dry ground was an island or a peninsula, the boy had not yet learned. The answer, in any case, might vary from season to season, depending on the yearly contest of flood and drought.

Lar's progress had been slowed by mires and willow thickets, and by the constant necessity of watching for bear, cat and snake. But ahead the terrain rose and opened out to a stretch of firm, dry grassland, like the farm pastures his father tilled far to westward. Rich, arable land, and yet not homesteaded—why?

Lowering the butt of his fishing spear to serve as a walking stick, Lar took up a swinging gait, scanning the horizon for tall trees or other vantage points.

Then, rounding an alder clump, he froze. A hideous sight reared just ahead of him: the bleached skeleton of a horse, upright and at the gallop, bearing on its back a grinning, skeletal rider clad in rusting scraps of armor!

Lar did not flee in superstitious terror. He regarded panic as beneath him, and his reason told him there was no immediate danger. He merely shrank back behind the screen of foliage and stood stock-still, listening. He heard only the rustle of leaves stirring in a breeze that had just arisen. No hoofbeats, no clank of arms. When the pounding of his heart subsided, Lar crept forth and looked past the alders once again.

The spectral rider was still there, galloping in place

through sparse meadow grass. There was only one movement to the tableau, that of the fluttering, windborne tatters of colorless cloth yet clinging to the bones and decaying armor-clasps.

Spying carefully, Lar could see that horse and rider were fixed to the ground and held upright by a vertical wooden stake; it passed straight through the belly and saddle of the horse and up the empty rib cage of the horseman. He shuddered to note that the skull itself was impaled on the stake, the pointed end of which had apparently poked through bone to raise the rust-eaten crown of the helm a few inches above its normal fit.

Lar knew that slow impalement was a mode of execution favored by the stern Brythunians. He guessed instinctively that the rider, if not the horse, had been placed in that position while still living. The thought sickened him, yet he could not tear his eyes away.

He walked forward, widely skirting the elongated, big-toothed skull of the war stallion while gazing up at the dead rider. And he saw with a thrill of delicious fear that the horseman was the leader of a troop.

Spaced about the clearing in a loose formation, nine other horses and riders were impaled, each as ancient and desiccated as the first. Some of them had sunk to the bases of their weathered stakes, where they lay as mere piles of rust-stained bones, while others sported crusty-gray leather hauberks and wore the green-brass hilts of rotted iron tulwars at their waists.

Most peasant boys would have been overcome by the weird menace of the place. They would have run home, babbling incoherent tales for their parents to dismiss laughingly or to silence with stern, frightened looks.

But Lar was different; he was a dreamer, and his mind had ranged wider than the minds of most boys of eleven winters. In early boyhood he had pondered deeply the meaning of certain remarks heard on late evenings before the fire, when the adults thought him safely asleep in his chimney-corner.

Now he moved among the skeletons, chill awe sweeping over him. At the center of the cavalry formation lay another relic, the ruin of a chariot. The team that pulled it had not been staked upright as had the others, yet it waited patiently in its traces—three tumbled clumps of bone, tangled with leather harness straps in the grass. The vehicle was a mass of collapsed timbers: gray, splitting spokes and spars bleached white as the bones around them, crusted with lichen and with curling flakes of once-gaudy paint.

Mingled in the debris were parts of an eleventh human skeleton, the skull incomplete, doubtless cloven by some long-since rotted blade. Lar liked not the look of the ancient headbone's unbroken half, noting a strange flatness and elongation in contrast with the other skulls on display, and an odd prominence of tooth.

But there, in the midst of it all, shining from beneath a tattered leather scrap that might once have been a shield or an awning, Lar's eye caught the glint of an untarnished surface. He peered into the shadow and gasped. A golden statue! Kneeling before the wreckage, remembering to watch for swamp adders, he peeled back the leather fragment. Dry bones clacked as he shoved them eagerly aside.

It was an oval gem case, molded and embellished to look like a golden serpent's head. To one who had seen but few pieces of worked metal in his life, the intricacy of it seemed miraculous. The eyes were great gems; when Lar gingerly rubbed the dust from one of them with a fingertip, the faceted surface gleamed deep green. The serpent's fangs were also jewels, tapering prisms as clear as icicles.

Looking over the chest, Lar could see hinges at its rear. He placed a trembling hand between the fangs and raised the lid. It was heavy and stiff with disuse, but he managed to force it back to an upright position. The inner surface of the serpent's mouth blazed in the sun's rays, mirror-polished white gold. The bottom of the chest was full of blood-red gems from among which the snake's gold tongue protruded. But the real prize rested on the two-pronged tongue—a golden, jewel-encrusted chaplet.

Lar knew of crowns and treasures only through the fanciful tales spun by his uncles on midwinter evenings. Still, he understood instantly the ornament's use. He longed to place it on his brow and view his reflection in the gleaming lid of the cask.

A sudden chill passed through him, and a terror touched his heart. He felt sure that if he dared look up, he would see the skeletal horsemen coming to life, flexing their chalk-white limbs, swiveling their creaky-hinged necks, wheeling their ghastly steeds toward him. He scarcely dared to raise his eyes. But finally he did, and saw that nothing was amiss. The riders were still there, the nearest looming over him as hideous as ever, yet motionless.

Iron clouds rolled over the marshland's distant reeds and trees, warning of a weather change. But nothing moved in the meadow except grass stalks. The wind among the bones made a faint sibilance in Lar's ears.

After all, he asked himself, what could be so evil or unholy about this place? Why should he fear to glimpse these vestiges of ancient power and mystic wonder? All his life he had heard the grandfolk prattle superstitiously against eldritch things; now he knew that he despised their cowardice! Not for him the cringing fears of ignorant serfs. He turned to the cask and reached inside to take the chaplet.

As his hand closed on the prize, he heard a metal latch disengage, and the lid of the chest slammed tightly down on his arm. He cried out in agony, feeling one of the ornamental serpent's needle-sharp fangs pierce his flesh to the bone.

Lar sobbed as he used his free hand to force the heavy, spring-loaded lid open, struggling to withdraw his arm. The deep perforation burned fiercely, like lye—yet already he felt a numbness creeping along the injured limb. His brain, too, was beginning to cloud.

As he pushed himself away from the chest and staggered upright, his dimming senses scarcely noticed that the serpent's jewel-pointed fang dripped not only blood, but yellow venom.

Three days later, his father found him staggering through a reed-choked slough near the leek field. He was dazed, and neither questions nor blows would bring him to speech. The old man hoisted his son on his shoulder and carried him back to their cottage, where the boy's mother waited.

"Lar! Oh Lar, my dearest child, why did you disobey me? Promise that you will never leave your mother's side again!" The distraught woman bathed and dried him, laid him on a pallet before the fire, and made a poultice for the festering wound on his arm.

Later, when the father had plodded off again to the fields, she tried to feed hot soup to her boy, but he would not take any. When she coaxed him, raising the wooden spoon to his lips, he seized her arm and bit it deeply. She screamed in his clutch; the wound burned like lye.

CHAPTER 1
The Dance of the Clubs

The dungeon was rank with the smells of human misery. Its fetid gloom made a tangible fog of despair that somehow was only deepened by the single source of light: a thin, dusty ray falling from a window grating high overhead. Where it struck the water puddled together with rotting hay on the floor, wisps of steam arose.

A score or more of the room's prisoners lounged or squatted in the shadows around its rough stone walls. Some of them were Nemedian serfs, swarthy-faced men clad in coarse, knee-length shirts corded at the waist with frayed rope. Others had more exotic rags and a more foreign look: jaunty street-thieves of Dinander, or wealthless travelers run afoul of municipal authority. The inmates varied widely in their physical health also, from the robust toughs loitering in choice positions near the cell door, to peasant

8

wretches broken by torture, moaning in the darkest corners.

Least fortunate of all was the one who sprawled facedown in the center of the wet floor, his limbs twisted under him and one dirty, sandaled ankle protruding into the barred patch of daylight. It was his plight that seemed to concern his fellows the most, and they called attention to it in loud voices.

"Jailer! Poor Stolpa's dead! Come haul him away!"

"Yes, come and get him. He's starting to stink!"

A stout, full-bearded prisoner ambled to the wooden door and gave it three hard kicks that failed even to rattle its heavy timbers. He leaned down and shouted through the peephole: "Warden! Come along here! The fellow's been dead half the morning. He's going to sprout maggots!"

"Get rid of him! Get him out!" A chorus of yells and hoots built to a raucous crescendo. All the able men contributed lustily, with one exception.

He was a northern barbarian—a tall, well-muscled youth of perhaps eighteen seasons, with shaggy black hair and the faintest shadow of a beard. His ill-fitting townsman's shirt and trousers made a parody of his hulking size; yet as he lounged against the wall near the cell door, his catlike ease belied the ungainliness of his garb. He kept his eyes steadily on the doorway, whispering at intervals to the man beside him, a broken-nosed ruffian who now and again added a jeer to the general outcry.

"They are coming!" The crook-nosed man's battered face suddenly grew serious. "Just look to your own part, Conan! The others will do theirs."

"Aye, Rudo. May Crom favor us!"

9

A loud thump sounded at the door. The youth eased himself upright as his cellmates' shouts died away.

"You scum!" a gravelly voice racketed through the peephole. "Let's have some order in there, or I'll shoot quarrels into the lot of you!"

The bearded door-kicker took a step forward in front of the spyhole, spreading his hands amicably, and pointed to the motionless one in the center of the floor. "Your Honor, Stolpa's been dead for hours, and the cell's crowded as it is. We'd like to have him out of here, please."

"Dead, eh?" the unseen warder rasped. "And which of you miscreants throttled him?"

The spokesman nervously clasped his hands. "No one, sir. He's been ailing for some time, as you know."

"Well then, let his ailing carcass rot. And yours with it, Falmar!" The voice murmured irritably aside for a moment, then came back to the eyehole. "How do I know it's not a trick?"

A stir of displeasure sounded among the prisoners, and crook-nosed Rudo stepped quickly from his place beside the barbarian. He went to the middle of the cell and, waving aside the bearded man, addressed the door. "Sir. With your permission. . . ."

Elaborately he swung back his buskined foot, aimed and planted a kick in the middle of the inert body, with force enough to drive it a handsbreadth across the slimy floor.

"Stolpa's suffering has ended, sir." Rudo faced the door and lowered his head slightly. "Ours is only commencing. Will you take him, sir?"

10

The prisoners waited, as still as stones. After a moment an indistinct question and answer were exchanged outside the cell. Then the voice barked in through the peephole, "All right. But you must fetch him out, in case he died of the creeping palsy. Two of you carry him forth, no more."

Rudo and Falmar stooped over the body and hoisted it up by its legs and arms. As the dull sliding of the doorbolt sounded, the inmates shifted nervously.

The heavy panel grated inward.

"Come on, then! Be quick about it." The harsh voice belonged to a man with a gray-jowled face, wearing the bronze helmet and red-leather vest of a municipal guard. He indicated the way through the door with a jerk of his crossbow, and the corpse-bearers lugged their burden forward. A second, leaner jailer grasped the door by its bolt brackets, waiting to close it on their heels.

As they passed through the portal, the prisoners' tense watchfulness finally disintegrated; they made sudden, swift rush for the exit. The northern youth sprang to the door and, seizing the nearest guard's arm so as to wrench it free of the door handle, dragged the man bodily inside the cell; meanwhile, the two corpse-carriers set violently on the senior warder. Their attack was aided by their dead burden, Stolpa, who sprang out of their arms in a miraculous, frenzied resurrection.

Inside the dungeon the young barbarian took precious moments to beat down the guard with savage blows of his elbows and fists. He seized the man's cudgel, wrenching and twisting at its lanyard until he heard joints crack in the wrist it was tied to; finally the thong pulled loose. Clutching the hardwood baton, he threw aside its former owner, relinquishing him to the driving feet and fists of other prisoners.

Then, shrilling a bloodcurdling war-whoop, he hurled himself into the stream of men pouring through the doorway.

By that time the wardroom was a mass of fighting bodies. The thick-jowled warden was down and disarmed, trying to crawl out from beneath the fight, his face bright with blood from a split in his scalp. At least four other guards had joined the fray; as the barbarian shouldered through the crowd, two more uniformed men mustered up the narrow stone stair from the torture-rooms.

The youth met the second of them at the top of the steps, his club already slashing in air. The stroke was partly wasted on the edge of the warder's helm; nevertheless, it sent the man tumbling back down to the torchlit doorway at the stairwell's bottom.

In an instant the first guard turned back to avenge his companion; the youth twisted aside, and the cudgel-blow struck him smartingly across the shoulders. The two fenced, oak clacking against oak, until the northerner landed a rap across the other's knuckles. As the guard's baton slipped from agonized fingers, a cracking blow across the eyes laid him flat. A straggly haired inmate swiftly fell upon him to appropriate his weapon.

Meanwhile, the barbarian drove toward the ascending stair, where more guards clustered. There crooknosed Rudo flailed at them with the stock of the chief warder's discharged crossbow, while other prisoners sought to grapple close and get inside the swing of the defenders' cudgels. Falmar strove fiercely against a burly guard, strangling him with his own stick; the scrawny Stolpa lay sprawled on the floor against the base of the stairs. This time his portrayal of a dead man looked even more authentic than before.

The young barbarian threw himself into the skirmish line, and struck viciously at the warders, who were already hard-pressed. Since metal hats covered their heads, he aimed slanting blows at their necks. He was quickly rewarded with a snap and a scream as a collarbone gave way.

A fierce battle-rhythm possessed the youth. His movements among guards and prisoners became a violent, intricate dance. When an enemy's cudgel nicked an arm or raked across his ribs, the flare of pain only quickened the tempo. Dodge aside, drive forward, parry, strike! Primitive blood chanted a savage war song in his ears.

The turmoil that raged around him seemed to slow and become trivial and remote. He felt all-powerful, invulnerable, his foes falling left and right before him like scythed stalks toppling in a grainfield.

Then the northerner was brought back to immediacy by urgent cries from behind. Dazedly, shaking off his battle-trance, he glanced around to see that more guards had come from the lower dungeon and sealed off the cell's exit. Some of the prisoners had either been driven back into the stinking hole or had never left it, due to cowardice or physical inability; now the mutineers' force was divided. Fletta, the tall, moon-

13

faced interrogator, stood at the cell door, backed by two guards and plying a copper mallet against the skulls of those who tried to exit the cell or clear its entryway.

A misfortune, clearly, and a dangerous one to turn back and try to correct now. Still, there was good hope for most of the prisoners to escape up the dungeon stair. Only two guards defended it, and they were retreating up the steps before the flailing clubs of Rudo and Falmar, who led the attack.

Then suddenly a new commotion sounded above. Fresh defenders came streaming through the archway, hurrying down the railless, curving stair. These were Iron Guardsmen of the province's elite army, clad in black-metal caps and cuirasses; as they approached the fray, they drew long, curved sabers.

Their commander strode through the arch at the top and watched them descend; he was a lean, distinguished-looking man with trim black mustachios. He placed his hand upon the hilt under his cloak, yet remained on the edge of the landing to survey the scene, turning aside only to whisper a word to a lesser officer who started down the stair. Then, calm and taciturn, he gazed down—directly it seemed, at the young northerner.

Thereafter the fight was short and brutal, the luckier prisoners falling before the warders' vengeful cudgels, the less fortunate methodically hacked or skewered by the Iron Guard. The northerner was hemmed in by guardsmen and disarmed by one who forced his thick, leather-vested body between the youth and his straining club. When he continued to struggle, a stinking shirt was clapped over his face from behind and he was dragged to his knees.

Yet he fought on against the cruel fists striking him from unseen directions. At any moment he expected to feel the chill of cold steel raping his guts, but for some reason his captors only pummeled and restrained him. His arms were bent behind his back, and there tied deftly and tightly. His thrashing neck was girdled by a large, sweaty bicep.

Around him he heard the last random thuds, moans and pleadings for mercy as the brawl ended. He was to be spared, it seemed; and so he strove all the harder, conjuring behind his sightless eyes vivid pictures of the tortures and indignities that might await him, if he lived so long.

Finally he could tell that the surviving prisoners were being herded back into the cell amid shouted orders and curses—yet he was kept kneeling on the floor in silence.

A level, businesslike voice spoke from somewhere near him. "This is the one called Conan?"

"Aye, sir, a Cimmerian. A dangerous fighter, and probably one of the ringleaders." The guard's voice quivered with anger and contempt. "With your indulgence, Marshal Durwald, he should be hamstrung, sir. Or killed straightaway!"

"Uncover his face."

The shirt was wrenched off, revealing to Conan the body-littered wardroom, the expressionless face of the black-cloaked military officer and the bloody-nosed visage of the municipal guardsman beside him.

The officer stared at him coldly for a moment. Then

he spoke tonelessly: "Put him in a solitary cell, to be transported later." Marshal Durwald swiveled on his heel, his cloak billowing behind him. Over his shoulder he added, while stalking away, "He is remanded to baronial authority."

CHAPTER 2
The Manse

As the chariot rumbled down the back streets of Dinander, furtive eyes followed it from the darkened windows and doorways of the town. Even at night, and even among offal-strewn alleys, its passing was carefully noted, as were all such comings and goings in this dull, provincial capital, whether for the sake of gossip, or political intrigue, or out of simple fear.

The war-chariot gave its occupants a violent ride across road paves purposely made rough for the traction of horses' hooves. Its iron-shod wheels jolted sharply over the cobbles in the clopping wake of the three matched roan stallions. At each of the shallow, open sewers that cut across the pavement, the vehicle dropped giddily, then banged high into the air.

It was a difficult ride for both driver and passenger perched side by side on the padded plank set athwart the fighting-platform. It was harder still on the one who lay prone on the chariot's timber deck, his hands bound behind him.

"Keep down, you stinking barbarian, or I'll club you down!" The driver's muttered threat was emphasized by a fist wrapped around a heavy knife-hilt, with which he smote the prisoner's writhing back.

"Crom! You're killing me!" The stirrings and complaints from the floor were muffled by a horse blanket that had been thrown partly over the chariot's human cargo. "I can hardly breathe!"

"Quiet, Cimmerian." The voice of the passenger, black-cloaked Marshal Durwald, was level and matter-of-fact. "This journey is by the baron's order. If you are seen, your usefulness to him will be ended; then you will find a fate that befits your station in the world and your recent crimes. Stay quiet, and you may fare better." He glanced down contemptuously. "Don't bother working at your bonds. We are almost to the Manse."

The driver whistled, jogging the reins to speed his coursers. After what seemed to Conan an endless time, he felt the chariot roll across a rough plank bridge, as smooth as satin by contrast with the pavement of the street. He heard a hail from above and the sound of a heavy gate swinging to. Then the lurching motion stopped.

The blanket was yanked away. With barely time to get his cramped legs under him, Conan was hauled out of the chariot and onto hard dirt. He fell to one knee, caught his balance, then stood straight.

The marshal motioned toward a postern door in a great building that loomed nearby; the charioteer prodded him in the same direction. Conan turned on him with a dark look, and the driver backed off a little, momentarily forgetting his captive's bound wrists. The northerner glanced around, stretched his sore limbs as best he could, then sullenly went along between his captors.

The edifice around them was more fort than mansion. Its curtain wall reared as high as the height of three men combined, and its gatehouse was crowned by an overhanging parapet. For further security, round defensive towers formed the corners of the square main building. The principal structures were of fitted stone, but against the inside of the outer walls huddled stables and other outbuildings of wood. The tall Manse commanded all; a little distance away one of its great double doors stood open, spilling a pool of yellow light across the broad stone porch.

But tonight Durwald, the marshal, stayed far from the welcoming light; he plied a key in the lock of an iron-bound door in a well-protected recess of the Manse's front wall. The door whispered inward and the three passed through into a large, lamplit closet.

Rows of boots and cloaks hung along one wall, a battered bench ran the length of the other. Through a doorway at the end of the room, Conan glimpsed an ornate entry hall with brightly colored tapestries and an imposing central stair.

"Close that," the marshal ordered. After bolting the postern behind them, the charioteer hastened to shut the door to the main hall as well.

Durwald gestured for Conan to seat himself on the bench. The youth hesitated for a moment, then complied, moving as smoothly as he could to hide the lameness of his back and limbs. The charioteer stood to one side, and the marshal, too, remained standing.

"A Cimmerian, eh?" Durwald parted his cloak back from his steel-cuirassed chest and regarded his captive narrowly. "Yet when taken into custody, you had coinage of Zamora in your possession, and gold drams from our capital of Belverus. You have traveled in the south, then?"

The youth gave a noncommittal nod. He knew there were bloody crimes in the Nemedian capital that might be laid on his neck, whether truly or not.

"Answer when spoken to! How long have you been in Dinander?"

"A dozen days." Conan lowered his eyes to the floor, where their gaze was less likely to betray him.

The marshal fingered his mustache thoughtfully. "Do you have any relatives or other ties in Nemedia?"

"No." Conan wondered briefly at this turn in the questioning.

"Are you sure? No female kin traded southward as brides?" Durwald inclined his head, closely watching the captive, whose face showed only surly resentment at the notion.

When no further reply was forthcoming, the marshal resumed: "Well, then, lad! Coming from the northern wastes, what think you of the wonders of our civilization?" He smiled under his mustache with a new, false air of heartiness. "Do you like the Hyborian lands?"

The youth considered for a moment, then turned his face up to Durwald's. "'Tis strange . . . never have I seen such wealth as in these southern cities, nor such filth and misery." He shook his head wonderingly. "In Cimmeria a whole tribe may hunger, but if they thrive, they thrive together. Here honest folk starve amidst wealth, and a greedy few fatten themselves at the expense of many."

Durwald's eyes narrowed in distaste. "Best to leave such notions in the northern snow-mires, lad. Sensible or not, they will only get your tongue torn out in Dinander." He squinted at Conan appraisingly. "But you have more than a passing acquaintance with the Nemedian language. How did you gain it?"

Conan spoke carelessly. "Nemedian squatters were among the border kingdoms' rabble who tried to steal Cimmerian lands. In my youth we took a band of them hostage." He flexed his shoulders, apparently confident that his youth lay sometime in the remote past. "Later I was among the war-party that marched them to Fort Ulau and bore back the ransom."

"Eastern Nemedians, those?"

"Vastian farmers."

"Hmm. Yes." The marshal nodded thoughtfully. "Have you, then, any objection to entering the service of the baron of Dinander?"

"Why not?" Conan looked up, his face growing blank and wary. "As long as I am not expected to slay my kinsmen or spy against them."

Durwald's face shaped a true smile for the first time. "Well then!" He turned to the charioteer. "He will need better clothes in which to be seen by His Lordship"—the marshal wrinkled his nose— "but the bath will have to wait until later, I fear. Swinn, find him something to put on."

The charioteer turned to the garments on the wall

hooks, searched among them and selected a green jerkin and tan trousers. He held them up wordlessly before Durwald, who nodded. "Now cut his bonds."

Swinn gazed doubtfully at the marshal, but only for a moment. Then he carefully laid the garments on the bench, drew his knife and advanced toward Conan. The youth arose and turned half away from him to place his bound wrists within reach.

The charioteer stood hesitating again.

"Do not fear," Durwald urged him. "If the northerner has any sense, he has guessed that whatever we intend to offer him is better than the dungeon and a lifetime in the copper mines. Go ahead and cut him loose."

Swinn did so, slicing the cords with a downward jerk of the blade. Conan brought his arms out in front of him, flexed them slowly while brushing away the cut ends of cord, and began massaging his red-wealed wrists. Meanwhile, Swinn cautiously moved up beside the youth to help him remove his clothing.

Conan's forearm darted out and struck him in the chest with an audible impact. "Back!" The charioteer reeled along the bench, steadying himself against the wall. Cursing, he shifted his hold on the knife to stabbing grip.

Durwald spoke up impatiently. "Swinn, leave him alone. You can put that turnip-slicer away now." He nodded to Conan. "Go ahead, boy. Remove those stolen rags yourself, if you insist."

The youth eyed the two others, relaxing his fighting-crouch and reaching to his shirt ties. "They are my own. Had I stolen, I would have stolen better than these!"

He stripped off the shirt, which was split halfway down the back from the day's cudgel battle. Then he lowered his tight, frayed trousers and kicked them to the floor. He showed no concern for his nakedness, but unavoidably he had a measure of pained regard for the bruises and welts that marked his body. His form was otherwise tan with sun and prison dirt, and splendidly tapered from the shoulders down, a remarkable physique for one indisputably so young. In spite of his injuries, he moved with the power and suppleness of a tawny leopard.

Conan donned the thicker and better-fitting garments, knotting the drawstring of the trousers and fastening the jerkin. Then he tied new brown-leather slippers on his feet in place of his soiled, travel-worn sandals.

"That is adequate. Come along." Durwald turned.

With Swinn close on his heels, Conan followed the marshal to the back of the cloakroom. There the officer pushed open a wooden door that revealed a spiral stairway in one of the Manse's corner towers. Conan had to duck as they ascended the narrow, worn stairs; from their upper course, a draped archway opened to a vacant sleeping-room whose plugged window-embrasures faced the Manse's front wall.

Durwald led the way through the room's far door and onto a mezzanine. This interior porch circled and commanded the ornate main portals and lofty entry hall, the upper vaultings of which were thick with shadow, Conan saw. The balcony's stout wooden railing, cut with deceptively ornamental cross-shaped loopholes, would provide a murderous bastion for archers called upon to cover the entrance and main stair. The three men walked a short way along the overhang, then turned through a taller door and into a large, ornately furnished chamber.

Just arising from high-backed chairs at a hexagonal writing table were two figures: a tall, elderly man with an iron-gray mustache, and a plump, round-faced retainer who moved silently beside him.

"Ah, Durwald. So this is the boy!"

The elder man half-turned to the door as he spoke. He was every cubit an aristocrat, clad in a fine leather kilt and a shirt of pleated silk, and armed with a silver-handled dirk, silver-scabbarded on a silver chain dangling from his hip. His face seemed the very sculpture of serene leadership, his gray mustache and side-whiskers softening the severity of his strong-arched nose and firm chin.

But as his head finished turning to fix both eyes on the new arrivals, Conan saw with unease that its noble symmetry was hideously broken. A livid, crookedly healed scar ran from one eye down to the corner of the man's mouth; in consequence his lip seemed to be raised perpetually at one side in an imperious smirk. The eye above it looked to be functional, if somewhat watery compared to its twin; now both eyes regarded Conan keenly with frequent, birdlike blinks.

The second man, by contrast, had an air of intense ordinariness. He wore his humble wool jerkin belted so tightly that bulges of soft fat projected above and below his waist. Close-shaven and spottily com-plected, he carried himself with something of a strut.

Durwald inclined his head in the aristocrat's direc-tion, then stood pikestaff-straight. "Yes, Milord

Baron! This is Conan, the lad of whom I told you. A savage Cimmerian, yet capable of understanding orders, it would seem. Conan, you may kneel before Baron Baldomer Einharson."

Conan gave a scant nod to the baron and remained standing, impassive.

Durwald's back stiffened with consternation as he swung to face Conan. "Cimmerian, you are required to kneel to your betters!"

The youth glanced around the circle of staring men. "Mayhap I will, when I meet one."

Durwald's hand found the hilt at his waist. "On your life, barbarian!"

"Marshal!" Baldomer raised an arm and spoke in a voice that, though hard-edged to command, was softened slightly by amusement. "Leave off; there is no need."

By the time the baron dropped his hand, a respectful silence was well settled in the room. "In any case, 'tis better that the boy lacks the habit of obeisance. That would interfere with his intended role."

The marshal looked from the sullen captive to the baron, then nodded. "Of course, Milord. Forgive me." He waited for a moment, composing his discomfiture, then asked, "You find his resemblance . . . adequate?"

Baldomer smiled. "Yes. He has the square-faced look that gives Cimmerian men such an air of ferocity . . . and their women such beauty." His brow wrinkled almost imperceptibly, as from a fleeting memory; then he smoothed his ravaged features as much as possible and continued his inspection. "With his hair trimmed to a decent length, and with the same pathetic attempt at a mustache as my son's, his likeness will be passable."

The plump man at the baron's elbow spoke, clasping his arms over his belly and leaning toward the nobleman officiously. "Milord . . . are you really suggesting that this burly brute could pass for young Favian?"

Baldomer laughed, turning his face aside so that he looked benign once again. "Well, Svoretta, my son and heir might have to wear padded jerkins henceforth to match his bodyguard! And both might have to wear war-helmets more often. But that would only improve Favian's public image."

While the others laughed dutifully, Svoretta pressed on with Baldomer. Clearly his subservience to the baron was less complete than theirs, and just as clearly he would rather have spoken in confidence.

"Milord, to introduce an unknown, unruly creature like this into your intimate household staff . . . I fear that it will pose a far greater danger than the one you seek to avoid. Speaking as your chief of espionage, I can say that the problem of maintaining secrecy in such an affair is practically insurmountable."

"Svoretta, this is nothing we haven't already discussed." The baron overruled his counselor abruptly but without gazing on him directly, as if accustomed to having him close at his side. "Whatever the difficulty of carrying out such a masquerade here in Dinander, it will be far simpler on the impending provincial tour. 'Tis then that we anticipate the greatest danger to my son's life—to my own as well—and the greatest need for a double." Baldomer's knuckles tapped absently on his kilted thigh as he spoke, his voice deepening.

"In these times of rampant rebelliousness among our peasants, my sole concern is the firm rulership of the barony of Dinander. That, of course, means the continued reign of the Einharson family. We must at all costs avoid the catastrophe of civil war—or worse, of some half-witted interference by our foppish King Laslo from his padded seraglio in Belverus!" Baldomer elevated his blinking gaze above the others' heads, his voice intensifying to an oratorical pitch.

"My own rule here must be firmly sustained! And more important, when my earthly tenure ends, those in command must be ready to effect the orderly transfer of power from one generation to the next. Obviously, that is possible only through the preservation of my sacred seed, exalted aforetimes by the gracious gods and passed down from my divine forebear, Einhar." The baron's head turned back to his listeners, his gaze flashing among them with a bizarre, alternating aspect of serenity and cruelty. "Therefore our course is self-evident. Do all of you pledge yourselves absolutely? It is vital that the life of my son and sole heir be preserved!"

Baldomer's speech was followed by an embarrassed silence; it lasted, however, for only an instant before the necessary nods, smiles and assents were given. The listeners had not failed to note how violently, even fanatically, the baron's fist smote his leather-clad thigh toward the end of his tirade.

The baron, by contrast, seemed unaware of any

awkwardness; his eyes were alert, scanning the eyes of the others for signs of resistance or doubt—lastly the downcast, shadowed eyes of the Cimmerian.

Finally Svoretta dared undertake to calm his liege. "Yes, Milord, I understand your priorities in the matter, truly I do! Of course I can humbly offer only one thing in support of your divine mission—my life!" He paused for the effect, his head bowed in an attitude of utter reverence. "Therefore I shall undertake to implement your . . . command and see that only good consequences result from it." His effort of ingratiation culminated in a deep bow and a lingering kiss to the baron's extended fingers.

"Good, then." Baldomer returned swiftly to his earlier, equable manner. He waved a slack hand toward Conan. "We can bring this one into the household as a personal bodyguard; plainly he is a fighter? Splendid! And we can keep him out of sight, or else downplay the resemblance, until he begins standing in for my son. He must learn to stay quiet —that potato-mouthed Cimmerian accent will never pass! And of course we must teach him noble precedence and horsemanship.

"I leave all that, and the clothing and housing of him, to you, Durwald. On second thought, my son's mustache will have to be shorn, since I do not think this stripling could manage to sprout even so much of one in the time remaining!" He shot them all a grave look. "The secret must not travel outside this room. Regardless of the suspicions or rumors that may arise, there is to be no hint or confirmation from any of you." He lowered his face slightly to catch the Cimmerian's noncommittal gaze. "Understood, boy?"

By leveling his look at Baldomer and nodding calmly, Conan surprised them all. "Aye. And what is to be my pay?"

Baldomer smiled thinly. "Must you trouble me with these petty things? Besides your life and your keep, one gold dram per fortnight should suffice. . . ." He reached into a slack purse on the table beside him, extracted a coin and flipped it to Conan.

Just then a green-velvet curtain parted at the back of the room, exposing a paneled door, and a young nobleman who edged through it a little unsteadily.

He was a large, tall lad, dressed in a silk shirt and a fur kilt lengthy enough to overtop his high, black cavalry boots. A long-bladed, jewel-hilted poniard was belted to his waist. His tousled raven hair and firm-jawed face bespoke Cimmerian blood as well as Einharson lineage, though both effects were weakened by the faint mustache at his lip. He was not unlike Conan in build, although he lacked some of the barbarian's height and more of his musculature. He sauntered in and stood by the table, resting one hand on it as he surveyed the room's occupants; whether he did this for dramatic effect, or to maintain his balance, was not entirely clear.

"Aha, a convocation! Men of responsibility pondering the weighty affairs of state!" The grandiose flourish of his free arm revealed, as did his slurred, flowery speech, that he was near-drowned in drink. "How is it, I wonder, that I was not summoned to this lofty conclave?"

The baron shot him a look of withering distaste. "Favian, when you are old enough to attend the counsels of men, and when you prove it by your honorable behavior, you will be summoned! Not before."

Favian straightened his back and faced up to the rebuke—without, however, relinquishing his grip on the table top. "Not even when the topic is so intimate to my welfare, Father? For I think I know what is being discussed here. Yon creature—" the young lord unsteadily raised his free arm, one finger wavering in Conan's general direction—"that is the one whose soiled breeches I am to hide behind, is it not?" He favored the barbarian with a bilious stare. "That unwashed thug is to usurp my public life! Well, am I right?"

Baldomer's face had gained color during his son's speech, but his voice remained cold. "In short, yes, you are right . . . at risk of repeating what you have already overheard while spying outside my door."

Favian's head recoiled slightly as from an invisible blow. If the accusation was unjust, apparently it smarted more painfully than a true one.

The baron spoke on: "Yet 'tis not quite so nefarious a scheme as you imagine. I merely intend, during a time of civil unrest, to take extra measures to preserve the safety of our line. None of your important functions will be interfered with"—Baldomer glanced among the other men—"none of your pleasures, that is." He paused to share a smile with the wary listeners at the lordling's expense. "Only in circumstances wherein you would be exposed to unnecessary danger will a substitution be made. On the coming tour, for example, I shall have you lads trade places in the traveling column. You might learn something from

30

riding with common soldiers, Favian, while the barbarian . . . can better cope with an attack."

"Well, that serves me nobly indeed!" Favian pushed himself away from the table, reeling, and moved forward. "For a baron's son to be thus coddled, and smuggled all about the province while a jumped-up jailsnipe enjoys his rightful fame!" He staggered dangerously and caught himself. "I tell you, Father, 'tis a dire insult!" The baron extended a restraining hand, but his son lurched past him toward Conan. "I can acquit myself better than any flint-axed savage! Just watch me!"

With this, Favian swung a clumsy fist at the huskier youth's head; meanwhile, as Conan instantly saw, he threw himself off balance and left no provision for his defense. The Cimmerian seized Favian's arm with a single motion of his own, turned him aside and propelled him away. The aristocrat struck the side of a chair heavily and sprawled against it. He leaned there helplessly, clutching for the poniard at his belt but unable to find it.

At the moment of the encounter, Swinn, Durwald and Svoretta had unsheathed their weapons. Now they converged on Conan—who awaited them, crouching, ready to snatch up a heavy stool close at hand. But once again the baron intervened.

"Hold! Let him go. My son is deep in his cups and less than discreet, as always. The northerner was only defending himself, as he is paid to do. Sheathe your blades."

Svoretta scowled. "Milord! Would you let scum like this believe he can strike a Nemedian noble with impunity?"

"Nay! 'Tis all right, I said!" The baron shook his iron-gray locks. "I grow tired, and our business is settled. Spymaster, see my son to his quarters. Durwald, take charge of the new man. A fair rest to you all."

"Good night, my liege," his retainers echoed.

Baron Baldomer turned, crossed the room and made his exit through the curtained door.

But it was Durwald, not Svoretta, who was then busied for a moment calming and expostulating with the drunken Favian. While he did so, the chief of espionage went to Conan, clutching the hilt of his sheathed dirk, with Swinn standing ready close by. The stocky spy-chief grimaced meanly, bringing his face so near the youth's that the two almost collided.

"And so, barbarian! Doubtless you think yourself fortunate to be the newest foible of his lordship's —nobly indulged and vaulted up above your superiors, even while still fresh, or rather ripe"—here Svoretta made his sneer even uglier, to suggest an ill odor—"from the prison pen!" He glowered at Conan, letting his pockmarked features creep into a stare of undisguised hatred.

"Well, I warn you . . . fancies and playthings come and go in the Manse, sometimes overnight! But one thing has endured in this barony . . . " he hissed out the last words in a whisper inaudible to anyone but Conan . . . "and that is my influence! And if I hear that you have grown arrogant, pressed your luck too far or taken one single advantage of your flukish position here, it will go even harder for you in the end. Harken to that!"

Svoretta fell silent, staring into the barbarian's face. Once, and once only, his shoulder twitched as if he meant to strike the younger man. But he held back the blow, perhaps because of the utter silence and stillness with which Conan returned his stare. Finally he uttered a foul curse and turned on his heel.

Chapter 3
The Schooling

The sun, from its zenith in the southern sky, burned down into the courtyard. Both its heat and the clatter of horses' hooves were magnified, trapped between the sheer side of the Manse and the high curtain wall. The steeds were well lathered after a morning's workout, and Conan's saddle-bow was coated with dust —as, he would have sworn, were his parched, thirsty lips.

"A little better, barbarian. You may yet learn to sit atop a horse." Durwald's voice was bored and slack, yet he waited upright in his saddle with no sign of fatigue. "See here, you needn't crouch and hunker so, nor lean so far on the turns. We Nemedian cavalrymen have a saying: 'Sit tall, and let the serfs and horses do the work.'" He laughed, stroking his mustache between two fingers. "With all that reaching and straining you would never pass for a Nemedian farmer, let alone an aristocrat!"

"In southerly lands they say that working with the horse saves its strength and speed," Conan grumbled in reply. "Besides, this saddle is infernally thick, and the stirrups are set too low."

"You will find the fixed stirrups useful if ever you have to swing a heavy weapon from the saddle." Durwald reined in his whickering steed at a stone drinking trough. "But enough for today; at least you begin to earn your calluses. Now for our midday meal!" He swung down smoothly from his mount. "Your weapon training will take place here this afternoon, under the fencing-master, Eubold. Trust him to put you through your paces."

Conan winced and guardedly let himself down the side of the horse. He imitated the other man by tying his reins to one of the rings set in the stone wall. Then he started across the dusty yard, walking stiffly from his previous day's beating, and the further punishment his weary thews had taken in the unaccustomed saddle. He could feel the sun scorching the back of his neck where his mane of hair had been shorn off.

"Where are you going, Cimmerian?" Durwald stopped short, turning to face him.

"Eh? To lunch."

"You dine in the servants' quarters, off the kitchen, lad." The marshal jerked his head toward the Manse's rear double doors. "Barbarous as you are . . ." he laughed and wheeled away . . . "you are not near savage enough for the officers' mess!"

Muttering a curse, Conan changed direction and headed for the broad doors on the balustraded porch.

Passing through them was like entering a dark cave; the sun's hot weight was lifted from his shoulders and he felt instantly and refreshingly cool. Yet from an archway at one side of the entry came another wave of heat and an infernal flicker: the fires of the huge kitchen hearth, crowded with steaming copper vats. Smoke meandered overhead among hanging sausages, hams and braids of onion and garlic, until it found its way out of a sooty hole at the ceiling's center. The room was rich with odors to tempt a hungry man's stomach, as well as some to turn it.

"Foraging for your lunch, barbarian?"

Of several heads bent over wooden worktables, the only one raised toward Conan was that of a curly haired young woman, a Nemedian farm girl of medium height and comely appearance. The lushness of her shape was shown off by a girdle of bright yarns laced around her narrow waist, joining her flimsy white blouse and knee-length skirt. She glanced at Conan appraisingly with eyes that had been artfully shadowed, probably by means of chimney soot.

"You come too late, you know. Most of the food is already sent upstairs, or gobbled down here." She flashed him a defiant look, then shrugged uncaringly. "But all right, go in and sit. I'll see what I can scrape up for you." Suddenly she laughed, gaily enough to draw glances from her workmates. "You look like a fierce one indeed, with strange, barbarous appetites. I wouldn't want you carving up one of my haunches to gnaw on!" She turned with a toss of a shapely hip and busied herself at another table.

Conan passed on through the kitchen. The adjacent room was gloomy, lit by a single barred window-slit

36

high in the wall. A long wooden table and rude benches stood in the center, and two sides of the room were lined with narrow, curtained sleeping-closets separated by wooden partitions. The one at the further end, alongside the cold stone wall, had been assigned to Conan late the previous night.

Ah well. No matter the chill, since this land was so much hotter in this season than his native Cimmeria in any season. He did not intend to stay in Dinander for the winter, in any case; mayhap not even for the night. Slowly, tenderly, he lowered his saddle-drubbed hindquarters onto the bench.

In a few moments the serving-wench appeared. She carried a wide wooden platter of food close against her belly, swaying her hips and shoulders gracefully on the approach. Conan's eyes were drawn up from the trencher's ample contents to the equally ample stresses and curves of her embroidered blouse. As she deposited her burden before him, thumping down an earthenware flagon of purple wine to one side of it, she leaned low enough to give him an even better perspective on her charms.

"There, barbarian! I hope that will be enough to stave off your northern appetites. If not"—she laughed good-naturedly—"give me some warning before you attack the horses with a meat knife, and I will look for more food in the pantry!"

"Ugh." Conan tossed a red-hot turnip into his mouth to crunch as he commenced tearing apart a thick loaf of black bread. "I could not stand to eat a horse, not after having been jounced about on one all morning!"

The maiden laughed, not loudly this time but

sweetly. "What is your name, outlander?" After a
glance at the curtained archway leading to the kitch-
en, she eased her round, wool-skirted thigh onto the
end of the table. "Mine is Ludya."

"I am Conan," he said, barely audible through a
mouthful of bread.

"You are . . . a Cimmerian, is that right?" She
rolled her eyes. "When I was a girl, I was not even sure
Cimmeria really existed. We were told the wildest
stories about it—tales of ogres, cannibals, draken and
even stranger things!" With a little shiver she folded
her bare arms across her girdle. "It sounded like a
dreadful place."

"There is no truth in that." Conan took a deep pull
from his wine-jack. "The teller must have confused
my land with Asgard and Vanaheim to the north,
where such terrors abound."

"Oh." Ludya's eyes widened a little as she considered this. "Well, when I came to the city I learned that
the Baron Baldomer, in his youth, brought back a
Cimmerian bride from his northern campaigns—the
Lady Heldra. I never saw her, but they say she was
beautiful and kind." Her gaze drifted away thoughtfully for a moment, then returned to Conan. "So now
the northern lands are much better regarded here.
The people remember Heldra fondly, they honor her
daughter, Calissa, and have even grown accustomed
to the prospect of being ruled someday by her boy-
child, Favian. You look very like him, by the way."
This she said with an appreciative flash in her glance.

"Hmm." Conan met her gaze, then chewed
thoughtfully. "He is no relation to me though, and I

have not heard of his mother, Heldra. Mayhap the daughter of an eastern chief, or else she was a far-roving warrior-girl."

Ludya sighed. "The thought of a mere barbar wench becoming baroness. . . ." Her brown eyes glistened. "It proves that a comely female can rise high in the world, though a man be bound by his family's station." She paused, plainly bethinking herself of Conan, and added quickly, "Excepting you, of course. You have done well, to become a guard in a noble household."

Conan busied himself with his meal, not looking up. "And what became of Lady Heldra?"

"Oh, she died." Ludya's gaze sank to the floor.

"She did? How?"

"She was murdered, poisoned by a tainted venison pie. The bane was meant for her husband, 'tis said." Ludya shook her head sadly. "There is so much of that here—murders, revolts and so forth. But Lady Heldra's death was at the start of all the troubles."

Becoming aware of a sudden absence of eating sounds, Ludya looked over at Conan. He was poking with his wooden spoon through the dainties left on his plate, which included a baked tart of uncertain composition.

He looked up at her. "Poisoning is the custom here, you said?"

"Oh, no—Conan, I'm sorry!" She was contrite. "I shouldn't have told you that. I prepared all these things myself. Here, I'll taste everything, as I do when I serve the nobles, to prove that it's safe."

She leaned down, picked up a piece of cheese and

bit off most of it, replacing a small remnant on the salver. Then she broke off a dripping hunk of the pie and scooped it toward her mouth.

At this Conan's doubtful look turned to one of amusement. Ludya noticed and, swallowing, arched her eyebrows at him. "Mmm. Spicy! Mind if I wash it down?" Leaning on one elbow, she reached close in front of him and bore his wine-flagon to her lips.

"Here now, that's enough!" Laughing, Conan wrapped a large hand around her wrist, drawing arm and cup away from her face. "You can stop now. I am convinced!"

Ludya laughed too, looking into Conan's eyes. A drop of wine was rolling from her lower lip and she caught it up with her quick pink tongue. It occurred to the northerner that her whole lush body was spread before him on the trencher-board like a magnificent dessert. For a moment her face lingered before his, edging closer. Then his mouth was tasting hers. His hands clasped her waist and pulled her against him; in a moment the ravaged food platter was shoved aside and they were nuzzling together in a tight embrace.

Somewhere beyond the kitchen arch a bell clanked flatly, once, then twice. Ludya stirred, but Conan grasped her closer, seeking her mouth hungrily. She whimpered and twisted in his arms. Then suddenly she was struggling violently against him. She gave an inarticulate cry, and shoving her body free of his, cuffed him hard across the mouth.

Astonished, he let her go.

"Stupid barbarian!" Her face was flushed with rage. "They rang for me! Do you want to get me flogged?" She rubbed her mouth with the back of one hand, tossed her hair to straighten it and turned away toward the kitchen. She was still patting her clothing straight as she pushed past a scrawny tow-haired boy who stood in the archway; he gave Conan a knowing, impertinent look, then came forward to clear the table.

An instant later the boy dodged nimbly to one side as the grim-faced northerner strode out of the room, his thoughts in a turmoil. The little vixen, how dare she use him so! And yet, he told himself, perhaps he had been too forward; who could know all the unaccountable local ways? Crom's curse on these Hyborians and the madness they called civilization!

The day's heat smote him again as he entered the yard. He scuffed across the dirt, a tempest roiling in his breast. Just ahead, in the shade of the smithy porch, waited a hulking man decked in gray-metal greaves, chain kilt, and cuirass, holding a battered helmet under one arm. His face had the fleshy, slack appearance of a strong warrior gone to seed.

Eubold, the fencing-master, no doubt, Conan thought. He was chatting with a shorter, thick-set man, barely visible in the shadows. As the second man turned and departed hurriedly toward the gate, Conan recognized him as Svoretta.

Scowling, Eubold watched Conan approach. "Well, barbarian, 'tis about time! You will learn not to keep your superior officers waiting, if only at the cost of some of that thick northern hide." The fencing-master's ill-shaven, leathery face creased further in distaste. "Tell me, have you ever swung a sword before?"

Conan gazed on the man sullenly. "I carried a

broadsword at the sack of Venarium several winters agone."

"Hm. The northern broadsword—a clumsy affair. All edge since the weapon is far too heavy to bring the point into play. You might as well swing a hatchet!" He started away across the yard. "Frankly, I regret my orders to teach the use of a more advanced weapon to a savage like yourself. But come along, you may learn something—at least some respect."

The sun was slanting once more into the yard, this time from the west, as Conan struck and hacked at the exercise dummy: a cowhide bag stuffed with hay, hung torso-high from a wooden post. His exertions had fallen into a steady, rhythmic pace, and this, apparently, was the source of much irritation to the fencing-master, who sat yelling orders from a stool propped against the Manse's shaded wall.

"Faster! Not like that, boy. Put some liveliness into it. That's a saber you're holding, not an oak cudgel!" His voice, Conan thought, had the sour croak likely born when the first infant drill officer, still wet from his mother's womb, commenced his foul ranting. "The secret of a blade like that is in its lightness, its quick recovery. You can lunge with it. Use the point —no need to dawdle about like a lead-footed ox!"

That Conan's strokes moved regularly through every aspect of a circle, and that the tough, slack rawhide was deeply slashed, its straw entrails strewn over half the yard, were facts the instructor chose to ignore. The youth, his upper body unclothed and his hair pasted to his forehead by sweat, continued striking deliberately. If he made any change in reply to the sergeant's railing, it was to slow his pace.

"And when you must hack and slash, remember to follow through with all your might. The curvature of that blade will let you take off a limb with one stroke, but only if you draw it through the wound without losing power." Eubold carved air enthusiastically with the side of his hand. "The sawing motion is what does the deep cutting!

"Of course you can learn little by hacking at a straw dummy. Even strung-up human carcasses won't do—too limp, no resistance. There can be no substitute for a live, moving target." Eubold's voice grew round and expansive, as if he elaborated his argument to a larger, unseen audience. "A man is nothing but a fragile tower of muscle and tendon, boy, a mere balloon of blood! When that frail tent of blood and muscle is upright and stressed, in motion against you, a sword can do miracles to it—shear it right in half if the bladesman is strong and clever!" The fencing-master folded his arms and continued musing aloud, leaning back and scarcely following his student's motions. "With any luck, the baron will order up some live captives for us to work with later —mutinous serfs, or young malcontents from the Temple School. That would be fine!

"But what now, barbarian? Are you still plodding along? No, no, that's not good enough. Again, there, and harder! Fah!" The tutor spat in disgust between his spraddled legs. "Curse you, northerner, you have paid no heed to me. This will never do." Abruptly he stood, kicking his stool aside. "We must have at it, then. 'Tis the only way you will ever learn." He strode forward, buckling the chin strap of his helmet and drawing on long leather gauntlets from his belt.

"A match?" Conan faced him, his blade slanting down loosely at his side. "Well enough! Where is my armor?"

"Your armor?" Eubold barked out a laugh. "True, you might be in need of some, to keep from sawing off your own foot. Otherwise, fear not. You will be in no danger unless I mean you to be." The fencing-master's sword leaped from its scabbard with a metallic hiss.

"Now then, this is the Nemedian saber, cavalry issue—a weapon that can stand against any Hyborian blade." He flicked the thin, slightly recurved edge in front of him, forth and back, while Conan raised his own saber on the defensive. "Thus armed, our troops might easily invest your homeland, Cimmerian—had we a sudden craving for frostbite and snow-lemming stew!" His laugh was drolly contemptuous. "Now first, when you slash, do it on the move, like this —hyaaa!"

With a grating cry the fencing-master launched himself forward, saber whizzing at a flat angle. Conan had to duck and sidestep quickly, his own blade screening his head.

"Now the backhand, thus!" The tutor stopped to pivot from the waist, his sword lashing out, and Conan was forced to retreat another step.

"'Tis clear that even a stumblekin like yourself can waltz away from my slashes all day. Hence the value of . . . the point!" An acrobatic lunge sent the fencing-master's blade spearing toward Conan. The

44

only possible response was body right, blade left —and the two swords clashed together where the youth's midsection had been.

"Ah, there you see where tardiness could easily cost you your life! Now more slashes . . . thus, and thus, and thus!" Eubold seemed to be growing slightly winded from the combined effort of fencing and talking; gradually he fell silent. Yet his saber-strokes continued relentlessly.

Conan, after a night and day of exertion finding himself half-naked against an armored man, was saved from the kiss of the lashing blade only by his inbred, feral quickness. He leaped and dodged agilely; nevertheless the grating clash of steel rang out almost continuously. He was forced more and more to rely on steel rather than swiftness to ward off Eubold's blade.

To the farrier and stable-hands who silently gathered to watch, the fight had no seeming of play or practice. The fencing-master might decide to soften any of his lethal strokes by using the flat of his sword, but there was no guarantee of it until the last vital instant. The student had no such option; his only course, if he did not care to stake his life on trust, was to kill his armored adversary.

The Cimmerian knew it better than the watchers did, and scarcely felt inclined to trust his foe. Well he recalled seeing Eubold chatting with his sworn enemy, Svoretta, before the start of the lesson.

At length Conan appeared to be weakening; for the first time, his blade lingered too low an instant too long. The panting Eubold saw the opening and struck. All his preaching of elegant swordsmanship forgotten, he dashed his saber down in a vicious, whistling slash straight at his pupil's neck.

Simultaneously Conan recovered his balance, and with a move that showed either subtle readiness or superhuman quickness, he drove his own steel up against Eubold's in a violent parry. An ear-stabbing clang sounded. Steel flashed brightly as both blades broke off near the hilt and went spinning away through the air.

After a moment's amazed silence, Eubold's voice bellowed hoarsely once again: "Why, you oaf! Those etched blades were worth ten of you!" The fencing-master let fly his broken hilt, sending it hurtling close past Conan's unprotected ear.

In a flash the youth was upon him, grasping the brow of his helm with one hand so that the thick, leathery neck was jerked back. With the heavy hilt clenched in his other fist, he belabored his tutor savagely about the chin and face.

By the time the onlookers dragged Conan off, Eubold was subdued.

Durwald came to take charge, ordering two men to haul the fencing-master away. In response to the officer's questions, the watchers spoke volubly of the fight. Their accounts to the marshal were confused, but by then their hands rested on Conan's shoulders more in congratulation than in restraint. Durwald gave the Cimmerian a sharp rebuke, with no decree of any real punishment, and dismissed him.

After a bath from a cold bucket, Conan went back to the bustling servants' quarters. He shared supper with the other household minions, whose names he

46

did not yet know. They were mindful of his newness and his recent fight, and their mealtime banter was strained, with only rare sallies at the outlander's expense. More than once that evening Conan heard whispers exchanged that ceased abruptly at his glance.

When most of the staff had retired, he arose from the bench and moved toward his own bed, but was stopped by a touch that fell silently on his arm from behind. A slim, feminine hand: Ludya's.

He turned to gaze on her face, upturned and dim-lit by the guttering candles. She was dressed in a scanty beaded costume, probably donned for her service at the baron's table. Conan started to step back, but her hand detained him. Wordlessly, still gazing into his eyes, she pulled her body up to his and ground her hips against him. He responded, seizing her in a savage embrace. After a few moments she led him to her sleeping-stall, where she received him passionately.

CHAPTER 4
The Shrine in the Crypt

"The basis of the science of noble precedence is the constant awareness of rank." Lothian, the baron's senior counselor and minister of protocol, inclined his gray old head as if afraid to look directly at his student. "Rank must be the first and predominant instinct in every member of the modern state, from the king on down to the lowliest . . . er, retainer." He stroked his carefully curled beard in a preoccupied way.

"Whether I can explain it adequately to a mere barb . . ." his gaze flicked nervously at last to the watchful steel-blue eyes of the youth who lounged on the broad divan opposite him. "That is, I cannot be sure that a foreigner like yourself, accustomed to the, shall we say, informal and diffuse style of government that prevails in a relatively, uh, primitive land, will be able to grasp this all-important concept. . . ."

Unsure of how to proceed, the counselor looked to the table at his side and at the red-scriven scroll outspread there. Together, the broad polished plank and the low divan almost filled the narrow room. They were blazoned by a strip of morning sunlight from a vertical arrow-slit in the wall, formerly a generous window but now filled in with masonry on either side to improve its defensive function.

"We have chiefs in Cimmeria too." Conan shifted, restless in his sprawling posture, feeling half-buried by the deep cushions of the divan. "That is nothing remarkable; as long as they lead us well, they remain chiefs."

"Ah, there is the difference!" Gaining confidence, Lothian leaned forward on his wooden stool. "In Nemedia, as in all Hyborian kingdoms, the blooded nobleman *must* lead well. He does so by definition, out of his own innate superiority." The elder spread his thin hands apart, their pale, papery palms upward, to show the simplicity of it all. "He never, obviously, can rule less than well. Therefore he always enhances his power and rank."

Seeing Conan's brow furrow at what should have been a self-evident proposition, the counselor shrugged resignedly. "If your homeland lacks such a concept, it is because your social organization has yet to develop sufficiently. Clearly, the upper level of your . . . native society has not risen to such heights of leadership."

"Nay, nor the lowest sunk to such depths of wretchedness." Conan nodded guilelessly to the counselor. "Having squatted three days in a Nemedian jail, I can affirm that!"

Lothian frowned. Rolling the two ivory handles on the table before him, he advanced his red-figured scroll with a rustling of parchment. If his inmost thoughts be known, the sage counselor found his appointed task nerve-wracking and distasteful. The role of tutor to a savage was an annoying one, a ludicrous reversal of the established order. Especially tutor to this rough fellow, with his imposing physical aspect and his reputation for brutalizing his teachers. Lothian's eyes flicked uneasily to the door of the chamber—left slightly ajar, thank the gods! He turned back to his pupil and spoke again, taking refuge in pedagogic cant.

"During the coming days we shall review the various aspects of noble precedence: chains of command, processional order, heraldry and rules of household. Much of this is common knowledge to the average Nemedian, you understand. These studies form the crowning wisdom of our modern science; more to the point, they are indispensable to you for security purposes, in your role as a baronial bodyguard." Lothian glanced up at Conan with curiosity glinting in his gray old eyes. "That is to be your function, is it not?"

"Aye." The Cimmerian returned the minister of protocol's gaze evenly.

"I ask only because it is a rather unusual rank. All the levels of nobility have their customary complement of guards and retainers, of course, but this employment puts you somewhat outside the ordinary scheme." Lothian lifted his eyes as if to question the matter further, then dismissed it with a shrug. Instead, he launched once again into the familiar harangue.

"The functioning of the whole empire centers about the king; it works for his protection and empowerment. Of course the monarch is almost never seen in a remote principality such as this. Nevertheless his spies abound, and his power remains absolute even here. We must be ever mindful of him, if only to offset the natural tendency of local authority to trespass on kingly office."

Conan's wandering gaze settled on his teacher. "You mean, the barons and Laslo don't get along?"

Lothian cleared his throat. "Well, there is a natural sort of tension, but one that works for the ultimate good of the kingdom. After all, no serf or subject can give his whole heart's devotion to the local ruler—the stern taskmaster who must personally oversee policing, tax collection, military conscription and so forth. There is unavoidable friction and resentment there. 'Tis far easier for the people to love the leader who rules from afar amidst fabled splendor, in glamorous Belverus.

"Therefore King Laslo is the common people's figurehead and champion. Occasionally he even caters to them by sending down an edict limiting the power of the nobles in some trifling way. Meanwhile, of course, the barons strive to increase their local autonomy. They band together to strengthen their voice at court, instead of warring against one another to enlarge their domains, as they would do in the king's absence." He smiled and inclined his head philosophically. "The system has functioned in recent years to make Nemedia a wealthy, stable empire."

Conan shifted his body in the yielding sea of cushions, trying through habit, and vainly, to get his feet beneath him. "Until the barons decide to rid themselves of the king. Or vice versa."

Lothian shook his head impatiently. "That is hardly likely; their shared reverence for noble blood and royal prerogative is too strong a bond." His silver-thatched brow knit slightly. "And yet there is danger from another quarter. By subversion, and by misrepresentation of the king's interest in local affairs—and, yes, with some energy rebounding from the, uh, decidedly firm stance taken by Baron Baldomer on civil discipline—a rebel movement has arisen against the baron's rule. You may have heard of it during your recent . . . detention?" The counselor's glance at Conan had an air of strained casualness.

Conan shrugged. "I knew that something was afoot, but I heard little of it. Most of the political criminals were kept below, in the torture-rooms. By the time they were brought to my cell, they were in no state to give fiery speeches."

"Yes." Lothian nodded to himself thoughtfully. "The revolutionary fervor is not truly abroad in the populace; a few incautious, half-mad troublemakers never pose a real threat. To hear Counselor Svoretta talk, every poacher is a rebel forager, every tavern-gossip a slinking propagandist. Dangerous prophecies to be whispered in the ear of a suspicious baron! Ah well!" The sage waved away his annoyance with a frail white hand, absorbed for the moment in thought.

Then, hearing a servant rattling crockery in the hall outside, the old man silently reminded himself of the need for discretion. Spymaster Svoretta's eyes and ears were posted everywhere, after all. He now glanced to the partly open door with a sensation of regret.

"In any case," he resumed, "the rebels seem to believe that if they throw off what they regard as a tyranny, they can somehow curry favor with King Laslo and be granted control of Dinander." He shrugged righteously. "Drivel, of course; nothing would have the Imperial Army down on us faster. But 'tis dangerous drivel if it weakens the people's belief in the men of Einharson and their supernatural warranties."

Conan propped himself up with an elbow against the carved wooden grapevines of the sofa's arm. "It is true, then, that the Einharsons claim some sorcerous title to their rule? I heard Baldomer say aught of it."

Lothian shrugged ever so slightly, with a glance to the doorway. "There are stories, yes. Whether they have a kernel of truth or are mere superstitions exploited by the family, it scarcely matters." The sage looked levelly at Conan. "If I were the baron, I would not rely too heavily on such beliefs to secure my rank. Adroit policy is more important."

"Aye . . . and a swift sword-arm." Conan clapped a hand on his own bicep to massage some of the recent kinks from it.

His tutor shot him a sudden, impatient look from under snowy brows. "Wrong, my child. A sword too swift will bring a man to ruin faster than anything else." He shook his ruffled locks, glancing disapprovingly at Conan's powerful body. "Better that some thought and wealth were given to learning and addressing the needs of the inhabitants of this barony, rather than to the hiring of additional sword-arms!"

Lothian turned back to his scroll with new energy. Perhaps this task would be tolerable after all; the young outlander seemed fairly tame and not entirely an inept pupil. He cleared his throat. "Now then. In street processions, the royal entourage will be headed by an honor guard of at least seven men, or if on horseback, by at least five. When a favored baron or knight accompanies the king, his own guards will nevertheless yield precedence. . . ."

As the sage counselor droned on, Conan lay in the creeping ribbon of sunlight and thought of Ludya. The cushioned divan beneath him had some of the marvelous softness of her skin, though it lacked her smooth silkiness. The prospect of further trysting with her was enough to dull his restless yearning for escape. Why not bide here in the Manse a while longer and restore his strength?

Yet it was important to be watchful and to spy out the devious workings of the place. Ludya herself was the best means to that, a simple, spirited girl after his own heart, yet well-placed and full of knowledge of the court. And, ah, the loving ways of these southern lasses! He settled back deep into the upholstery, lulled by memories of her caresses. His mind grazed warmly in remote, sunlit pastures.

Suddenly a harsher touch prodded him, and he jerked instantly awake. His hand shot out to intercept the one that menaced him, even before his blurred eyesight could focus on his looming foe.

Blinking, he saw that the hand in his grasp held nothing more deadly than a plumed writing quill. He glanced up to the startled, pained face leaning over him, that of Lothian, the scholar. Gingerly Conan relinquished his grip on the thin old wrist lest the birdlike bones snap in his clutch. He hauled himself upright in the clumsy seat, slightly abashed.

The sage counselor backed away, rubbing his chafed limb and gathering his flustered dignity about him. "As I thought, napping in class! Well, young ruffian, be assured that tomorrow I shall test you thoroughly. Then we shall repeat however much of today's lesson you slept through." He waved his unimpaired hand sharply in the air. "Now, off with you! Go!"

Conan left the tutor massaging his wrist, and headed for the lower precincts of the Manse. While treading the worn spiral steps, he pondered. In spite of its lack of bodily strains and bruises, Lothian's teaching would be the hardest of all his duties to face. What a sledge-load of manure!

His weapon training, by contrast, had grown routine, even interesting, since being taken over by Durwald. And his horse pacing was tolerable under the lax supervision of Arga, the farrier. After the perils of the first days, Conan was beginning to feel more at ease among these Nemedians, vain as they were of their petty local crotchets and customs. It might do to linger here at the Manse, but not without a ready escape route and some material provision for his survival. He glanced carefully through the arch before entering the ground-floor corridor. He assumed that his movements around the place were watched.

Going to the kitchen, he did his share in helping to lay out the servants' dinner, then did more than his share in consuming it. The other menials had grown to accept him, even to like him. This was especially true of Velda, the fat, bawdy chief cook; the sly tow-headed boy, Glin; and Lokey, the half-witted kitchen hand whose forehead was still flat on one side from a mule kick received in childhood.

Conan's preemptive appetite posed no threat to any of them since food was ever-plentiful in the lower reaches of the house, as it was wasted royally by the nobles above. And in these gatherings, Ludya's familiarity helped to draw the stolid Cimmerian forth. She teased him merrily during the meal, as usual, and he enthralled the diners with heroic legends and gruesome accounts of northern ogres and trolls.

Later, when all were abed—and after a brief, restless wait in his own sleeping-closet for discretion's sake—Conan went to Ludya's side. They embraced, and conversed in whispers while lying close together, and embraced again. Ludya confided her fondest ambitions to him.

"Even in class-bound Nemedia, Conan, it happens from time to time that a girl of lowly station is favored by a man of position and taken by him to wife. Here, unlike some of the southern kingdoms where queens and priestesses hold sway, rank accrues only to the male. But a woman, if she is both beautiful and strong in spirit, can rise greatly. Like the Lady Heldra." Ludya's voice was a sighing warmth in Conan's ear.

"Great good fortune," he murmured back, "as long as one doesn't end as she did, with poison in her craw or a dagger in her back!"

"I serve the baron's table, Conan, and of late I have felt the young Lord Favian's eyes on me. He is an impulsive fellow, and yet he nears marrying age."

Conan's voice rumbled in the narrow bunk. "I would warn you against Favian. He is an intemperate chap, and violent in his cups."

"Not like you in the least, is he, Conan?" Ludya teased. "But truly, nobles must not be judged by the same mete as ordinary men. Rank and responsibility weigh heavily on them and impel them to excess. Favian merely bridles under his father's strictness, as any son would."

"Now there is a thought! If you want to rise in the world, why not catch the watery eye of the old man himself? Go straight to the top, marry the baron and make yourself Favian's mother!" Conan's husky whisper managed to convey a cynical distaste.

"Oh no, Conan! 'Tis a well-known state secret that Baldomer has no use for women." Ludya's voice shifted from protest back to confidentiality. "In the last Brythunian border war, just before Favian was born, he sustained two grave wounds: the one to his face and another lower down, here!" Ludya's hand moved expressively beneath the bedclothes. "'Tis a dangerous custom, the wearing of kilts by Nemedian nobles. He was sorely impaired; that is why he so cherishes Favian as the last Einharson heir.

"But I know you were jesting. Really, Conan, how could you suggest such a thing? Me seduce the baron, indeed!" She laid a hand on her bedmate's cheek in a mock slap. "Baldomer is mad and old, and not nearly so good-looking as Favian." She pecked a kiss on Conan's cheek. "Why, Favian is just as beautiful as

57

you are . . . maybe even handsomer. I can't make up my mind!"

Late that night, groggy with sleep and ebbed tides of pleasure, Conan raised himself from the warmth of Ludya's bed. He crawled to the end of the stall and drew on his clothes quietly to avoid waking her. He peered through the drapery, then went silent into the dim moonlit common-room.

His destination was not the burlap and hay of his own pallet. For that he would not willingly have abandoned the Nemedian girl's linen and soft furs, nor the fragrant warmth of her body.

He padded to the kitchen archway and felt his way cautiously through the room beyond, lit by the faint red glow of banked cook fires. An almost imperceptible fringe of light outlined the half-open door to the corridor; when Conan edged up to the opening and eased his head through, he saw the night sentry standing against the wall beside the Manse's rear entry.

The guard was a veteran in full uniform, including steel helmet and breastplate. Burdened so uncomfortably, he would not stand motionless for long Conan knew. He stepped back inside the kitchen and waited.

Indeed, in a little while he heard the scuff of leather soles in the corridor. They passed the kitchen, turned around and passed it again. Conan chose that moment to steal into the passage. Before the guard ended his circuit and turned back to face the corridor, the youth had flitted behind him through another archway.

The Cimmerian made his way slowly and noiselessly through pitch-black storerooms, using skills honed in night-stalking panther and minx through northern woods. Now he employed these talents in pursuit of a more fabled reward: the vast treasure that all castles harbored and all barons hoarded. Legendry told him it was so; he believed unquestioningly, and the promise of claiming his share of it made him bear all the vexations of the place.

Another hope was to find some escape route that might prove safer, when at length he needed it, than a desperate dash through the open palace gates by daylight. Although he had found no hint of such a route yet, a previous night's wanderings had taken him to the highest roof of the Manse, to an aerie above the very helmets of the pacing sentries. There he had breathed the heady airs of summer night, smelled the perfume of blooming jasmine, and gazed out over the slate and thatch of the town roofs to the moonlit band of river. Close beneath him, he had seen how tightly secured and well-patrolled was the baron's keep during the dark hours. Still, there would be a way.

The once-glimpsed stair, which Conan now found by touch, ascended toward an unexplored quarter of the Manse. But as he started up the narrow steps, he heard the scrape of a door at the top. A crease of light appeared and widened, sending forth yellow rays to pierce the dusty expanse of the storeroom; Conan ghosted off to take refuge behind a bale of coarse cloth.

The source of the light proved to be tapers of crimson wax, set in two of the three sockets of a gleaming silver candelabrum. As the wavering rays descended toward Conan, he was forced to crouch low out of sight. But the scuff of feet on the steps bespoke the presence of only one person, and so, as the light passed him by, Conan risked a look. The candles' glare illuminated an heroic if worn and war-ravaged profile: Baldomer's.

After the baron's passing, Conan glanced up to see that the door was shut. Then, moving silently and lurking among the shifting shadows thrown back by the swaying double flame, he followed. The Cimmerian felt intense curiosity over Baldomer's presence in the castle's nether rooms at this eerie hour. The nobleman's garb was strange for the excursion, consisting of a long, pale nightshirt, his leather kilt belted over it, and upon his breast a heavy, gleaming amulet in the form of a star, with six dagger-pointed blades.

The night-walker moved on steadily, as if sure of his purpose; yet Conan wondered that he seemed to be heading for the blank end of the vast, vaulted storeroom. No passage was visible in the wavering light. Was Baldomer going to visit a treasure-hoard secreted inside one of these dusty bales or kegs, or mayhap beneath the heavy flags of the cellar floor?

Walking staight to the back wall of the chamber, the baron set down his candelabrum on a crate at one side; then he laid his hands on a cobwebbed wooden loom across which a dusty, half-finished tapestry stretched like the sagging web of a titanic spider. Leaning and straining, the nobleman shoved the heavy frame aside to reveal a breach in the wall beyond a low, dark archway barred by a metal grating.

Without working any lock or bolt that Conan could

see, Baldomer grasped the metal crossbar and pulled; as the grating swung open, it sent a rusty, rasping groan echoing through the dim emptiness. The baron picked up his candlestick and stooped to enter the cramped tunnel, the light sinking and dwindling immediately. It was almost out of sight when Conan ventured forward to follow.

He nearly tumbled down the steep, uneven steps waiting inside the archway, but he caught himself by wedging his palms between the narrow walls. He descended swiftly and silently, anxious to overtake the last faint glim of candlelight disappearing beneath.

The level corridor at the bottom was a burial crypt lined with open alcoves. Reflections of retreating candle-flame gleamed against its wet, slimy cobbles, and the joints of the masonry walls were green-bearded with sparkling nitre. Conan feared that the baron might look back at any moment and see him skulking along the straight, narrow passage; fortunately, stone monuments bulked out of the alcoves at intervals, large enough for him to hide behind.

These were the sarcophagi of Dinander's past rulers, Conan surmised. Involuntary contact with the marble casks confirmed the impression gained from the light of the distant candle-beams, that the sides of each one were intricately carved with runes and heraldic symbols. Laid atop each coffin were a rusting sword and suit of mail, probably once the favorite battle-dress of the noble cadaver tucked away inside.

Conan felt uneasy about these relics; he avoided touching them, for he possessed the primitive's dread of tombs and anything that lingers in them. Though some of the armor might be inlaid with silver or gold, this foul grave-trash was scarcely the treasure he sought. Nevertheless, each time the light was raised high in the passage ahead, he found it necessary to shelter behind the coffins and press up close against them.

After a long, tense stalk down the arrow-straight corridor, Conan began to wonder just where beneath the Manse or its grounds he was; the tunnel seemed to extend too far to be a part of the building's foundation. Then he saw an end to the journey, for the will-o'-the-wisp candlestick came to rest. It was deposited atop an especially large, ornate sarcophagus. The box lay transverse across the corridor where it abutted a wall just ahead.

Halting, the baron knelt with a genuflection that was screened by his body and invisible to Conan. Then he reached forward among the armor debris laid on that largest box-lid, taking up what looked like the rust-eaten skeleton of a great longsword. With careful reverence he propped it against the wall behind the sarcophagus. When it was placed thus, its hilt, star-shaped because of its crossed double hand-guard, stood up behind the marble coffin lid like a holy fetish above an altar. It resembled the amulet around Baldomer's neck, Conan realized; indeed, it was probably the model after which the charm was fashioned.

The baron took up the candelabrum and placed it in front of the hilt, so that the star was visible through the vacant center of the silver-branched utensil. The flickering tapers at either side illumined it, their flames playing brightly within the gems still gleaming from the ornate, decaying hilt.

The light in the gloomy passage seemed to grow brighter by virtue of Baldomer's careful placement of the sword. To Conan the weapon seemed inhabited by a radiance of its own; there was something uncanny in the way the flames danced and shimmered on the ancient metal, and for a moment he could not tell whether the sword he gazed on was old or new, corroded or freshly polished. He blinked repeatedly, squinting at the odd illusion.

Baldomer knelt before the tomb as before an altar, folding his kilt beneath his bare knees on the stone. Meanwhile, Conan crept forward for a better view, until he was lurking behind the last sarcophagus short of the candlelit one, mere paces from the baron. He peered over the coffin carefully so as not to disturb the debris atop it; some of the armor in this deeper and older part of the crypt was more intact than was the newer rusted plate. Fashioned of heavy bronze rather than of steel, it was tarnished bright green, but still serviceable.

Baldomer now spoke in a prayerful chant that reverberated along the narrow confine. His utterance was couched in archaic dialect containing obscure hints and allusions, but Conan could follow the gist of the ritualized statement.

"Sacred sword of Einhar! Blade of my father's father's first father, I commend myself and mine unto thy power! Still we sing the storied times when they wielder was king. Still we remember the old days, and honor the old ways. Kin of thine shall never brook the insolent eye, nor the treasonous tongue, nor the hand that moveth sluggishly to obey. All such are the rightful prey of the blades of Einhar's sons!

"O Sword of my father, our rule is by thy license. I pray thee, keep vigilant on our behalf. Watch over our clan; temper our spirits harshly with thine iron strength. Stand thee ready to lead us in the exercise of our noble privilege, carved aforetimes from the bones and blood of men!"

As Baldomer spoke this sanguinary chant, the hallowed sword appeared to blush ever brighter; Conan could now distinctly see candle-flickers playing along a gleaming blade, where before had stood a mere rust-eaten twig. The undeniable evidence of sorcery made him restless, and he glanced nervously over his shoulder to spy for other lurking shapes among the crypt's huddled shadows.

Then a further thought struck him: Baldomer's candles were burning low. The baron must soon finish his observance, and when he did, he must needs make his way back via this same corridor. Even if Conan managed to hide behind a coffin and then follow the noble out, he would reach the catacomb's entrance to find the grating closed and the heavy dross of the storeroom shoved once again in front of it.

The thought of being entombed with the dead of the ages in this magick-ridden crypt made the Cimmerian shudder. Keeping his eye on the kneeling, intoning noble, he crept back along the passage. Once he put a safe distance between himself and the light, he paused to watch the baron halt his utterances and, a moment later, arise and reach between the dwindling candles for his ancestor's sword. Satisfied that the strange religious observance was ending, Conan groped the rest of the way along the passage and at length back through the darkened storerooms to his bed.

But one thing of value he took with him from the crypt: a fragment of knowledge. For as he had lurked in an alcove near the end of that ancient corridor, he found that it contained, in addition to a coffin, a concealed door. Cleverly shaped of stone, the portal filled and sealed the niche almost completely, but not quite; for through the crack beneath it blew a draft, a warmer current invading the dank, noisome air of the tomb. Putting his face near the floor to sniff it, the northerner had smelled the jasmine-scented breath of summer night.

INTERLUDE
The Plain of Smokes

From the Varakiel a forest of smoke-pillars rose skyward. Through sultry, yellowed daylight a motley army moved, stretching in a ragged line across field and copse, scrambling over hedges and splashing through shallow canals.

Peasants they were, sturdy men and apple-cheeked women in the rude garb of their daily toil. Yet they marched as an army, swinging their threshing flails and hayforks like swords, their faces wearing a hardened warrior's lack of expression. Their home fields and crofts were left far behind, else they danced up in flames with the others gouting fire on either hand.

In places along their line where a cottage or a hayrick was set newly alight, groups of marchers lingered nearby; weapons laid aside, they crouched in waiting circles. As rats, cats and sundy vermin were driven out of hiding by the scorching heat, the waiting ones seized them up and devoured them. In these attacks the pillagers threw off any sign of their humanity; ofttimes two or three of them clutched together at the same struggling carcass, rending it alive with eager teeth.

When human refugees were caught, similar struggles ensued, but the feasting was of a different nature. As many as half a dozen of the marchers would fall greedily upon the victim and drag his or her wrists and ankles to their gaping mouths. But instead of tearing and devouring their prey, each captor would bite down once, hard. The victims, after their initial shrieks of agony and fear, would lie stricken on the ground. In time then they would arise, weak and faltering, to shuffle after their attackers. Finally each would take up a weapon, to become a part of the ever-advancing line.

So the campaign proceeded from swamp to plain, from onion field to ox pasture. Through it all, there sounded no drums or trumpets and there galloped no dispatch-riders. Seemingly the conquerors went on of their own accord, with no sign of leadership but one: down a rough dirt path that ran diagonally across the line of mounting smokes, a chariot rumbled.

It was a rude vehicle cut down from an ox-wain, decked with bright metal fittings, gaudy draperies and other petty spoils of the rural campaign. To its heavy poles had been yoked three sturdy farm horses, a brisk and healthy team, though not well matched in size or color.

Inside the rumbling conveyance rode three figures. The driver, a brawny man, wore the leather apron of a smith, with smudges of soot still shining on his thick arms and unshaven jaw; the fellow beside him was blackly bearded and also burly, a swamp-dwelling trapper judging by the rich and somewhat unripe appearance of the animal furs in which he was decked from neck to toe. These two stood in the front of the chariot, wordless and expressionless, stiffly balancing the weight of their bodies above the jolting axle.

The third passenger lay at leisure on a bed of cushions behind them, his weight so slight as to be ignored by the laboring team. For he was a mere boy, though he reclined in a plundered shawl of gold-embroidered purple, and wore on his brow a gold chaplet arrogating to royal rank. It was none other than the swamp-child, Lar, arisen from his sickbed and clearly exalted to some strange rulership. Of all those who stalked the plain under his command that day, his was the only face that wore what could be recognized as a distinctly human emotion, and that an incongruous one: he gazed over the whole scene with a look of imperious boredom.

As the charioteers rolled past peasant troopers who strode the fields, there was no exchange of signs or hails, nor even a glance of shared recognition. Both went their own way in cold, mindless efficiency. The chariot splashed across a shallow stream and followed the dwindling track into a brushy copse of elms and laurels. As the woods crowded closer and darker, the path grew fainter. The team finally scuffed to a halt before a hut of moss-green stone.

Marchers had already found and entered the place, as evidenced by its broken door and by the flames that gnawed tentatively at one corner of its mossy thatch. The burly guards stepped out over the sides of the chariot, and the young princeling stretched and sat up in his bed. Even as he stood erect, two armed peasants emerged from the hut dragging a third person; a scrawny, elderly man with a wild look in his eyes and a wilder disarray to his gray, bushy hair.

"Nay, infect him not!" Lor's voice piped abruptly, for already the captors were raising the old man's wrists toward their gaping mouths. "First I would put him to the question." Casually he hopped down from the chariot and ambled over; his two helpers went to crowd up close behind the captive.

"Well, old witch-man, your petty sway in this district is ended! An elder and greater magick comes to lay claim to you and yours." The boyish reediness of the lad's voice gave the portentous words a quality incongruous with the scene. He flicked a beckoning finger impatiently, and his henchmen forced the old one down on one knee, so that his face was on a level with the boy's.

"Tell me, old man, did you have time to send word to your far-flung brethren?" He glanced to the empty straw-filled cages at one side of the cottage. "I see that your pigeons have flown . . . bearing news of me, no doubt. What did you tell the others about this new faith which sweeps the plain?" He strutted and preened before his captive, like a child playing at men's conquests. "Will your warlocks guild be foolish enough to oppose me?"

The old one, grimacing in dismay, kept his yellowed, decayed teeth clamped shut behind his white-puckered lips. The bone-and-tooth beads around his neck and the grimy medicine-bag suspended thereon showed him to be a rural wizard, as did the herbs and fetishes hung from the eaves of his smoldering roof. He showed no sign of any vast or preternatural power as his watery eyes flashed doubtfully at his inquisitor. Still, he made no answer.

"Enough! He will not speak." Lar glanced up at his escort, one hand slipping casually inside his gaudy robe. "Cut him!"

Obediently and expressionlessly, the burly trapper produced a short, gleaming blade from his furs and jabbed it into the old warlock's side. Issuing a sharp yelp of pain and surprise, the captive writhed between the men who pinioned his shoulders.

At the instant the old man's mouth opened for the cry, Lar's hand leaped from the folds of his garment to the captive's face. So swift was the motion that it was hard to see, but it appeared that the youth tossed something into the withered old mouth—something small and blackly gleaming that seemed to wriggle like a thin, sinuous tadpole as it passed the ramshackle gate of the wizard's rotted teeth.

The old one clamped his jaws shut, his pain quickly forgotten, eyes wide in astonishment. Lar's hand fell back slowly to his side as the blacksmith's thick, sooty paw was insinuated under the old man's chin to keep his mouth closed.

The princeling stared closely at the wizard's face, now mutely eloquent. In the course of a moment it passed from surprise to alarm, through choking panic, to agony. Then the pale eyes bled tears, and rolling skyward in torment at whatever unseen predations and violations were taking place inside the gray old skull.

The witch struggled between his captors, his legs

kicking violently enough to tear the moss of the cottage yard. With his mouth clamped shut within the blacksmith's sooty, viselike grasp, he could only emit stifled nasal grunts of pain, these gradually diminishing in intensity. And even after the warlock's struggles subsided, his head still nodded in exhaustion, his labored breaths sighing through his nose.

In a moment Lar waved an impatient hand and the smith's grip was withdrawn. The princeling leaned closer, putting his ear to the old man's mouth, which now lolled slightly open. He waited in a pose of alert listening, though all that could have been heard by the others was an exceedingly faint and scarcely articulated hissing, seemingly nothing more than the victim's feeble, glottal gasps. But the youth lingered patiently, nodding as if at some sage piece of advice imparted by a kindly gray-haired grandfather.

Finally, straightening up with a satisfied look, he reached a hand to the oldster's mouth and removed something from it, which he once again secreted in the breast of his mantle. Carelessly he turned and strode back to the chariot, tossing his minions one further command as they threw down the dying witch-man and hastened to follow.

"Watch the roads."

CHAPTER 5
Sword and Lash

"By Mitra's holy beard, lad wherever did you get this torso?" Dru, the armorer, lifted his largest black-armor breastplate away from Conan's naked chest. He replaced it on one of the heavy dowels set inside an oaken armoire. "Nothing here is going to fit him!"

He turned to Baron Baldomer, who stood at one side in black-and-gold casual equipage, his arms folded on his chest and a slight smile softening the wildness of his face. Dru said, "Milord . . . I cannot alter anything we have on hand. I must turn a new piece of plate."

"They grow them big in Cimmeria." Baldomer reached forth a hand and squeezed the muscles of Conan's shoulder. The youth bore the touch for a moment, then twisted away uncomfortably. His massive chest was smooth-skinned and almost hairless, although marked by newly healed welts and some shackle scars at the neck. The baron eyed him appraisingly. "The feral northern vitality . . . it shows in my son, too, but not so much as in this boy."

"We could as well let the youth hammer out his own steel plate," said Arga, the farrier, matter-of-factly. "Conan tells me his father was a smith. His folk use small forges, but they make good-sized, hotly tempered blades." The farrier kept his eyes downcast, sheepish about showing off his knowledge before the baron. "It must require a strong, untiring pair of arms at the bellows."

"Thus accounting for this boy's massive physique." Baldomer glanced amusedly at Conan, who said nothing. "Well, I have more urgent need of him than smithy toil." He addressed the armorer. "How long did you say a new plate would take?"

"A week, Milord, at least."

"Hm." The baron's brow furrowed. "Perhaps you could work from one of Favian's old outfits."

Dru nodded. "Perhaps, Milord. Though much of the young lord's weight is distributed . . . lower down."

"Come." Baldomer turned and strode out the double doors of the armory. The other three followed, last of all Conan, still shrugging his jerkin over his head.

Their lord led them briskly through the main entry hall and up the central steps. For the first time, Conan found himself on the broad expanse of marble stairway, and he took the opportunity to gawk; the room's stately alabaster pillars loomed tall from this angle, and the gold-and-scarlet tapestries blazed in sunlight from the windows set high above the Manse's front portal. It was afternoon, and the hall was empty except for Iron Guardsmen, who flanked its doorways, their eyes riveted straight ahead.

Moving swiftly, Baldomer crossed the mezzanine and entered a corridor that Conan recognized from his former explorations. Wheeling to a halt before a black-polished door, the baron gave two hard raps. Without waiting for a reply he struck the latch with the heel of his hand, pressed the door open and entered. The others followed him at a respectful distance.

The chamber, low-ceilinged and spacious, had no other occupants—only carven furniture, a great bed whose blankets were wildly disarrayed, and walls adorned with cavalry gear and bright tapestries. At a nod from the baron, Arga went to the window and dragged apart the thick curtains, letting in beams of dusty daylight.

Baldomer strode to a black-lacquered wardrobe opposite the bed and threw open its doors. Multicolored folds of clothing inside emitted musty scents of sweat and talcum. "Hmm. I know there are several suits of mail in here. One of them should be usable." He began sorting through the close-packed sleeves; after a moment's hesitation, Dru started working from the other end.

Shortly the armorer reached both arms into the cabinet and produced a cuirass; it was fashioned of brass, unadorned, and showing many scrapes and shallow dents. Its leather fastenings were sweat-stained and frayed, and the brass-ribbed leather battle-skirt hanging underneath it was in no better shape.

"Lord Favian's old training gear . . . not really enough to work with, I fear, Milord."

"No. It won't do." Baldomer was fingering a flimsy sleeve of scarlet fabric thoughtfully: a woman's diaphanous gown. He pulled it free of the other clothing, crumpled it in his fist and tossed it to the floor. "Keep on looking."

After a smart but undersized mailcoat had been rejected, the baron produced an impressive-looking armor suit from the back wall of the cabinet. It was a steel breastplate trimmed with black leather after the fashion of the Iron Guard, but more carefully crafted, and inlaid with silver. The matching silver-spiked helmet hung on a peg above it. "Here now, what about this?" He held the plate up against Conan's chest.

"A fair fit, Milord, with some alterations. But that is Lord Favian's new formal suit of mail, turned by me last fall at Milord's command for the Baronial Conclave." Dru's gaze at Baldomer showed some concern. "I doubt that your son has anything else so splendid to wear."

"Our need is more immediate." Baldomer did not spare him a glance. "I authorize you to fix up something for Favian from the standard guard uniform. And see that it's padded at the shoulders to make his figure better match this lad's. Here, boy, try this on."

As Conan began donning the heavy breastplate over his jerkin, Dru continued to protest. "But, Milord . . . is it really necessary to outfit a bodyguard so resplendently, with the provincial tour slated for so soon?"

"Better not to ask, armorer." The baron silenced

him with a steely look. "And I bid you make no mention of it. To anyone . . . understood?"

"Yes, Milord." Dru stepped back, looking cowed.

"Now then. Raise your arms, boy. Yes, the straps will need lengthening, but it should do nicely. What's that?"

The baron turned as the chamber door banged open behind him. Arga and Dru stepped forward to their baron's defense, but when they saw that the intruder was only young Favian, they stood at ease, looking slightly abashed.

Favian was booted and leather-clad, fresh from the saddle. His lip was newly shaved by his father's decree, making his resemblance to Conan more noticeable. He stared at the party in surprise for a moment; then his eyes narrowed, and his broad, handsome countenance darkened. "So, Father, a new enormity! Stealing my face and my name is not enough for you. You find it necessary to ransack my closet, too! Truly, how can you explain this?" He flashed the baron a defiant look as he slammed his unstrung hunting-bow onto a rack by the door.

After a slight initial coloring, Baldomer's features composed themselves to as much icy regularity as his scarified face allowed. "A mere security matter, Favian, that is all. Besides which," he continued more vehemently, "my place is not to explain my actions to you. Remember, every decision I make is for your own good and that of the baron."

Favian stepped forward into the center of the room. "Yet you violate my privacy. You have given my best armor to this barbar-boy; next you'll probably have me clapping on his filthy dog-skins. Well, I won't have it!" He moved toward the wardrobe, reaching out to close one of its doors.

The baron stood fast, blocking his way. "What you will have or will not have is no prerogative of yours, Favian. Remember, you have nothing in this world but what I have given you—and nothing I cannot take back, should you prove undeserving!"

"Father, this is too much!" Favian turned from the unmoving baron and approached Conan. "You, there —get that armor off your stinking carcass at once!" While Conan glanced to the baron for assent, Favian shoved belligerently at the northerner's chest, scarcely budging him. He did so again, harder, as a measured provocation.

Then, suddenly, the lordling produced a riding crop from his sword-belted waist and lashed at Conan's unprotected head and shoulders. The Cimmerian raised an arm in defense and with a lightning-quick grab, seized the lashing tail of the quirt. He yanked it out of the young noble's grasp and tossed it into a corner of the room.

"Oh you will, will you? Miserable serf! Well, mark me, I am not drunk this time . . . and not unarmed, either!"

The room's confines rang with the sound of Favian's rapier clearing its scabbard. With hardly a pause in its streaking motion, the blade lashed out low at Conan's unshielded legs, but the northerner was already dancing back. He skipped clear of two more wild slashes, then vaulted over the bed to keep from being cornered.

"No, hold!" Baldomer's low command was addressed not to the fighters, but to his two retainers,

Arga and Dru, who stood by indecisively, their hands on their dagger-hilts. An instant later the baron unhooked a scabbarded straightsword from the wall and tossed it to Conan. "Here, bodyguard, defend yourself!" The Cimmerian caught the piece smoothly, raising it before him just in time to meet Favian's blade as the young nobleman came vaulting over the bed.

"At him, son!" Baldomer called lustily.

The lordling's stroke knocked the scabbard free of Conan's blade to clatter across the floor. The blows that followed rang out rapidly and deafeningly, for it was easier to parry than to dodge in such close quarters. Conan saw that his heavy old sword was dull and notched; it had been a mere set-piece for years, and the leather winding of its hilt was dry and loose in his hand, allowing the metal edges beneath to saw and cut at his skin.

"Favian, pace yourself! Don't waste your strength," Baldomer urged his son. "The Cimmerian has endurance. Draw him out and await your chance."

Conan's worst discomfort was the ill-fitting chest armor that restrained his breaths and bit into the flesh under his arms. His movements were sorely limited, yet he was not hard-pressed.

For Favian's attack quickly lost energy against an armed and armored opponent. He spent ever more time in feinting and threatening and ever less in sparring. Not once did his blade strike the gaudy cuirass. It seemed that his only forceful strokes were low, vicious cuts at Conan's legs.

"That's it, son! Keep your wits. Wear him down."

Without fighting to kill or wound, the northerner

began using his training to trip or disarm his adversary. Stools and tables crashed out of the combatants' way, or splintered before their rushes. Just once, Conan's blade locked into the curve of Favian's, threatening to wrench it out of the Lordling's grasp —and before the edges scraped apart, the Cimmerian glimpsed real fear in his opponent's eyes.

Then Baldomer's exhortations faded to silence, and Favian was holding his blade vertical before him, looking nervously amused, calling in fencer's sign-language for a halt. Conan lowered his weapon.

"Well, barbarian, I see that you have benefited greatly from our training." Breathing heavily, the lordling sheathed his blade. Then, to Conan's momentary alarm, he reached forward and clapped a hand on his shoulder. "I should have taken you on a fortnight past, though poor old Eubold met with little luck even then." He gave Conan a rueful smile. "You have passed my little test. If I am bound to have a bodyguard, it may as well be one as nimble as yourself!"

Favian glanced around the company, his look daring anyone to assert that he had meant the fight in earnest. Dru, looking embarrassed, busied himself righting furniture, while Arga took Conan's sword to scabbard it once again on the wall. The youth surrendered the weapon wordlessly. The baron quietly gave orders to his retainers and left without good-byes, his face closed and remote. Conan shucked his armor and handed it to Dru, but as he was about to depart with the two craftsmen, Favian detained him.

"Now that we have crossed swords, Cimmerian, what say you to a drinking bout?" Favian went to an undamaged locker near the bed and brought out an earthenware bottle and two noggin-cups. He flourished the pair of pewter-sealed human skulls in front of Conan's face. "Frankly, I find tippling a nobler sport. I would rather lose my head to drink than to steel any day!"

Much later in the afternoon, when his once-sullen tongue had been oiled by liquor, Conan finished regaling Favian with the story of his jailbreak. His green jerkin was winestained and his gestures lavish. "When they dragged me from the place, I expected to be stuck in a gibbet, not in a noble household! 'Twas as good a piece of luck as a foreigner could wish in this tight-knit country . . . but mayhap an added trouble for you." He tipped his cup up, then thumped it back to the board. "I never wished that, Favian."

"Fah! Think nothing of it, Conan." The young lord waved a hand breezily in his new fashion of camaraderie. "Could I fault you for looking like me, or for being thrown into my father's dungeon at the wrong time? No reasonable fellow would hold that against you. What was the cause of your arrest, by the way? I never did find out for certain."

"I was guiltless, I swear." Conan shook his bleary head. "'Twas only a curfew scrape."

"No consorting with rebels? Sedition, perhaps?" The noble youth watched his drinking partner closely.

"Nothing of the sort. Although there was a bit of skull-thumping when I was taken . . . all on account of your city guards' rudeness."

"Aye." Favian nodded. "The municipals are on edge of late, because of rebel stirrings. And the

80

whispers of snake-cult activity, too. Not that there is any real danger to my family's reign. But the harsher the measures you take at the first hint of unrest, the less trouble you will have later on."

Favian tilted a flask sloshing yellow liquor first into Conan's cup and then, more sparingly, into his own. "Svoretta says the trouble is caused by rural serfs who want to skimp on their fees and tributes." He raised his skull-cup toward the dimming rays from the window, letting the sunset gleam in its red crystal eyes. "That, my friend, is where I could shine. If Father would let me lead a horse detachment into the countryside, I would show the ignorant turnip-eaters the price of dissidence! A lot of rebellion there'd be then! Or better, give me a chariot; I could drive one of those to Helheim itself!"

Conan watched his host through a spiritous haze. "There couldn't be much of a revolt underway. The peasants in the lockup didn't seem any too fierce. Perhaps a show of fairness would get better results. . . ."

"Peasants? Fierce? Why, of course not!" Favian overrode his companion's words with drink-slurred cynicism. "If they were fierce they wouldn't be peasants. That alone is what makes us Einharsons rulers: sheer ferocity, in spite of all Counselor Lothian's pleasant-sounding theories." The young lord tossed the contents of his cup down his gullet and regarded Conan with a sardonic look.

"From the time that my ancestor—noble Einhar, or his rotty grandsire, whoever began it—from the day he first took up a blade and learned the craft of butchery, using it to elevate himself above his fellow

81

men . . . from that day, the sword has been the ultimate expression of our fine nobility. All of it is based
on the murderous art of war. Ever must we use that
skill, or induce others to use it for us. The moment we
forget, we place ourselves in dire jeopardy!"

Carried away by his own rhetoric, Favian arose
from his stool and took up his scabbarded sword from
his bed. Removing the sheath and tossing it back onto
the disarranged quilts, he clutched the weapon by the
middle of its blade and held it up before him.
"Strange to think, is it not, that this gruesome tool is
the highest implement of human will, the tiller of
man's destiny! Yet it is this flesh-slicer, and only this,
that steers the course of empire, and sustains us
Einharsons in our modest glory!"

"Only the sword?" Conan felt impelled to interrupt
before Favian worked himself up into another fighting
frenzy. "What about your exalted bloodline, then,
and the supernatural wardings that protect your
clan?" He watched his host across his raised cup.

"Wardings?" Favian glanced at him suspiciously
and tossed the sword casually aside. "What know you
of those?"

"Only what the baron once told me," Conan muttered. "And what is rumored around the castle."

"Ah, yes, rumors do seem to get around the
Manse." The lordling turned his noggin-cup thoughtfully in his hand. "Well, Conan, soon I shall reach the
age of initiation into the mystery of my family's
heritage. Then I may find out whether Einhar's curse
is merely a hobgoblin with which to scare credulous
fools or whether there is real power in it." He eyed his

drinking companion speculatively. "But you, Cimmerian, will never find out—if you are lucky, that is, and if you do your bodyguarding well."

Favian stoppered the flask and gathered the cups across the drink-splashed table. "Now, fellow, I make ready for my supper, and you must hie off to yours. But we shall talk again. And should my father forge onward with this imposture he has in mind, I pray that your good luck continues."

Conan left the interview with his wits fogged by Favian's heady beverage. It took all his concentration just to find his way downstairs, nor did stuffing his belly at the servants' table seem to help the state of his brain.

Ludya did not appear, and Conan did not take his usual part in the mealtime chatter. He sat silent, dully pondering what he now knew of Favian: the young nobleman had a volatile character, every bit as complex as the baron's, and mayhap just as mad in the final reckoning. His understanding was burdened by one further insight, which he knew the father shared: the knowledge of the son's cowardice.

After the meal, Ludya passed swiftly through the room without any greeting for Conan; her eyes went over him with no acknowledgment. To his half-stupefied senses, that was the final blow. He crawled away to his bed, blearily cursing all civilized men and women and their mad, unpredictable moods.

Late in the night Conan was dragged out of a murky pit of slumber by faint sounds from the common-room: scuffing footsteps and imperfectly muffled sobs.

He rolled swiftly to the foot of his bed and parted the curtains. The candlelight was faint, but he saw that a half-clad figure was just disappearing into one of the alcoves: Ludya's.

In a moment he was across the room. He entered the dark closet and stood over her pallet, where she lay huddled, weeping quietly. "Ludya . . . what is wrong, girl? Have you been hurt?"

Her sobs became more audible as they mingled with her speech. "No, Conan, go away. Don't worry about me. Please!"

He knelt to put an arm around her. "What is it, child? You can tell me . . . Crom!"

As his hand brushed the hot, swollen welts on her back, she whimpered in pain. Conan gingerly probed the extent of her injuries and felt the slickness of blood on his fingertips. "We must have these wounds dressed. Ludya, come." He put his unstained hand to her tear-damp cheek. "Girl, who did this to you? Tell me."

She sobbed for a long moment, making no reply. As he opened his mouth to speak again, his attention was caught by the clink of mailed boots in the adjoining room.

Heavy footsteps marched close to the alcove and halted with the clack of a metal-butted half-pike grounding on stone. A military voice, firm and toneless, called out, "The maid Ludya—is she here?"

"That is her bed, sir," confided a younger male voice.

Conan drew aside the curtain and saw two Iron Guardsmen standing before the alcove, one holding the pike and the other a flickering candle. Faces peered from between the curtains of the other sleeping-closets, but no one spoke.

"The wench Ludya will accompany us," the pikeman ordered Conan.

"She cannot come. She is unwell." Conan stepped forward, keeping the curtain closed at his back to block view of the girl.

"She must come along, by the baron's order. Move aside!" When Conan stood firm, the pikeman widened his stance and lowered his barb-bladed weapon to the ready. The second guard set his candlestick on the dining table and placed a hand on his sword-hilt.

At that moment Ludya pushed through the curtain at Conan's side. He tried to restrain her, but she staggered past him toward the guards. She was pale and silent now, clad in slippers and a scanty shift. She clutched a fur blanket about her, but it left exposed one bare flank and part of her red-striped back. When Conan glimpsed this in the flickering light, rage buzzed inside his skull like a seething cloud of hornets. Any remnant of his earlier intoxication was by now wiped away.

The guardsmen fell into place, one in front of the shamed girl and one behind, and they moved off through the archway. When the pike-wielder heard Conan following them into the hall, he turned and leveled his blade. The barbarian faced him in the doorway, unflinching. After a moment's silent stare, the guard turned and hurried after his comrade and the retreating candle.

The Cimmerian followed the three closely through nighted corridors and up the servants' stair to the residential wing that was newly familiar to him.

Several doors stood open there, and the guardsmen escorted the now-quiet Ludya through one of them: Favian's.

The pikeman turned and blocked the entry with his pikestave, but he did not drive Conan away from the doorway; the room within was fully visible to him. On the edge of the disarranged bed sat the young lord, half-dressed in a rumpled nightshirt and riding kilt, his head hanging and his elbows propped on wool-skirted knees. The baron stood at the center of the room, clothed hastily but formally, his hair standing up untidily on the scarified side of his head. His rigid face and posture betrayed his anger, as did the rapping of his knuckles against his kilted thigh. At his side, in the dark garb of a night-prowling spy, stood Counselor Svoretta.

When Ludya was thrust before the men, she sank to one knee in obeisance—or weakness. The second guard stayed with her, standing stiffly at her back. Baldomer bent and grasped the hair at one side of her head, tilting her tear-stained face up to the candle-light, then let it fall again. "So this is the wench, a mere table servant! What was she doing here?"

Favian raised his head and spoke in a weary, wine-bleared tone. "She would dally with me, she said, as most any of them gladly will. And yet she failed to please me. High notions this one has, indeed, for a low scullion." He raised his head to view the abject girl, a drunken sneer twisting his face. "Then she spoke impertinently to me, and so I scourged her. A commonplace enough happening; what of it, Father?"

Baldomer pivoted, drawing himself up in indignation before his seated son. "Favian, need I tell you why I am upset, or that I will not have unclothed wenches driven like cattle through the halls of this Manse? This is my home, I remind you, not a Zamoran brothel! It was your mother's home." The baron paced stiffly a few steps across the marble floor, then back to the bed, where he half-leaned over his son and shouted at him. "If you must vent your lusts so ignobly, then I bid you, use a trace of discretion! A display like this is scandalous and vulgar, bad for the morale of the entire household."

"All right, Father, I apologize—since you choose to make an issue of it." Favian shook his head in exasperation. "Can we please just have an end of it now?"

"An end? Very well!" Baldomer pulled himself erect. "But from this moment you are placed on restraint. And the woman cannot continue here; she will have to be killed."

"Father!" Annoyance and a little disgust tinged Favian's protest. "Why not just send her off somewhere?"

Now that he had his son's full attention, the baron's demeanor was somewhat more settled. "House lackeys must not be encouraged to fraternize with the nobility. It is a breach of precedence." He waved his hand at Ludya, who was stifling sobs once again. "And what if she comes back in a year with an infant on her hip, claiming your paternity and a lifetime share of support?"

"Father, why should that be a problem now, when it never was before . . . ?" Weary of argument, Favian arose from the bed and threw up his arms in futility.

"All right, all right, slay her if you must! But leave me alone now, will you!"

The door-guard, thrust back bodily into the room, interrupted them. "Milords, this man . . . followed us from the servants' quarters. . . ." His speech was sporadic as he struggled with Conan over the haft of his leveled pike. Before he could say more, the Cimmerian hooked a leg behind his opponent's knee and shoved forward against the weapon. Still clinging to it, the guardsman toppled to the floor on his back. The other guard drew his sword and faced Conan as the barbarian stepped into the room over the fallen man.

"Boy!" Baldomer barked at him. "Control yourself!"

By a deliberate effort, Conan halted. He stood with his hands at his sides, though his fists remained clenched. "Milord Baron . . ." his tongue stumbled over the unfamiliar terms of respect . . . "I tell you, the girl means no harm." To his faint surprise, he could hear his voice rasp with emotion. "She has suffered much already; let her be!" As he spoke, the two guards positioned themselves in front of him, their weapons pointed at his throat.

"What interest can you possibly have in this affair —" the baron began.

"Milord." Svoretta stepped close to his master, though his words were audible to the others. "Since his arrival at the Manse, the barbarian and the wench have consorted together very closely indeed!" His pause lent added meaning to his words. "I charge the existence of a conspiracy to manipulate the will of the young Lord Favian—to suborn him against you by means of the girl's affections, to blackmail him, or possibly to steal from him."

For a time the only sound was Ludya's forlorn weeping. Favian's eyes rose slowly to meet Conan's. "And today I tried to make my peace with him, yet here again comes the stealthy savage, stealing this time into my very bed!" He shook his head angrily. "You are right, Father. The girl must die! Had I known of this little scheme, I'd have flogged her doubly, no, triply."

Baldomer's voice, smooth with complacency, joined his son's. "You see, Favian, how untidy these matters can become. If she were allowed to live—"

The nobleman was interrupted again, this time by the rattle of curtain hooks at the back of the chamber. An embroidered hanging parted there, to reveal a dim-lit doorway through which a young woman stepped. She was red-haired, with a pale, broad-cheekboned face that looked strikingly beautiful in the half light. Her slender form was wrapped in a green-velvet robe that she held together at the throat with one hand.

"Father, how can you torment this poor child?"

The baron raised an arm to forestall his daughter's approach. "Calissa—do not interfere here, girl. This is a matter between father and son."

"Nay, 'tis not!" She came barefoot around the end of the bed and stood beside Favian. "Just now I heard you call it a household concern. Well, my mother ran this house when she was alive, so I will have a say in it too." Calissa's robe fell apart a little way at the throat, exposing an alabaster curvature of chest that she did not bother to conceal. "Just send the serving-maid home; surely she has a home!"

While Baldomer faced his daughter with an air of mingled consternation and tolerance, Svoretta made answer to her. "My Lady Calissa, I fear 'tis not that simple. The damage is already done, and we must take a firm stance on this sort of thing—"

"Nonsense, Counselor. Your spies in our household should inform you better than that." Calissa turned to her father. "The girl Ludya is well liked by the rest of the servants. If you slaughter her for this mischance, you will be troubled henceforth by mutterings and terrors among all the scullions. Worse, you will have to deal with the ill will of that formidable individual —whoever he is."

Calissa's gesture indicated Conan, who stood tensed on the balls of his feet, eyeing the two guards positioned between himself and the rest of the company. From their ready postures and sweat-filmed faces, the Iron Guardsmen looked none too confident of their superiority.

"Oh please, Father, if this is just one of my brother's boyish indiscretions"—Calissa placed a hand on Favian's shoulder, which he shrugged off impatiently —"then there is no reason for any more suffering." She stepped forward and knelt beside the trembling figure on the floor, laying a protective arm over her. "Ludya . . . where is your home?"

The girl's voice was broken and barely audible. "Varakiel. The marsh country to the northeast."

"Do you have people there? Do you want to go back?"

Ludya seized Calissa's hand and bathed it in tears. "Oh please, Milady, please!"

The older girl helped her rise from the floor. "Come, let me tend your hurts. We will send you home soon, child." She led her charge toward the curtained doorway.

Conan called from his place at the other end of the room. "Ludya—"

Svoretta's harsh voice overrode him. "Milord, what of this incorrigible oaf? I warned your lordship of the trouble he would bring."

The baron turned a cold gaze on Conan. "Learn your limits, barbarian—before I limit you to a steel cage in the torture-rooms." He glanced after the departing women. "And forget the girl; you'll not be seeing her again."

CHAPTER 6
Nectar and Poison

Yet Conan did see Ludya once more before she was spirited off to her remote home district. For it was Arga, the farrier, who oversaw the hitching of the donkey cart in the gray-lit stableyard at dawn. And he, while instructing an elderly hand to accompany her, stoically pretended not to notice the hulking young ruffian who crept to her side where she lay bundled in the straw-bedded wagon.

"Ludya, girl, will you be all right? Are your homefolk kind? Only say the word and I'll trounce these noble guards and minions, and carry you away myself!"

Long Conan waited for her reply, and in vain. He watched her wan, expressionless face in the pale light whilst awakening birds chorused faintly in the trees beyond the wall.

"Ludya, do not despair!" As she lay there unresponding, Conan searched for words by which to soothe her inner hurt. "Your dream of advancement here was in vain. These courtly fools were never worthy of you. You'll be better off far away from this wretched Manse, girl; you'll be happier, much happier than—"

"Cease!" Her red-rimmed eyes flared suddenly at him, her bloodless lips forming an angry rapier-curve. "You are right, I have no further need of lords and noble lackeys." Her contempt was obviously meant to include him. "But I am not finished here, not by a long chance! There are other ways for one to rise in Nemedia."

This wrath in her, utterly strange to Conan, might have been hysteria, or worse. Yet there was a coldness to it and a fixity in her gaze as she spoke. "This unhappy land seethes with rebellion. I go forth now, but when I return, it will be with fire and sword" —her pale hand stirred weakly, folding an edge of her shawl across the lower part of her face—"to cleanse away the foulness festering here!"

Conan stared down at his recent lover, holding his dismay within himself. "Rest with your family awhile . . . "Across the yard, Arga finally turned away from the stable-hand, shouting an order for the guards to throw open the gates.

Numbly Conan reached down to brush the maid's slim fingers in farewell; then he faded back into the shadows of the smithy porch. But as the driver took his seat and the wain jolted forward, Conan called softly after her, "Crom heal you, my poor, mad Ludya!"

* * *

Conan did not allow his dolorous parting from Ludya to shadow his thoughts for long; he let himself be swept up with the other occupants of the Manse in readying a gala entertainment. The preparations were all the more feverish because the celebration was a farewell feast, to be given the day before the baron's departure on his tour of the provincial holdings of Dinander.

And so Conan spent many hours in the hauling of stools and trestles up and down stairs, unfurling and beating the dust out of tapestries heavy with gold threads, and performing other tasks less fitted to his size and dignity, such as the polishing of chamber pots and the husking of vegetables. By noontide of the great day, the kitchen cookfires were hot enough to make the Manse's basement swelter like an inferno, its great copper vats frothing and bubbling all at once. By midafternoon of the next day, the giddy aromas of spiced fruits and broiling game were enough to madden a creature more tame and civilized than the Cimmerian.

As he was filching sweetmeats from kitchen trays, at risk of raps on wrist or skull from Velda's long brass ladle, Counselor Svoretta sought him out. Curtly the spymaster told him to don his newly tailored suit of mail and stand ready for orders; until told otherwise, he was to stay out of sight during the festivities.

Much later, the day flown and the sun vanished in the west, Conan crept upstairs via one of the Manse's corner towers. He could not bear to wait any longer in his cramped, sweltering sleeping-cabinet; there he had nothing to occupy his thoughts but memories of

Ludya and his restless doubts over whether he had already lingered fatally long in this domain of madmen. He must escape the prison of his gloom.

The Manse's festive atmosphere was evident in its ravaged kitchen, its bustling corridors, its stairways smelling of spilt wine and echoing with boisterous talk. He avoided the larger rooms, making his way to a remote corner of the mezzanine where he might overlook the party and remain inconspicuous. He felt sure he could pass for a guard in his polished black-and-gold helm and newly tailored cuirass, imposing but still too tight in the shoulders.

Brushing past murmuring lovers in the narrow, dark side-chamber, he slipped out onto the inner balcony. As he had hoped, this part of the gallery was not thickly populated. Moving to the rail, he encountered a wave of heat and a smother of smoky fumes, for the chamber below was alight with a lavish array of candles and oil pots. The entry hall was thronged with guests seated at red-draped tables, promenading through the main doors and loitering on the broad stairway.

Most of these appeared to be merchants, farm-squires, and their highest-ranking retainers. Appearing excited and a little astonished at this rare glimpse of baronial splendor, they loitered, gabbled noisily and overindulged in wine. More eminent guests, the minor nobles and guard officers, seemed to gravitate toward the entry to the inner Hall of State. Thence the tinny chirping of military trumpets issued, and there, presumably, the baron and his counselors held court.

Widely in evidence among both groups of revelers were uniformed men of the Iron Guard. Standing stiffly at intervals along the walls and up the stairs, and spaced more sparsely around the mezzanine, they seemed almost equal in numbers to the guests. Serving on highest alert, they went fully armored, with halberds grounded between their toes and rapiers sheathed at their belts. Conan realized uncomfortably that while his own steel carapace ornately enfolded his vital parts, he possessed no offensive weapon, not even an eating-knife.

Meanwhile, his armor was growing hot in this high, stuffy part of the room. The visor of his helm, though broadly pierced, obstructed both vision and breathing. He raised it impatiently, then instantly regretted his action as a youthful voice called out to him from close at hand.

"Ho there, Lord Favian! So you choose to loiter out here with us rough-and-ready types!"

It was the inevitable confusion of identity. Pretending not to hear the hail, Conan turned away, reaching up to shut his visor. But a hand grasped his arm to arrest his flight; a rawboned, ill-tended paw, dark with sun and farm grime.

"Favian, Milord," the husky adolescent voice croaked, "'tis lucky to find you here." At Conan's murderous glance the hand was quickly withdrawn, but the speaker continued to peer ingratiatingly into his face. "I . . . I am Ralfic, remember, Sire? We had a jolly time at my father's manor. South of town, last season . . . don't you recall, your Lordship?"

Conan regarded the gangling youngster furiously; the lad was nearly his equal in years, though surely not in travels and combats. His face was pitted by some past siege of pox, his clothing foppish, his hair obviously cut with the aid of a porridge bowl. The Cimmerian counterfeit finally, grudgingly, conceded to his fate. He answered the younger man with a nod and a grunt, trying to bark it up from his belly like a true Nemedian noble.

"Yes, Milord . . ." the boy gazed at him uncertainly. "Well, our little carouse was great fun, was it not?" He grinned suddenly, exposing snaggled eyeteeth. "I cannot blame you, Milord, if your recollection was dimmed by all the ale we guzzled. Those peasant weddings are a rout, 'tis ever true"—he rolled his eyes ceilingward—"especially when the brides are young and innocent, and greatly in awe of their noble masters. Eh, Sire?"

Conan deepened his scowl and grunted again non-committally while darting a distracted glance around the balcony. The youth's braying was attracting interested stares from other idlers, some of whom were now drifting toward him, sipping cups of mead. These they had obtained from a kilted, brown-vested servant who bore them on a tray balanced high over his shoulder.

Ralfic, although cowed by Conan's stare, clearly sensed that something was out of joint. The cornered Cimmerian searched for a quick means of escape, knowing that, were he trapped into speaking a single word of Nemedian, his inept masquerade would collapse all the faster.

"Remember that young lieutenant we thrashed, sire . . . what was his name? Arnulf? The one we diced with all night, who would not pay his bet?"

Desperate now, Conan was clenching a hamlike fist with which to brain Ralfic when the serving-man

97

interrupted them. "Milord Favian! Your pardon, sire." He handed the startled Cimmerian a cup of yellow mead, then spun and departed, his tray empty under his arm.

"Aha, a wise lackey, to give his last cup to the noblest lord in attendance!" Ralfic crowed loudly enough at his own jest to draw nods and laughter from those nearby.

Thirsty as he was, Conan saw a better use for the drink. "Mmm. Uh." Raising a hand to his face, he grimaced, clumsily feigned illness. Then he thrust the sloshing cup into Ralfic's hand and quickly turned away.

"Why, thank you, sire," Conan heard the yokel saying as he fled. "A toast to you, Lord Favian. Purge your stomach in good health, sir!"

Conan was at the door of the blessedly dark, silent side-chamber when a hoarse scream rasped out from behind him. Tempted for just an instant to ignore it and make good his escape, he nevertheless turned back toward the mezzanine. This time, as he shoved his way back among the gawkers he remembered to flick down his visor.

There lay Ralfic against the wooden rail, clutching his belly. His mead-cup was shattered beside him, and bloody froth drooled from his gaping mouth. Where the dregs of his drink had fallen, they smoked and seethed on the polished wood floor.

Other guests bent over the dying farm-squire, and guards were shoving past frightened revelers toward the spot. Without waiting for them to arrive, Conan charged in the direction the poisoner had taken. He followed jabbing fingers and excited cries toward a passage near the head of the main stair, certain that he glimpsed the treacherous servant's brown vest disappearing into it. By the time he had pelted down the corridor, striding heavily in his armor, other guards could be heard clattering some distance behind him.

He knew the Manse well enough by now to guess in which direction the assassin had fled. Veering through an archway near the end of the passage, he dashed down a straight flight of steps, taking four at a time. Somewhere in the silent halls ahead of him there sounded footfalls, hushed voices and a low moan.

When Conan rounded a corner into the main corridor, he found the end of his chase. The poisoner lay dead, a dagger standing out sharply from his brown vest. Over him bulked Svoretta, wiping blood from his plump hand with a kerchief.

The chief of espionage stared keenly at Conan for a moment, as if trying to pierce the faceless steel helm with his gaze. "Well, Lord Favian—we know your true provenance better, of course, but I shall call you by that name for security's sake." The plump retainer glanced quickly up and down the corridor. "What you are doing here I know not, in view of your orders. But stand ready; your work may well begin tonight!"

Two guards came lumbering into the passage, and Svoretta at once demanded a report from them. When they told him of the poisoning and of Ralfic's death, he nodded knowingly with a sidelong glance at Conan.

A moment later there sounded new, hasty footsteps,

and other men appeared: Baron Baldomer himself, looking wildly exultant, and a pair of guards behind him.

Svoretta reported the events to his master. "A known rebel, Milord," he said, nudging the body with his toe. "I happened on him in the corridor, recognized him and slew him. Then I learned that he had already done his evil work in trying to give poison to your son. Luckily, he failed."

"Aye, luckily indeed!" Baldomer gazed on Conan, his healthy eye for once almost as bright as his wounded one. "Come aside with me, boy."

Motioning Conan apart from the Iron Guardsmen, Baldomer addressed him briskly as Svoretta stood by. "You see now how wise I was to hire you, lad! Already you are serving your purpose, flushing our enemies forth. Now go to my son's room and bide there till morning. We shall lodge Favian elsewhere tonight for his safety. But be wary; this night's danger is not ended!"

Nodding curtly to signify his obedience, Conan turned. As he made his way upstairs, he was able to shoulder brusquely past guards and anxious party-goers alike, pretending muteness and deafness to their nods and salutations by virtue of his helmet's lowered visor. All the while, his mind was equally opaque with thought, pondering the assassin's sudden appearance and his equally sudden death.

There was no guard posted near Favian's door to witness Conan's approach, and no one lurked inside the room when he entered. Drink there was, set out in a crystal flask on the ornate table, but after his recent encounter he feared to taste it. And in spite of the lateness of the hour, he did not rest himself on the lordling's broad, soft bed. Instead, he removed his helm and armor, laid them on the cushion to resemble a supine body, and draped them with a satin quilt.

After possessing himself of one of the less decayed pieces of weaponry from Favian's wall, he snuffed out the candles. Unencumbered now by armor and able to move silently across the darkened room, he chose a padded chair on the interior side of the chamber, opposite the window. There he settled down to wait.

Two phantoms hunted through the dark palace halls. Savagely they sprang out of shadows, striking cruelly at one another with blades and flails. In transports of wrath they grappled and rolled across a dim-lit floor, tangled together in lashing dark cloaks. On falling into a stray beam of moonlight, they glared upward suddenly to reveal . . . not human faces, but the drooling , ravening jaws and bloodstruck eyes of wolves.

A dream. Nothing more than a sodden, fevered dream, Conan slowly came to understand. His reaction to it as he dozed had not reflected the intense, terror-stricken feelings it had inspired, he realized. For his chin still lay heavily on his chest, scarcely supported by his slack neck muscles. His nether limbs were still piled against the hard angles of the chair, cramped and chilled in the posture of unintended sleep. He pried open his reluctant eyelids to discover where he was.

Suddenly then he came alive, his heart lurching, wakefulness jolting through every limb, although he still did not move. For there, outlined against the paleness of the window, was a sinister shape which mirrored the skulking figures of his dream: hooded and silent, gliding slowly through the nighted room, an undeniably real menace, creeping slowly nearer. He watched it loom over the vacant sleeping-couch, saw a sharp motion, heard a muffled cry.

He was up then, moving lightly and swiftly on the balls of his feet. His weapon abandoned, he flung himself on the nameless creeper, bare hands poised to crush and rend. His victim sagged with a gasp before his onslaught, arms flailing, offering little resistance. Conan saw no sign of a blade, yet could not be sure because of the thick garment muffling the intruder.

Forcing the other's body down beneath his overmastering weight, he made a swift, groping inventory through the folds of the cloak. The only weapons he found were the age-old ones of womankind: soft breasts, silky tresses of hair, smoothly curving belly and thighs. Cursing under his breath, he dragged his writhing bundle toward the window and turned the pale face up to a beam of moonlight. It was Calissa, the baron's supple daughter, clad in her dark robe, the cowl raised.

He shifted her leaning weight as if to set her upright, then thought better of it. Clamping a hand to her chin, he whispered into a delicate ear, "In case there is any doubt, Milady . . . I am not your brother." He waited for her reaction, but as there came only a passive flexing of her limbs, he spoke on. "If you set up a howl, I shall have to muzzle you. I mean you no harm, but I would rather not be denounced as a ravisher of noblewomen." Experimentally he loosened his hand, letting her head turn slowly to face him. Her motions had a strange, deliberate calm. He asked, "Can you hold your peace and listen to reason a moment, before rousing the whole Manse?"

She gazed up at him unanswering, but with seeming composure in her symmetrical features. Firmly he brought her to her feet, loosening his grip on her lithe limbs.

Her response startled him. Instead of drawing away, she eased up against him, her face softly brushing the side of his neck.

"Whoa, girl, what do you mean by this?" Nervously he brushed her creeping hands once again, checking for weapons. Satisfied that her probing fingers were innocent of any but amorous intent, he let his own touch roam across her softly flexing shoulders and lissome back. In a moment his mouth turned to greet hers.

Her embrace grew warmer, her lips more questing; they opened to his, promising him everything without uttering a word. Yet a corner of his mind still nagged uncertainly at him, and at length he broke off the kiss. "You are . . . companionable tonight," he muttered, slightly breathless. "Who were you expecting to find in that bed, anyway?"

He felt her back stiffen slightly; she ceased her embraces and drew far enough away to regard his face in the faint light. Her voice came forth smoothly, with surprising calm. "You presume much, bodyguard! A shame to let your suspicion stifle your passion . . . but I will answer, if you insist.

"I came here to have an intimate conference with my brother; instead, I found a cold, armored shape in his bed—and behind the visor of his helm, no face!"

Her level, cultivated accents stumbled slightly at the recollection. "And then you, falling on me like a fiend from the shadows . . . ! Still, I know that you have not done away with Favian. I wondered before at your presence among us, but now I understand why a wild creature such as you has been brought to the Manse."

"Because of my fitness for a certain role, you mean." Conan glanced to the room's rear door, left ajar by Calissa. "That role may not be finished for the night. We should not dawdle near your brother's bed. One of us—he or I, I am not sure of which—is a lodestone for an assassin."

"My chamber would be more comfortable," she told him, laying a hand on his arm.

Her room was almost adjacent to Favian's, lying across a narrow passage in the false rear wall. The door had a good chaste bolt to seal it from within; when they had locked it, her moonlit sleeping-couch provided them a comfortable place for repose more satisfying than sleep.

"So you knew of the poisoning tonight?" Conan asked his hostess at length.

"Yes. Although I did not understand how it could be an attempt on my brother's life when, at the very same moment, he was partaking of less potent mead on the dais beside me."

"The cup was meant for me." Conan shook his head impatiently, as if to sweep webs of treachery aside from his vision. "Then, to hide his plan, Svoretta killed the killer."

"Are you suddenly so important to the workings of this palace, bodyguard?" Calissa's purring voice held, along with skepticism, a note of wistful jealousy, Conan intuited.

"Nay . . . only an irritant to Svoretta." His voice probed slowly through the dimness as he worked out his notions: "By killing me, the spymaster persuades Baldomer of the rebels' power, and so enhances his own. Even in failure, his ploy served that purpose."

"That could be true." It was Calissa's turn to shake her head gloomily. "Svoretta has been the guiding force here ever since my father's war wounds nearly killed him, changing him so much. The spymaster leads the strongest faction at court, and his clandestine powers are even greater. Now, with snake-cult stirrings added to the rebel ferment, he will accrue more of a following."

"Lothian, for one, opposes him."

"Aye, Lothian!" Calissa laughed cynically. "Our harmless, maundering, childhood tutor. Why, only tonight my father threatened to clap him into irons for daring to counsel restraint in moving against the rebels. Another delight of this evening's entertainment!"

"I'm glad I missed it . . . I wish had missed more of it," Conan amended himself.

"Oh, Conan. But it was a splendid evening, truly, in spite of all the intrigues." In a gush of enthusiasm, Calissa seized his reclining shoulder with an eager hand. "It was like my childhood days, when the Manse was surrounded by gardens and alive with the best bards and dancers. Every night there was a feast. Merchants and squires dealt freely here then, not just scowling men-at-arms! The land was happier, too."

Deciding to ignore her slight to men-at-arms Conan urged Calissa on. "That was when the Lady Heldra was alive?"

"Aye." She nodded sadly. "Long ago. Even Favian is too young to remember it well. Things have changed so since then. My father. . . ." Her voice trailed off.

"The baron was not so harsh a ruler aforetimes?" Conan asked.

"No, he was a fair-haired knight, a hero. And Mother was like a sylph, teasing him out of his deepest glooms. Oh, she was not weak; they matched each other at javelins and rode together to the hunt. But in her woman's way she brought a warmth to the house and to this whole realm. Her death was a great loss, a great crime. . . ." Calissa paused again. "If she had lived, I would be a better woman."

"And yet your family is a long line of fierce warriors, hardened to death and suffering, is it not?"

"Yes, so it is said. That old legendry stands us in good stead from time to time, when it is needed to muster the peasants out to fight. Nemedia is a turbulent land, with barons who wax surly and greedy. Unlike some provinces, Dinander is not safely hedged by mountains and rivers." She shook her head, drawing her long hair across her shoulders; the red of her tresses was so deep that it seemed black in the dimness, its color visible only where moonlight brushed its soft waves. "Still," she went on, "any good ruler would rather live at peace. To my father, this heritage of blood and steel has become an obsession, I fear."

106

"And with it, the mystic guardianship of the Einharson forebears?" Conan asked.

"Fah, superstitious nonsense!" Calissa's eyes flared at him from beneath her tent of moon-burnished hair. "I care nothing for that! I hope Favian will forget that rigamarole too, once he becomes baron. I can help him rule wisely; I have ideas for improving trade in the province, and for tithing the landholders more equitably—things my father would never consider, because they swerve from tradition. As a female, my voice in matters of state is ignored; they do not even intend to include me in tomorrow's provincial tour! But through Favian, I will have some influence."

"And so you creep to your brother's bed to counsel him privily by night." Conan stroked the noble maid, who had stretched out alongside him in her restlessness. "A wonder that you dare to. He strikes me as a turbulent fellow, more engrossed in his drinking and raping than in good government."

She flashed an irritated glance at him, but then nodded reluctantly, even wistfully. "Aye, 'tis true, we are not so close as we once were. As Favian approaches his majority, he tries out more and wilder excesses. As I do, too. But all of it is mere bridling at our father's overharsh control of us!" She adjusted her position on the cushion, propping her fists beneath her chin before speaking further.

"If Baldomer would just accept Favian and reassure him, and let him take on the trappings of power a little at a time. But try as he might, Favian never could please father. Now, I fear, he has given up entirely." Calissa stretched beneath the soothing pres-

107

sure of Conan's hands on her robed back and laughed softly, with a note of sadness. "Strange, the great baron treasures his son and heir above all else, and launches elaborate schemes for his protection, yet he treats him with contempt, never showing him the least hint of fatherly love."

"Be that as it may," Conan muttered, "if I am any judge, Dinander is in for a wild ride once Favian's hand wields the whip."

"Bodyguard, you are a mere savage. And a youth at that, with no understanding of rulership." Calissa spoke chidingly, yet she lay still under his caressing hands. "It is in a great lord's nature to behave . . . erratically, because of the pressures and prerogatives of his office. How can anyone be expected to use power ably if she or he never tests its extremes, even those extremes that command the life and death of one's followers?"

Her words, he noted, were occasionally interrupted by little purrs of satisfaction at his continuing massage. Even so, she spoke on casually of worldly matters. "You will be surprised, no doubt, to hear that some of the most righteous and well-loved rulers are also the most eccentric, even licentious, of men. Of these, our own King Laslo in Belverus looms foremost, with a harem of varicolored and variously sexed slaves for his amusement. Few of us highborn folk are free of these foibles, as you will learn. Few of us are easy in mind.

"By contrast with some others, my brother's carousings and philanderings are mild. Besides, young women of almost any rank seek him out first. He is comely"—she twisted her slim back to gaze up at Conan—"even as you are."

"Aye, no doubt you like my mein." Conan's fingers reached forth to brush aside dark strands of hair from Calissa's eyes. "How much of your liking, I wonder, is due to my likeness to him?"

"Careful, bodyguard! Even you can push matters too far. But now this idle gossip should cease." She rolled over on the couch. "And here, this smothering cloak impeded us before. Off with it!"

Calissa arched her back, squirmed out of her enfolding robe and tossed it to the floor. As she did so a wondrous, moonlit landscape opened before Conan's eyes.

CHAPTER 7
Favian's Ride

"Yonder lies Edram Castle, in the meanders of the Urlaub River." Durwald, the marshal, sitting straight in his saddle, slowed his horse to pass the word to those riding in the chariot close behind him. "We should easily be there by sunset."

"Yes, sire, thank Einhar!" Shaking the reins, Swinn, the charioteer, ran his team up along the high bank of the road to improve his view of the valley. "At least the hills and haunted fells are behind us, with their accursed rocky goat-paths!"

Conan, grasping the bronze rail to steady himself, stood up from his seat on the leather-padded plank athwart the chariot. Looking over Swinn's rounded shoulder and across the rumps of the horses, he saw the structure that Durwald referred to: a low, broad water-castle at the center of the valley below.

Built of yellow stone, it was laid out as five interlinked round towers topped by conical roofs, and enclosing a central courtyard. It stood on the opposite bank of the Urlaub, in a sharp bend of the blue, snaking river. Its position commanded the waterway on three sides; it also controlled a triple-arched stone bridge that spanned the river almost under the shadow of its turrets.

A strong keep for a rural squire, Conan decided. And a rich one, judging by the lush green farm fields on either side of the river and the dense sprawl of cottages just before the bridge. It would be a long way upstream to the first river ford, he guessed, so whoever held Edram Castle held a stranglehold on the valley and a reliable source of tariffs and tolls.

The place was not far ahead by the road, which dropped swiftly from its present crest to wind through sparse-forested foothills and out into the level valley. At the very least, the castle promised a more comfortable sleeping-place than the drafty hill-cavern of the previous night, with its starlit serenade of owls and wolves among the crags and its long, weary watches against the threat of brigands.

Not that the nobles, with forty of Baldomer's picked horsemen formed up behind them, had much to fear from robbers or rebels. Assassination was the baron's pet worry—concerned as he was not so much with his own life as with that of his son. Among the cavalry rode Favian in the guise of a common trooper, surly and aloof from his fellows and scarcely heeding his nominal officers. Ahead of the horsemen rolled the chariot driven by Swinn, Conan idling within and garbed in the lordling's armor. In the vanguard rode Baldomer, black-clad astride his white stallion, with

Durwald and two other officers keeping him close company. Svoretta was absent, having remained behind in Dinander to twitch the ropes of rulership in the baron's absence.

"Here, Swinn, move aside!" As the chariot lurched forward, the castle was lost from view behind tree-clad foothills, and Conan gruffly addressed the charioteer: "Let me drive the beasts for a change. I've watched you do it these past ten leagues; it can't be difficult." Reluctant to rest his aching nether parts on the jolting bench again, he pressed toward the front of the rattling platform to displace the driver.

"Nay, barbarian!" With a flick of the reins, Swinn changed the chariot's motion suddenly, causing the northerner to stagger back to his seat. "I may have to bow and scrape to you when the crowds are watching, but not here! Anyway, driving these battle-cars is a touchy skill. And a noble one, at that."

Conan grunted ill-naturedly and started to arise again, but he thought better of it as the road began to drop steeply down a rocky hill and into a narrow, grassy glen. "If cart-driving is so noble a pastime, why do all the nobles hereabouts prefer to lounge on horseback?"

Swinn laughed. "Lord Favian himself would rather be here in my place. He is the expert charioteer in the royal family. Why do you think he is so ill-tempered of late?" He tossed a glance backward at the formation of cavalry behind them, with the princeling riding stiffly out of earshot. "Having you go as a passenger in his stead will make him seem a dolt to his future subjects."

"Well then, we can try to please him better." The road had leveled again, and Conan now felt safe in standing. "I will learn horse-chasing someday; it may as well be now!" He made a grab for the reins, jostling the stocky charioteer to one side.

"Here, now, barbarian . . . aah . . . ugh!" Resisting Conan's shove, Swinn jerked suddenly rigid, then sprawled against his surprised passenger. Looking past the charioteer's shoulder, Conan saw that a long arrowshaft had driven deeply into the man's back, piercing the black steel armor as though it were parchment. As he watched, astonished, another shaft struck the charioteer's rigid body from the opposite direction; it had sufficient force to pass through both breastplate and breast, dinting Swinn's scapular plate outward with its point. Other projectiles were thudding into the wood of the chariot or clattering against the metalwork. One of them smote the back of Conan's helm, rattling it against his skull and causing white starbursts to bloom before his eyes.

A little way down the road a horse screamed and toppled: Durwald's. The chariot lurched and bounded as its team left the road to avoid Baldomer's stallion, which was staggering aside, an arrow standing out from its splendid white neck. Shouts and screams sounded before and behind the car as shafts rained out of the brushy woods that fringed the clearing. Belatedly a cavalry officer began rasping orders to the milling horsemen in the rear.

Conan was encumbered by the body of the charioteer, whose eyes were already glazing over. Letting Swinn slump heavily to the floor, he jerked back the reins in an effort to control the horses. Frightened, they reared and jostled backward, tilting the chariot up sharply and almost spilling Conan out among the wildflowers and fieldstones of the glen. Clinging to the rail, he let go the reins, nearly falling to his knees as each of the three horses tried to bolt in a different direction.

Then a hand steadied his shoulder and a voice rang in his ear. "Get your feet under you, if you want to ride! I'll soon have these brutes in order." It was Favian, capable-looking in his plain black cuirass and uncrested helm, who had leaped from his mount onto the platform. After kicking out the riding-bench, and Swinn's body after it, he groped among the horses' lashing tails to find the reins.

"Here now! Hang on tight and give me room!" The leather straps suddenly came alive in Favian's hands. With the horses surging forward as one, the chariot bounded across the road and into the meadow on the far side.

Conan stood gripping the rail, his knees bent to absorb the ever-increasing shocks of the wheels. He had assumed that the lordling would turn back up the road to flee the ambush, but he saw with alarm that they were rolling instead straight toward the brushy forest margin whence the arrow-fire was heaviest. As he stared, a shaft flew out of the foliage at him, swishing between the heads of horses and riders alike, almost tickling them with its feather fletching.

"Thank your northern snow-sprites for the jouncing of this wagon," Favian declared. "It makes us a trickier target!"

Conan said nothing, instead unclenching one hand from the rail to grasp the sword at his waist.

"Nay, nay, you fool, not the saber! The javelin!" Urging the horses to greater speed, Favian shouted exuberantly at his passenger: "That is a one-handed weapon with the range you'll need. Aye, there you are!" he added as Conan reached behind him, where the short spears were butted upright in quivers at the chariot's sides. The Cimmerian hefted one of them and braced another ready in the hand that still clutched the rail.

"All right, man! Now duck low!" Instead of wheeling the rumbling vehicle around to halt before the trees, as Conan expected he would, Favian astonished his passenger by continuing straight ahead into the brushy woods. The sunlit wave of green lashed into the Cimmerian's face, sliding across the defensively raised shaft of his javelin. Abruptly then, tall trunks and shadows loomed on all sides, sheltering cloaked figures who fled left and right before the plunging horses.

One of the dim figures wheeled, raising his longbow to speed an arrow at the chariot. Reflexively Conan's arm lashed out, and his javelin flew, piercing the man's unarmored chest. The ambusher crumpled and fell aside, the Cimmerian never noticing where the arrow went.

"Hiee, you have the knack!" Favian's shout was wild as he veered his team around a looming tree trunk. "I shall hunt them out and you shall slay them! There's one!"

Conan readied another spear, but it was not

needed, for the fleeing man tripped on a fallen branch a dozen paces ahead of the horses. In an instant the animals were on top of him, stamping his body deep into the forest loam. Conan felt a sickeningly soft impact as the metal-clad wheel passed over the victim.

"Hee-yaa, another dead! They are scattering, the cowardly traitors! But be careful here." Favian crouched low and Conan sprawled helplessly against the rail as the chariot bounced over a fallen trunk bulking almost as high as the tall wheel hub. Then followed more giddy lurches and dips; the horses were plunging through a tangle of brush and downed trees, making it hard for Conan to regain his feet. The last impact was over human bodies, to the accompaniment of screams, as Favian ran his chariot over two more cloaked forms huddling behind the windfall.

Then, gathering speed, they were out among widely spaced tree trunks again; even so, Conan frequently found it necessary to duck under lashing foliage. Hearing shouts and hoofbeats from behind, he risked a glance backward to see that Baldomer's horsemen were entering the forest, riding down other ambushers. Yet the riders themselves were vulnerable; as Conan watched, one took an arrow in the throat and two more were knocked from their saddles by low-hanging limbs.

"Fear not, the glory will be ours!" Favian gave his full attention to the glade ahead. "A chariot can go places a horseman would never dare, because it is so much lower to the ground!"

So saying, he lashed his team down a tangled,

tortuous rabbit trail in pursuit of a pair of fleeing ambushers. Conan clutched the rail and crouched low as the horses strained and surged before him, their tails close to flicking him in the face. Under Favian's demonic guidance, the wheeled platform seemed to spend more time in the air than it did on the ground, caroming past man-sized trunks and bounding over massive roots, threatening at each jolt to catapult its passengers high into the treetops.

"Hiee, that's it! Turn and fight, you skulking coward!" Favian bore down on one of the fugitives, who had stopped between two trees to aim an arrow at his pursuers. But the jolting chariot was an unstable target and the shaft went wide. The lordling, in his turn, slewed the battle-car close under the trees to give Conan a clear stab.

The javelin took the man in the armpit as he turned to run. Conan did not intend to relinquish the spear, for his others had been lost in the wild chase, and so he held on to it, dragging his victim a dozen paces through the forest before the weapon pulled free of the body. Then he raised it to face his last quarry.

This one had gained the top of an ancient, fallen log too high for even the baron's son to surmount. The hooded figure held no bow and gazed back for only an instant before vanishing on the far side. From that glimpse, Conan gained a strange conviction; he felt it as a pang deep in his stomach. The oval face coldly regarding him had been that of a female.

"Damned rebel snake-kisser! I'll have your head yet!" Favian, still hot in pursuit, drove his team on a long detour around the upended roots of the great tree. There he halted, cursing, at the brush-choked bank of a stream that splashed among boulders at the floor of the forested ravine. Conan stepped down from the platform and walked to the torrent's brink. There was no sign of the woman; the talking of the water masked any sound of her flight.

As he returned to the chariot and helped Favian attend to the half-dead, frothing horses, gruff voices and the cracking of twigs heralded the arrival of mounted troopers. They came at a walk, winding through the trees with no great urgency other than that raised by the visible agitation of their leader, Baron Baldomer, who sat astride a common soldier's horse.

"Favian! Here he is! Come on, men, this way," he cried with a wave of his arm. "Boy, what do you mean by chasing away so far afield?"

"Father, we were slaying rebels—" the lordling began.

"Well, I will not have it! You yourself might have been slain, and the royal line of Dinander cut short!" The baron jerked his horse aside in irritation, halting the animal before the chariot. "Henceforth stay at my beck and call."

Marshal Durwald, also riding a commandeered mount, reined up close behind him. "It was a respectable feat of charioteering just to get here, Milord! After all, the young lord did scatter the rebels, and he dispatched quite a number of them along the way."

"Aye. This barbarian shows an able hand with the javelin." Baldomer nodded in grudging respect. "No doubt you did the driving, Favian? I thought as much." He frowned, shaking his head. "Well, someday you must learn to be a true commander and lead your troops honorably, from the back of a fine steed."

Making no answer to his father, Favian went to fill his helmet with stream water for the horses. But as the lordling turned away, Conan saw that his features were distorted in anger, and wet with unmanly tears.

Meanwhile, a lesser officer came riding up through the trees to make his report to the baron. "Eleven rebels dead, sire. None left alive for questioning, sad to say. We think that five or six others may have escaped, but it will be dangerous to track them in this forest."

"Nay, there is no need. Squire Ulf knows the district and will tell us how best to strike at them." Baldomer turned to Durwald. "These were a desperate lot. Likely these were the snake-cultists we have heard tell of, judging by their hoods. Wouldn't you say?"

The marshal nodded uncertainly, watching the baron as if to gauge the risk of frankness. "'Tis hard to tell, indeed, Milord. The cloaks were obviously meant to hide their identity. But the few heads we now have may lead us to more in coming days." He raised a hand to tug his mustache. "I saw no sign of cult fetishes or distinctive markings among the dead rebels."

"They were brigands of the worst stripe, 'tis clear, since they shot our horses!" Baldomer shook his head in righteous wrath, his scarred eye glinting fiendishly. "The swine will pay for their murder of those fine, costly animals!"

"Indeed, sire. They were not simple thieves, or they would have spared the horses."

"Ah well, there is no telling what incites these turbulent types to revolt and take up heinous religions." Baldomer wheeled his horse impatiently. "But come, let us get back to the road and on our way. Drive this wagon out of here if you can, Favian; follow us closely. Squire Ulf will be able to tell us more about these rebels once we reach Edram Castle."

CHAPTER 8
River of Blood

"And so you see, it was a costly skirmish on both sides." Baldomer paused in his account to sip wine from a silver goblet. "We lost a dozen of our troops and some of our best horses to their first arrow-flight. Yet in turn we routed the ambushers and slew most of them. Even my son, in his disguise as a commoner, took some small part in the fray." The baron spared a glance across the littered board toward Favian, who sat within an arched window of the circular dining hall.

The lordling, resting taciturn with one foot propped before him on the brick sill, did not return the look, nor did he make reply. Nursing his wine-cup, the young aristocrat continued gazing out across the slow-rolling river. He cut a dashing figure even in the office of a common cavalryman.

His double, Conan, sat easily at the broad oaken

table, tearing at the remains of a roasted boar the others had long since lost interest in. The Cimmerian had recently accomplished a brief, stiff masquerade before the rural populace. He had passed from his chariot through Edram Castle's yard and up into the keep, suffering no further attempts on his life. Now he remained with the nobles, decked in his borrowed armor but with no pretense at nobility.

Their host, the rotund Squire Ulf, shifted his leather-armored body in his capacious chair to face Baldomer. "Aye, Milord, your grave inconvenience is a sorrow to me. 'Tis a shame, I fear, to this entire district. Would that my men and I had ridden forth earlier and met your party higher in the hills. Would that I myself had taken the arrow that slew your noble steed!" He clutched the flesh of his broad belly as if it had been pierced by a clothyard shaft. "But the infamy is done. I promise to initiate harsh measures against the rebels at once!"

"We might assist you in that," Baldomer said, with a glance aside at Marshal Durwald. "You have some idea, I take it, as to a local source of this mutiny?"

"Oh, aye, Milord!" Ulf nodded vigorously, setting his stubbled jowls aquiver. "Heresy and treachery lurk in many quarters these days, especially since the resurgence of the snake-cults; I have more to tell you on that score later." The stout squire shook his long, unwashed blond locks in fervent commiseration with his baron before continuing.

"Even locally there are nests of viperish disloyalty. One village in particular, a mere half-day's ride from here, I have long yearned to chastise myself, even before this latest offense. If you could send part of your elite force to help in the task, Milord, 'twould be most welcome. I can say with some certainty that these miscreants had a hand in the cowardly attack on your party."

"Ah, that is what I like to hear!" The baron nodded approvingly, with another sidelong glance at Durwald. "A plan of action, without posing endless riddles and hypotheses. We would be glad to assist you, Squire."

"Aye, Milord, but we should act carefully." Durwald regarded the fat squire with some doubt. "If you recall, we noticed that the weave of the ambushers' cloaks had the look of city workmanship, perhaps from Dinander or Numalia. It may be that the rebels preceded us here from the west."

"Aye, but undoubtedly they had local support —else why did they not fall on us deep in the hills? And where did they flee?" Baldomer shook his head, a frown setting his mouth askew. "Nay, Marshal, there are times when it is best simply to act, swiftly and decisively, with no hint of hesitation."

He swiveled his vulpine gaze back to Ulf. "I shall send a score of horse-troopers to aid you, Squire. My son, Favian, shall lead them—properly this time, in the uniform of a cavalry officer, with a keen blade in his hand and a strong mount between his legs. You will ride along, Durwald, to oversee the boy. Take the barbarian, of course, to make sure no harm comes to my heir."

"Aye, Baron," Durwald said resignedly.

"Thank you, sirs!" Squire Ulf bowed unctuously, his small eyes calculating swiftly. "We should dispatch the troops before dawn tomorrow. I myself will abide with you here at the castle, so as to ensure your safety and comfort."

Baldomer nodded magnanimously and surveyed the room. If he expected his son to thank him for the boon of a cavalry command, he was disappointed. Favian only glanced briefly at them all with a look of disinterest, then returned his gaze to the river.

After a moment of awkward silence, Durwald spoke. "You said you had further information, Squire, on the activities of the snake-cult?"

"Better than that," Ulf gloated. "I have a captive!" He clasped his hands together, savoring the others' earnest attention. "Recently I sent a party of tax-gatherers eastward to Varakiel to collect overdue shares from a balky landholder. They found his tracts abandoned and his croft aflame, with no sign of the serf-master himself. But in the forest nearby they spied the marauding rebels, and captured one. A devout snake-worshiper by any measure, though perhaps caught up only recently in the hysteria."

"And where is this prisoner?" The baron rose from his seat, restless for action. "How soon can we see him?"

"This very moment, if you like, Lord Baldomer. We kept him alive especially for you." With a grunt of effort, Squire Ulf hove himself up from his seat. "Though I warn you, he has not proven cooperative; the power of Set is strong within him. Both water and fire have been applied, and each has failed to drive the devils out."

"I hope you have left enough of him for us to question," Durwald muttered. He rose to follow his baron and Squire Ulf toward a side door of the dining hall. Conan went too, taking with him a couple of ripe quinces from a fruit bowl on the table. Behind him, Favian left his window seat to trail along after them.

The hall opened onto a broad parapet stretching between two of the castle's five towers. The sun shone bright on yellow bricks fretted with the black, angular shadow of the battlement. The sky was clear blue, dotted with white puffs of cloud driven before a fresh breeze; beyond the river stretched fields of emerald green, with the yellow thatches of the town huddled at the bridgehead.

Ulf led them past a large, wheeled ballista, one of several standing ready to sink riverborne boats or drive attackers from the bridge. Waddling past racks of stones and tar pots kept nearby as ammunition, the stout squire approached the next tower. He halted before a pair of sentries standing rigid at each side a bolted, metal-clad door.

"We use the north tower as a guardhouse," Ulf explained to his guests while undoing the latch. "The foundations of Edram Castle are too wet from river floods to provide us a livable dungeon. But I think you will find these facilities well-equipped."

He pushed the door inward on its grating hinge-post and ushered them into a room that felt warm with the heat of a brazier. Shards of daylight fell in through arrow-slits in the walls. Stable harnesses and metalworking implements, incongruous here in the guard tower, arrayed the curving walls; other devices of obscure function littered the floor.

At the room's center hung a great spoked wheel, suspended at an angle by a chain from the ceiling; lashed to it, spread-eagled, was a half-conscious peasant youth. Where his rough garb had been cut or torn away, his skin bore marks of scalding, charring and other abuses. His wan boyish face stared upward with a fixed expression, unresponsive to the men's arrival.

"He makes no utterances except that of weird curses," the squire explained. "Yet when he had strength, he fought like a very fiend." He waved a hand invitingly over the brazier of fluttering pink-and-gray ashes. "Here, Milord, try your skill with the hot pincers. Mayhap you will have more success than we did."

The baron ignored Ulf, eying the captive with skepticism and evident disappointment. "A mere child! Not a very formidable rebel."

"Have him say '*Kaa nama kaa lajerama*,'" Favian remarked from the doorway. "No follower of the snake-god can utter those words and live."

Marshal Durwald leaned over the prisoner, swiftly assuming the experienced interrogator's role of a succoring friend. "Come, lad, do not fear! I am not here to hurt you." He pinched the boy's cheeks together so as to force open his jaws, and peered inside. Abruptly he released him, and wheeled upon Ulf in outrage. "Here now, how is he supposed to tell us anything? Some fool has disfigured his mouth!"

"Nay, nay, that is part of the snake-cult ritual!" Shaking his head anxiously, the squire seized an unheated pair of tongs from the wall and leaned over his captive. "They slit their own tongues, so they can utter the sacred syllables of Set." He delved into the slack mouth for the tongue, but instantly jumped back and dropped his tongs as the victim came snarling to life at the intrusion.

"*Hathassa fa Sathan!*" the pale face spat at them. "*Sa setha efanissa, na!*" As the peasant lad cursed, the watchers gained eerie glimpses of his forked tongue, lashing like that of a serpent. Though the voice rasped with startling vehemence at first, the blaze in the pale eyes swiftly faded. The head thumped back weakly on the wooden spokes, and the slim body sagged even lower in its bonds.

"What did he say?" Baldomer asked, gazing around at the others' blank looks. "Does anyone know the language?"

"'Tis no local dialect, Milord. Nor even a human one, I would guess." Ulf shrugged. "I do not know his meaning, but I know one thing: I shall check my boots carefully for vipers in the morning!"

Conan, lingering near the half-open door, had long since lost the appetite for his second quince; now he set it aside on a charred table. He pressed forward behind Favian, a little surprised at the anger tapping in his temples and not sure of just what action it boded. Memories of the lockup in Dinander were rankling at him, renewed by the unmanly doings before him in this smoky cell.

But one glance at the prisoner showed that there was no point in intervening. The last remnant of life had quit the emaciated serf, whose eyes now glared sightlessly upward. Feeling soiled and somewhat queasy, Conan turned and made his way out onto the sun-bright battlement.

The next morning a double chain of horsemen rode abreast across the meadows of the Urlaub Valley. They did not follow the river upstream, for it meandered too widely to mark a sensible route. Nor did they use any road, for their ride had detoured in the first hour after dawn to the fringe of a forest tract. There they gathered twigs and bound them together into faggots, which they tied in bunches behind their saddles.

Conan, by virtue of his noble armor, was exempt from carrying wood, as were the officers. He rode in his cavalry officer's equipage with Durwald and Lord Favian, near the center of the line. The two less-aristocratic riders flanked the young lord to protect him, and Favian in turn was sullen, so there was little conversation.

But the lordling made a show of commanding the others, frequently ordering a brisker pace and savagely rebuking any trooper who failed to stay in line. The twenty cavalry supplied by Baldomer were better at maintaining their ranks than were Ulf's men; these struck Conan as lax and surly, especially the weasel-faced guide who rode beside Durwald.

As the morning sun angled toward noon over the hazy eastern plain, the cow pastures beneath the horses' hooves changed to lush grainfields. A curving line of trees and brush ahead signaled the position of the river. One of the Dinander cavalry, a farmer by origin, voiced dismay at the broad swath of rich oats they were trampling down. At this sentiment the others laughed and hooted.

Harshly, Favian commanded them to silence. But it mattered little; a moment later, at murmured instructions from Durwald and the guide, the lordling called the troop to a halt. He signaled Ulf's men, who

128

carried torches and a firepot, and waited while they set their brands alight. Then he drew his sword and shouted the order to charge.

At first it was impossible to see their goal; the guide reassured the officers at the top of his voice that it lay straight ahead. Conan let his horse dash forward on faith with the others, concentrating on keeping his perch in the awkward, bulky saddle.

The drumming of the hooves was muffled by soft soil and knee-high grain, but there was no real obstacle to their flying advance. The rich fields of river bottomland, lacking hedges and walls, were divided only by low, weedy mounds that flew beneath the horses' swift leaps.

Suddenly, just ahead, roughly clad figures were seen looking up from their labor in the fields at the approaching tumult. The peasants dropped their hoes and fled in panic. Conan, to his surprise, heard the steely whisper of swords being drawn all along the plunging line, amid the baying of vengeful cries. A moment later the unresisting farmers had been cut down or ridden down without so much as a slowing of the horsemen's charge.

Ah well, these Hyborians play rough, Conan told himself. They were even quicker to slay one another than they were to slay strangers, he had observed. He felt relieved that none of the wretches had come before his own steed's churning hooves.

Nevertheless he was in the thick of it, and had better be alert. Having drawn his blade along with the others, he now had to lend more attention to staying astride his plunging steed one-handed.

Soon the riders found themselves among scattered orchard trees and outbuildings. Their formation curved and widened to encompass one flank of the village, which lay ahead on a slightly raised area of ground near the riverside. The surprise of their appearance was total, it appeared, for more frightened figures could be seen ahead scurrying for shelter. The pace of the horses slowed, but their gallop grew rougher and louder on the hard-packed earth.

The center of the column thundered into the main square of the town, with Favian yelling and brandishing his sword in the lead. Conan followed some distance behind, his horse veering to avoid the fallen bodies of villagers cut down by the first wave of attackers. Screams and terror-stricken cries sounded beyond as other peasants were overtaken by horsemen or flushed out of hiding.

Conan knew he had been a fool to expect some sort of baronial proclamation or organized search. This was forthright slaughter, with men, women and children alike tasting the steel. The local squire's troops were particularly zestful at it, even hacking with lusty shouts at tethered, yelping animals. The men of Dinander slew more efficiently, urged on by Favian's shouted commands. Red images of the sack of Venarium flashed before the northerner's eyes, but here the zest was somehow tainted. This wretched place did not even offer the promise of plunder.

Conan would not have imagined that the killing of Nemedians would ever be a source of concern to him; now he felt growing unease. But he did not intend to forfeit his life, either to rebels or to Baldomer's troops. He dismounted from his horse to reduce his jeopardy and led it through the smoky turmoil, telling himself that this was not his fight.

The torches had finally come into play. The green crops in the fields could never have been set alight, but the parched edges of thatched roofs flared brightly at the merest touch of flame. Under Favian's supervision, a handful of troopers was setting the bundled twig fascines alight, forcing open the doors and shuttered windows of the huts and hurling the torches inside. This brought cries of alarm from those still cowering within; any who emerged were cut down by waiting pillagers or flying horsemen. Conan looked in vain for a sign of armed resistance. He decided that this miserable hamlet could hardly be the den of rebel activity that Squire Ulf had described.

Then his attention was caught by something else: a face glimpsed through the gap between two burning huts. In spite of the smoke, it was eerily familiar.

Abandoning his horse, Conan rushed between the buildings, one arm raised to fend off the hot vapors pouring out of the smoldering eaves. Beyond the row of huts he paused, blinking watering eyes, and then spied several figures disappearing into brushy willows near the riverbank. He followed, holding his sword at the ready.

Only a few paces into the brush, a peasant attacked him. The sandaled, jerkined man wielded only a pitchfork, whose wooden tines Conan battered aside with a swipe of his saber. His blade's recoil caught the man at the base of his skull. As his opponent went down, Conan realized that he had used the flat of his sword, likely doing no permanent injury. Still, the fellow did not stir as Conan stepped over him.

A little way beyond, at the swampy river-edge, four more fugitives were struggling with a tiny boat of wood and hides concealed among the reeds. The eldest of them turned to regard him: a fit-seeming woman clad in a familiar-looking cloak, her cowl thrown back to reveal her long-plaited blond hair. It was yesterday's ambusher, he knew—the one who had escaped him in the forest. She was accompanied by three children of the village.

One of them, a gangling, smudge-faced boy, turned from the coracle and started toward Conan, clutching a broken-bladed knife. The woman grabbed the child by the collar of his serf-shirt and dragged him back to her side. "See to the boat," she told him in firm Nemedian accents. She reached to her waist, drew a long, straight dagger and coolly awaited her pursuer.

A new crashing sounded in the brush nearby; Conan turned to see one of Baldomer's troopers, a middle-aged, mustached veteran, leading his horse through the reeds. "Ah, a country lass, and nearly flown the nest! We shall have her to ourselves, eh, fellow? . . . uuh!"

The man staggered back, his horse whinnying in fright, as Conan's saber struck him beneath the ill-fitted lower edge of his breast armor. The veteran raised his weapon valiantly, showing stoic resistance to the pain of his sundered abdomen; but he had lost any chance of survival at Conan's first, speed-blurred attack. The Cimmerian's second stroke, a deft slash to the unarmored back of his leg, made him topple; then a deep, carefully aimed stab through the neck-hole of his cuirass left him lying in the mud, twitching his last. The horse shied back into the brush, rolling its eyes fearfully at the smell of its master's blood.

Conan turned back to the girl, only to see that she and the others had freed their boat and were pushing off into the open channel, out of his vision. "Wait," he started to call, but the word died in his throat. He strode to a place where the brush sprouted thinner and watched the coracle drift out of sight around a stand of trees downstream. Intent on her steering, the woman in the stern did not look back.

He turned his gaze upstream. Along the pebbled shore where slower currents moved, the clear water was clouded by lazy, red tendrils: blood from the massacre of the town. Looking farther up the curving stream-channel, the view was even grimmer; where the water reflected the red leaping flames and smoke-veiled sky, the whole reach of the river seemed to be stained crimson.

Then another feature of the scene caught the Cimmerian's eye, causing him to stand cursing while almost laughing in bitter disbelief. At either side of the river, low wooden docks had been constructed. Each bore a rude windlass, the one on the village side now brightly aflame. Towropes, probably slashed by the invaders, trailed far out into the rolling current, while in the shallows at the foot of the village there floated a wide, flat-bottomed wood boat, staved in and swamped. A ferry it was, one that must have served farmers in this part of the valley. Doubtless it had accounted for the healthy growth of the place, until now.

Muttering darkly, Conan turned from the river and

strode up the bank. As he went, some of the haze of the town's burning seemed to hang before his eyes and tinge his vision redly. He found his way through the weeds and broken sheds near the water's edge, moving toward the cries and fire-roarings of the town.

He paused just once behind a burning cottage; there he dragged one of Squire Ulf's ravagers off of a struggling village girl. He slashed the man's throat with the keenest part of his saber, near the hilt, and left the body in the weeds while the maid scampered away downriver.

Then he strode onward amid smoke and swaggering forms. At the heart of the inferno he found Durwald, still sitting atop his mount, watching Favian hoarsely urge the attackers on. The lordling was telling his troops to heap fresh faggots and debris onto the flaming huts, to make sure they were burned to the ground.

Conan strode to the marshal and glared up at him. "Durwald, I know why we are here!"

The aristocrat gazed down on the Cimmerian and his blood-smeared, restless blade with a melancholy look on his face. His own sword lay ready across the pommel of his saddle.

"A ferry! That was the rebellion Squire Ulf so deplored, the uprising that marked this place for destruction—a wooden boat competing with his bridge and cutting into his tolls and revenues!"

Durwald shook his head in mute annoyance, saying nothing.

"Will you stand for it?" Conan raged at him. "Are you a warrior, or a butcher of innocents?"

The marshal reined his horse away from the shouting Cimmerian, his face betraying no emotion. His eyes were red and streaming, as were the eyes of most of those present, but whether the tears came from the smoke hanging heavy in the air or from bitter shame, none would ever know.

CHAPTER 9
Death's Eager Bride

The city gates of Dinander reared tall on either hand. Built of heavy square timbers bound with black iron straps, they loomed as formidable as the dark stone walls that flanked them. Doubtless they were as efficient at holding unwilling citizens in as they were at keeping invaders out. But today the great doors stood wide, and the main avenue beyond was scattered with townsfolk sporting festive garb in the early afternoon sun. These pressed back swiftly out of the roadway, their faces stiff with respect and habitual fear, as Baron Baldomer Einharson's column of horsemen entered the city.

The baron, riding just behind the four armored cavalry who formed the advance guard, sat imperiously astride a high-stepping sorrel gelding in lieu of his slain stallion. Close after him rolled a chariot carrying Chief Marshal Durwald and driven, as any country lout would openly have declared, by the baron's dashing son, Favian.

But the country lout would have been wrong, for the charioteer was truly a northern barbarian decked in Favian's best armor. Baldomer's real son rode near the head of the main cavalry column, the steel beaver of his helm clamped down across his handsome, mortified features.

The purpose of this double imposture would surely have puzzled the simple-minded countryman. There rode Baldomer, plainly identifiable, a ready target to his ill-wishers. His finely turned and brightly polished armor was scarcely more proof against a skillful bowshot than was the bulky plate of a common cavalryman. Why, then, should he conceal his son's identity, and not his own?

The answer, the simple farmer would have concluded, had more to do with the tortuous, mysterious workings of the noble mind than with plain sense. Aristocracy moves in strange ways, he would have muttered to himself.

And yet Lord Baldomer seemed content—if ever such a tranquil emotion could be read into his craggy, wild-featured face. Sitting straight and tall in his war saddle, he surveyed the sunlit-and-shadowed rows of his subjects. Hampered by the press of watchers, he gradually let his mount fall back alongside the chariot, which was navigating the streets adequately well under the Cimmerian's raw hand. At length Marshal Durwald, speaking from his passenger bench in the rumbling car, addressed the old warrior.

"Word of your early return must have preceded us, Milord, for your subjects to turn out like this." The marshal scanned the lines of citizens thoughtfully, nodding from time to time to a prominent townsman or his rosy-cheeked wife. "Either the courier we sent to Svoretta let it slip or the spymaster made it known through his agents."

"Aye. Would that the chief of espionage were not so shy of public appearances that he could meet us openly at the gate! Even old Lothian would be a welcome source of news." Baldomer kept his face immobile and aloof toward his watchers as he spoke. "Still, 'tis no great harm to be greeted by my subjects. I shall stop in the central square to inform them of the successful provincial tour, and of our decisive stroke against the rebels."

"It might be wise not to make too much of it, Milord," Durwald advised, a bitter smile crossing his face. "It was, after all, a small skirmish, not clearly aimed at any rebel faction."

Baldomer shook his head sharply and deepened his frown. "The death by sword of two of our crack troopers proves a significant military presence. And did your own officers not count the bodies of seventy-eight armed rebel sympathizers, man, woman and child? I call that a formidable victory."

Conan, his attention held by the task of guiding the chariot through the milling crowds, nevertheless gave an ear to the talk. He had been ill-tempered of late, especially today, as the impatient jerking of the reins in his hamlike fists revealed. The press of the street was growing thicker, and he was ever alert for a new ambush or an assassination attempt. The reserve and forced gaiety the Cimmerian sensed in the lines of watchers made him wonder whether the people really celebrated their baron's return, or his absence. For whatever reason, all the folk of the town seemed to be packed into the main street on this day.

To call Baldomer's abbreviated provincial tour a success was a gross lie, or an even grosser delusion, Conan knew. During the week in which their decimated party had lingered at Edram Castle before turning back to Dinander, he had never heard what report the baron had been given of the village massacre. He knew that the luckless river town was no rebel stronghold. And yet he had seen the girl there. . . .

"Remember, sire, we found no lair of snake cultists during our assault." Durwald was still arguing with his obtuse baron. "They are the fastest-growing menace, and the one that should be dealt with promptly."

"True enough, Durwald. Now that I am returned, I shall ready a larger force with which to eradicate them." Baldomer paused in his talk, gazing ahead across his horse's tossing mane into the market square. "But what have we here, a wedding?"

Conan gave close attention to the handling of his team as the crowd widened and the avenue opened out before them. He had already driven the chariot past the Temple School, its marble porticoes lined with young male and female acolytes, and moments ago he had cleared the gray, battlemented municipal barracks, from whose murky grilles the stench of the town's dungeons wafted, especially sour in his memory. Now, just ahead of the procession, lay Dinander's cobbled central plaza.

Here tables heavy with food and drink had been set out, and the loiterers affected even more lavish dress, bright with lace and embroidery. Their activity centered about a spired, broadly arched building: the town's guild-hall.

"'Twould appear to be a marriage in the family of one of the chief artisans," Baldomer said from the saddle. "A goldsmith or jewel-tinker, to judge by this costly outlay."

"Yes, my liege." Durwald leaned near the chariot's trundling wheel to address his master more discreetly. "Now I recall that the banns were recently posted for the marriage of Evadne, daughter of old Arl, the silversmith, to a petty landholder."

"Evadne . . . is she not the one who teaches metalcraft at the priest-school, in defiance of the guilds' ban against females?"

Durwald nodded. "Aye, a headstrong wench."

"Indeed. I think I know what is afoot." Baldomer scanned the plaza grimly from his saddle. "It is an old trick of rich and disloyal families to stage their weddings when their baron is away, and so avoid the exercise of lordly privilege." He turned in his saddle and delivered a curt signal to Favian, leading the main body of cavalry. "Form up, there! You, boys, pull over to the steps," he ordered Conan. "'Twould be unmannerly not to stop and pay our respects at this celebration. Remember, you are my son."

Conan swung the chariot toward the steps of the guild-hall, scattering nervous watchers and toppling a decorative flower stand along the way with his brisk, inexpert handling of the team. Favian, as his cavalrymen clattered past on either hand to form a protective cordon, grumbled a curse at the Cimmerian for this display of poor driving in his name.

Conan, biting back an angry retort, stepped down from the platform and awaited Baldomer. To his surprise, the baron did not dismount, but spurred his steed straight up the low steps toward the building's stately entrance.

Conan strode after the horse's flicking red-brown tail as it passed through the high, intricately sculptured archway; his careless ill-temper, he realized, probably lent him a convincingly noble bearing. Durwald and Favian followed close behind, the latter leaving the visor of his cavalry helm down.

The interior of the guild-hall waited cavernous and dark, with a nest of bright candlelit hues at the depressed center of its floor, where the ceremony was underway. Those gathered in the gallery evinced a short, astonished silence at the baron's clopping invasion, before the obligatory bows rippled through the assembly. These were halfhearted, with some of the celebrants even risking disgruntled whispers to their neighbors or stiff-necked stares at the mounted lord. Others gazed at him with no evident emotion but fear.

The focus of the room's attention was, or had been, the brightly gowned man and woman at its center. They knelt facing one another, undergoing a marriage ritual danced by a garlanded priestess in tribute to the local harvest goddess, Ulla. Now, whether at the baron's intrusion or at the completion of the ceremony, the couple turned to face the warlord. The young, boyishly handsome groom's bearing toward his feudal lord was proud and a little resentful, Conan could see. The woman, although her face was thickly veiled in gem-sparkling lace, showed an impressive, calm resolution as she rose to her feet.

For some reason her bearing held the Cimmerian's attention. His lordly counterpart was likewise attracted to her, as he could tell sidelong from the forward attitude of Favian's visored head.

"Greetings, subjects!" Baldomer sat erect in the saddle, his voice ringing out sharply in the hushed gallery. "A sad thing it is that my travels on urgent state business have made me late for your nuptial feast! Nevertheless, I intend to be the first to wish you a long, fruitful union. Health, too, to your kinfolk gathered here." Shadowy in the candlelight, the baron's face scanned the inner circle of the newlyweds' families with unconcealed contempt, or so it seemed to Conan.

"I assure you that my royal line means to confer on your houses every honor and privilege that our city's customs dictate. My son, Favian, agrees with me in this." Conan started briefly at the weight of Baldomer's gauntleted hand on his shoulder, as the warlord leaned down from the saddle to clasp him in a show of fatherly pride. Uneasily the Cimmerian felt the gaze of the entire assembly shift toward him, not necessarily with affection.

"To this end," the baron resumed, "I proclaim to you: today, upon my homecoming, the doors of the Manse shall be laid open for a continuation of these festivities. My servants will set forth food and drink for all. Come as my guests. The presence of this young fellow and his stately bride is welcomed, nay, commanded!"

Baldomer finished his decree and began reining his horse around in the crowded space; meanwhile, murmurs and halfhearted shouts sounded in the gallery. Given the festive nature of the invitation, the response was far from the enthusiastic one Conan would have expected. The buzzing of the throng spread and deepened as the mounted baron herded his retinue before him through the archway and out into the sunlit plaza.

Once again the noise and bustle of entertainment filled the Manse. Down its stone hallways wafted the smells of cooked food and the tinny, martial-sounding echoes of trumpet music. Again Conan sat excluded from the feast, brooding in young Lord Favian's beshadowed room. He waited with his chair drawn half behind a window curtain, gazing out across the dusty sill. He watched pale ghosts of the festivities in the courtyard below, shadows thrown onto the inside of the outer wall by the torchlight and candlelight issuing from the Manse's open doors.

The flitting shapes portrayed the indecisive state of his thoughts, dulled by frequent sipping from a wine-flask beside his chair. He pondered many things: the loves and the enemies he had found in recent weeks, the splendor and ambition that lurked in the Manse, the wrath and shame of the evils he had witnessed here and elsewhere. Dissolved by wine, the turbid confusion of his brain had finally begun to drain down to hard particulars: how much longer to remain here, how much wealth to take when he left, how many lives to leave intact. . . .

His musings were interrupted by a noise in the corridor outside. He placed his hand on his saber-hilt. The weapon was already clear of its sheath, propped against his chair arm. Yet the fumbling at the latch was unguarded, and Conan watched the faint outline of the doorway with no particular dread. If his heart quickened at all, it was only in hope of a repetition of the last tender meeting that had occurred in this chamber.

But when the door swung wide and the fumbler strode in, the candle that wavered in the intruder's hand showed that it was Favian, unhelmeted and clad in his second-best armor. He reacted in a slow, tipsy way to the sight of the outlander sprawled on his bed-furniture, then waved an arm toward the open door behind him.

"Begone, savage! This room's rightful owner has arrived, and he shall scarcely be needing your services tonight. Back to your stinking cellar!"

Hardly warmed by this speech, Conan did not move to obey. "I was told to wait out the night here. With the Manse full of revelers, your father and his spy-chief think the danger too great for you. Better that you crawl off to some other bed."

Instead of taking offense, Favian showed astonishment. "My father told you . . . ? Why, the old demon! He would never stoop so low!" With an air of distracted rage, the lordling took two steps toward

Conan and stood lowering at him. "Cimmerian, you may have stolen my place and my name—my chariot, my clothes and my honor as well! But my manhood you shall not have!" He set down his candle and stood unsteadily, waving his fist in the air like a knight's flourished mace. "The oaths are cast, the decree is made, and the bride is commanded here to my pleasure. 'Tis my natural right and privilege—wellnigh the last one remaining to me. I will die rather than relinquish it!"

Faced with imminent assault by the intemperate lord, Conan arose and stepped back. "What mean you, drunken rogue?" He clutched his sword ready at his side, avoiding the empty-handed Favian more for his madness than for his menace. "A bride is to join you here tonight?"

"Aye, barbarian—by my noble right, the right of the seignior. What think you is the occasion of tonight's revel, anyway? Thank the gods there is still one lordly freedom my father cannot deny me, if only because of his own handicap." Favian stood arrogantly straight at the room's center, his gaze fixed scornfully on the Cimmerian. "As sole functioning heir of the Einharson line, I have first claim to each new virgin of the province on her wedding night."

Conan shook his head in astonishment, his sword sagging at his side. "Why, 'tis vile! What young woman would permit such a thing . . . and what groom?"

"Permit? What choice do they have?" Favian laughed disdainfully. "But you would be surprised, barbarian! Most girls yearn for it—the well-bred ones especially. They cherish the brief moment of splendor throughout the remainder of their staid, boring lives. And what commoner does not welcome a royal graft into his stunted family tree, if his bride is lucky enough to be chosen?"

Conan's head still shook, half now in bitter amusement. "A wonder that your father so guards his noble seed in your loins. Likely his heirs are spread over half of Nemedia!"

Suddenly ignoring Conan, Favian harkened to approaching steps and scrapes of armor in the corridor. "Enough prattle now, and away with you! I hear the favored one being brought hither to my tutelage. A proud and surly student, she strikes me to be. But she will learn well under her master's rod." With no further seeming of threat or insult toward Conan, he extended an arm to usher him out. "Come this way; an encounter in the corridor might be . . . confusing. This passage leads to the rear postern stair." Drawing his hesitating bodyguard by one arm toward the room's hidden doorway, Favian flung aside the curtain and unlatched the panel.

The Cimmerian, his head buzzing with drink and confusion, let himself be shoved through without protest. In the narrow passageway beyond, as the door slammed and latched behind him, he found himself without light.

Well, no harm; he remembered the place from his earlier visit. With his armored elbows brushing both walls and his still-drawn sword probing before him like a cane, he moved toward the rear of the Manse.

The darkness was not total, he came to realize. A

dim thread of light crossed the passage just ahead
—from Calissa's door, he knew. On coming to it, he
found that the portal was not tightly secured. The
inner bolt was wedged only partway home, leaving the
panel minutely ajar and allowing light to escape.
Sliding his sword-blade into the crevice, he flicked up
the hinged metal bar and pushed the door open.

The source of the light, he saw, was a three-
branched candelabrum resting on a dressing-table at
the opposite side of the room. Its triple radiance was
reflected in the hazy, polished silver of a mirror hung
beyond the table. Also thus hazily reflected were the
pale, rosy charms of Calissa, who stood at the table
laving herself from a golden basin. Her flimsy
sleeping-gown was thrown down from her shoulders
to hang loosely about her waist, and her hair cascaded
in a rusty-red plume down her shapely back.

At the faint creak of the door she turned to regard
her visitor. Her face showed gentle surprise rather
than alarm, and she made no effort to cover herself in
modesty. "Favian, dear brother! We have had no
chance to talk . . ." Her face reddened then as she
realized her mistake. Swiftly she took up an embroidered linen towel with which to cover her bosom,
patting her skin dry where it glistened with
washwater.

"Your brother is dallying with another beauty tonight, Calissa." Conan sheathed his sword and eased
the door shut behind him, taking care to set the bolt
securely this time. "He ousted me from my night-
watch in his room."

The noblewoman said nothing. Contriving to keep

her towel across herself, she drew up the front of her nightdress and shrugged her arms into the sleeves. Her newfound shyness was not well served by the mirror at her back.

"Why cover up such splendor, girl?" Conan went across the woven carpet toward her. "'Tis nothing I have not seen before, and from a good deal nearer vantage. . . ."

"Stop!" Groping behind her, Calissa snatched up a pair of haircutting shears, pointing them meaningfully before her. "Whatever license I may once have allowed you, you do not command me! Remember, you are still a minion in this house!"

"Aye, whatever you say." Conan stopped in the middle of the room, watching her push strands of raven-red hair out of her face. "But then, joinings between lords and their minions seem to be the way of this place."

"Enough!" Calissa stood against the dressing-table, waving her scissors as if to hold him at bay. "Should my brother decide to take every slattern of the town to his bed, what am I to do about it? Women are as nothing here. I am not at fault for his low tastes!"

"Why, girl, you are jealous! I did not know . . ." Conan started toward her again, then thought better of it and stayed in the middle of the carpet. "'Tis a trial for you, I see, to be joined to such a mad family."

"Madness! Speak not of madness, lest you call it forth from places you did not expect. Remember, I, too, am an Einharson." Her eyes blazed darkly at him from her pale face. "But then, what does it matter, really? Madness is the common thing in the world. 'Tis widely abroad in the land. The madness of war and civil strife eventually sweep over us no matter what we do."

"You have heard more talk of rebellion, then," Conan offered. "Is it whispered here at court?"

Calissa laughed. "Are you so blind that you do not see the stirrings, even amidst all this ghastly merry-making? The murmurs and the surly looks, the cruel remedies bandied by the nobles, the bridling of the commoners under my father's ever-harsher demands? And now we hear these stories of snake-cults gathering power in the east."

"Aye, did they tell you of the ambush? 'Twas a crack company of archers that set on us in the woods," Conan told her gravely. "They might have slain us all, had we rallied less swiftly. . . ."

"Fool, they will not stand a chance!" The noble girl was shaking her head in exasperated impatience, her hair thrashing darkly behind her. "My father, and you, and all his other troopers, will crush them, as the warlords of Dinander have dealt with such outbreaks over the centuries." She paused, placing a hand on her forehead. "What I despise most is the turmoil and the suffering, and the way our province will be thrown backward once again, with all the gains of my mother's day lost. The serfs will be as slaves, this city little better than a prison. How I dread it!"

Conan regarded her silently for a moment. "Aye, girl, I understand. I would not want any part of it myself." He paused as if silently debating within himself, then resumed: "Have you ever thought of leaving here? There are other cities than Dinander, most of them comelier and better-smelling."

"Nay, Conan, you do not understand." Wearily she

tossed her scissors onto the dressing-table, where they clashed against bottles of ointment. "No matter what happens here, I must see it through and try to salvage something. My father will need me, and after him, my brother, though they would never admit it."

He nodded gravely. "As long as you do not expect me to do the same."

"Oh Conan, no. 'Tis better if you leave. But come here." She raised her arms to him, resting them on his black-plated shoulders as he faced her. "I am sorry I rebuked you so. As you say, these strange alliances are in the tradition of the Manse. All we can do is to make the best of . . . ummm." Her words were smothered as his mouth moved against hers.

A few moments later she disengaged from him, panting. "This is most awkward. Let me help you remove your armor—part of it at least!" She reached to his waist, her slim hands fumbling at his straps and buckles.

Conan's doze was interrupted by distant cries of wrath and pain. Slumbers in the Manse were never deep, he had learned; in a breath he was awake, squinting in the faint light of the last guttering candle stub. Surely the shouts had been more than an evil dream; surely they had issued from some nearby chamber.

Easing himself from the coverlets and the warm, silky weight of Calissa's limbs, he arose to don his boots and armor. There was no repetition of the blood-chilling yells, yet now he fancied that he heard clanks and footfalls in distant corridors—other sleepers roused by the same disturbance, perhaps. Strapping on his saber, he moved silently to the concealed door of his lover's room.

The narrow passage between the walls was dark, but he quickly located the entrance to Favian's room by touch. Unfamiliar-sounding voices, male and female, clashed faintly beyond it, and something in their tense, sharp accents signaled danger. Bracing his back against a wall of the narrow corridor, Conan placed the sole of his boot upon the door and pushed, forcing the panel inward with relentless, mounting pressure. Finally the bolt gave with a splintering crack, and the door swung open to thump against the wall.

Beyond the half-open curtain, murder glared up at him luridly: on the floor sprawled Favian, shirtless, his kilted, cavalry-booted legs tangled in a silken bedcover, his face and bared chest kissing the crimson pool outspread from his slashed throat. He had died in surprise, clearly, in the midst of his lordly pursuits; one of his slack hands still lay amid the coils of a many-tailed whip. His blood shone fresh in the brightly candlelit chamber, its scent coppery and cloying in the heated air.

Of the three persons standing at the room's far end, two were males: commoners in festive garb, yet armed, their swords drawn but unstained. The third, a woman, was busy wiping her glinting knife, and the red-smeared hand that held it, on the limp rag of Favian's discarded shirt. Clad in a torn yellow robe which Conan immediately recognized, she spoke hurriedly with the others. In spite of her brusque, businesslike manner, she was without a doubt the innocent young bride Favian had earlier awaited so eagerly in his chamber. But as she turned to stare at Conan's figure in the broken doorway, he knew with dawning certainty that she was already well-familiar to him—as the rebel girl he had glimpsed first in the forest ambush, later in the doomed river town.

CHAPTER 10
Succession by Steel

As Conan had burst open the door, the female assassin had turned. Her two companions fell silent to gawp at him, probably thinking him the ghost of the dead Favian. Now one of them started forward reluctantly, lifting his sword, but he let himself be stayed by the woman's swiftly extended hand. She regarded Conan gravely, as if preparing to address him—when he felt a touch at his side and heard a quick, stricken gasp in his ear.

"Ah, Favian, no!"

It was Calissa, who had awakened and crept silently after him along the passage. As she started to push past him into the room, he caught her and pressed her back into the darkness. While she wailed and struggled, he reached out and dragged the door shut after them, jamming it closed on its broken latch.

"Come away, girl, this is no place for you!"

"But my brother—he is slain!" Calissa gasped. "Why do you not arrest those assassins, kill them? I know that woman . . . Evadne . . . she was one of the Temple School rebels. Go back!"

"I would sooner protect your life." He was forcing the distraught noblewoman down the corridor before him. "Red mutiny is afoot tonight, Calissa. I will be surprised if this is the mere extent of it."

"No, stop! Let me go!" she shrieked. "Coward, do your duty!" She raged against him, her red hair lashing his face, her voice breaking roughly with sobs. "Ah, but I see why you refuse to obey me. You are in league with them!"

Conan had borne her back through her dim-lit door with no sound of pursuit behind them; now her face glared up at him, pallid and tear-stained in the wavering candlelight. "You, my brother's trusted bodyguard—you abandoned your post at the vital moment! And then you came here to seduce me, and keep me from his side in his final hour!" She threw herself on him, bruising her fists against his steel-plated chest. "Murderer! Villain!"

"Hush, girl, you are mad! Crom knows I had no love for your brother, but . . . ." Realizing that she was clutching for the dagger sheathed at his waist, he thrust her back into the center of the room. "Calissa, calm yourself!"

"Nay, deceiver! Vile lecher! For all I know, you slew him yourself!" She was on him again, clawing at his eyes. "Guards, come seize this traitor!"

He shoved her back once again, and she tumbled onto the divan. After lying there panting for a moment in her disarranged nightgown, she lunged to the bedtable and rummaged for a weapon. The turbulent sounds coming from other parts of the Manse had increased, although they might not be in response to her outcries.

"As for Favian, he died of his own vices; I had no part in it." The Cimmerian's voice was low and bitter. "But you, Calissa . . . you make yourself too dangerous to protect! Bolt the door after me, and farewell!" He eased the panel shut behind him, hearing bottles smash against it as he closed off the tumult of her curses.

Groping his way down the passage, senses swimming in the darkness, his heart alternately plummeted and soared in his chest. Calissa was just as mad as the rest of her family, sad to see! But he, the Einharsons' pawn, was free of them at last, all his oaths discharged. He could leave now, if only he could carve his way out of this viper's nest.

He bethought himself of the rebels. Certainly, they had his sympathy, against the likes of the baron. And this Evadne . . . now there was a fine figure of a woman! Yet somehow he felt no great desire to kiss her bloody hand. All these Nemedian wenches were too treacherous for his liking; he was best away.

For that matter, should he not, while the Manse was in confusion, try to collect the back pay owed him? —with a comfortable bonus for severance, perhaps? He bethought himself of the money chest he had seen in Baldomer's chamber. His resemblance to Favian might help him in the theft, if he acted soon; yet perhaps 'twas wiser just to fly by night, and avoid even more painful severances.

He came to the door at the end of the passage; working its flimsy latch, he pressed it open and peered through. On the far side hung a curtain, screening the doorway from a sleeping-chamber. This in turn adjoined a lamplit spiral stair.

There was no one to be seen, and still no sound of imminent pursuit; even Calissa's angry cries had subsided. But from below came shouts and the sound of weapons thumping at the doors. He slipped past the curtain and, mentally gauging directions in this unfamiliar corner of the Manse, turned away from the stair to pass through the empty second-level chamber.

The chamber's far door opened onto one of the broad halls, but no sooner had he set out along it than he was opposed. Around the corner ahead of him two men came running, obviously pursued. The first Conan recognized as Svoretta, the chief of espionage, his portly figure black-caped and wearing a soft-brimmed hat that concealed half his face. Close beside him came Eubold, the fencing-master, armored from neck to waist and laboring breathlessly.

"Well, barbarian, you are a welcome sight!" Panting, the spy-chief slowed as he drew near. "Your ward is dead, I am told! But fear not, you still can be of service to us!" He halted, casting an uneasy glance behind him, then turned a guileless look on Conan. "Unless, of course, you have cast your lot in with the traitors . . . ?"

"Nay, not with traitors." Conan regarded Svoretta stonily as he drew his sword. "Hence, never with you!"

The whistling slash of his saber should have killed the spymaster in his tracks; yet the portly man moved swiftly under his cape. His own unsheathed sword, carried slyly out of sight, lashed forth to meet Conan's; it was a longer, straighter blade than the cavalry weapon carried by the northerner, made slim to pierce the joints of armor suits. In riposte it darted swiftly toward the Cimmerian's unshielded neck, causing him to dodge back.

The fencing-master was quick to draw his sword and join Svoretta, and so the Cimmerian battled the two of them. He did so with a blinding rain of strokes, weaving a clashing, glinting hedge of menace in the yellow light of the hall lamps. A powerful cut drove Eubold's saber down and aside, forcing it out of action for a moment; it was as a follow-up to this, seemingly an afterthought, that Conan's blade licked under Svoretta's cape to emerge red-splashed.

The spy-chief staggered, grunting in guttural pain, his hands clutching at himself beneath his tunic. His eyes widened in horror to discover the extent of his wound. Fumblingly he dropped his sword and with a paralytic sideward lurch, pitched to the floor.

"If I trusted you to die by yourself, I would let you do so," Conan told his fallen foe, who lay straining to breathe, gasping in slow, toiling shudders. "Yet I would rather not live out my years in fear of your poison-cup, or your henchmen at my back." Ignoring the watching Eubold, he raised his saber high over the spymaster's neck, then brought it down, using the arching strength of his entire body. At its chopping crunch, the fallen man's motions ceased and his head rolled free.

Conan looked to Eubold, who had not renewed his attack; the fencing-master stood well clear of

Svoretta's spreading gore, gazing back up the corridor where three armed men jostled into view. Rebels they were, sporting the now-familiar combination of wedding-guests' raiment and ready swords. They conferred calmly together, advancing at a walk.

Eubold turned to face Conan. The scrapes and bruises his face had gained during their first encounter had almost healed, although their last yellowing traces lent a jaundiced look to his sweat-gleaming stare. He raised his sword none too heartily; his eyes darted involuntarily to his companion's cloaked, blood-smirched body on the floor.

"Well, fencing-master, I see you are ready to tutor me once again." The Cimmerian lashed his blade forth and back, slicing air audibly. "I have learned much since our last meeting, as you can see."

Spitting a curse, Eubold turned and pounded away toward the three advancing rebels, preferring their mercies to those of his former pupil. Conan watched him go, disappointed but reluctant to follow.

Closing swiftly with his adversaries, the fencing-master drove between two of them with wild slashes and parries, wounding the sword-arm of one; but he failed to break completely through their rank, and the third man ducked and stabbed low to pierce his leg. Then, moving at their leisure, the three surrounded the limping tutor; gradually overwhelming his desperate defenses, their blades scored further cuts.

Conan did not stay to watch the inevitable end; he wanted no more to fight these rebels than to join them. While they were still enthusiastically and bloodily occupied, he turned to sprint in the opposite direction.

That route, as luck would have it, angled directly toward the center of the Manse, whence echoed more cries and clashings of steel. A recklessness blazed in the outlander's heart, fueled in part by the prospect of taking loot amid the havoc. But no stray imaginings could have prepared him for the encounter that awaited him then: mere paces ahead, Baron Baldomer Einharson strode forth into the corridor through a side door of his apartment.

The baron may have understood the feral hatred that blazed from Conan's steel-blue eyes; whether he did or not, he was followed by a fully armored man of the Iron Guard, who clearly knew no qualms as to Conan's identity or allegiance. At a gesture from the old warlord, the helmeted trooper blocked the passage and swung his sword in a level stroke, meeting the Cimmerian's upraised weapon with a ringing clang.

Thus battle was joined. The two warriors hovered an arm's length apart and hacked resolutely at one another. The guardsman's blade dashed time and again toward the youth's unhelmeted, black-tousled head, only to be ducked beneath or beaten aside; Conan's saber struck repeatedly at the neck and groin of the guard's cuirass, with no more effect than to brighten the polish of the supple black steel. The trend of the wordless, desperate combat was an unclear as its purpose, and the baron deigned neither to speak nor join in; he watched the contest coolly while buckling on his armor-scaled gauntlets.

Inflamed with battle-lust, Conan soon wearied of the futility of fencing with the armored man. Darting inside one of the ponderous sword-swings, he grappled with him chest to chest; an instant later he used

159

the guard's own top-heavy momentum to throw him off balance over his hip. As his foe clattered to the floor, Conan was astraddle him; savagely he wrenched and twisted at the helmeted head, clubbing with his sword-hilt at the leather-sheathed joint of the man's spine 'twixt helm and scapular plate. In a few moments the guard lay quiescent, his head cocked aside at an unnatural angle.

"Ah, my son! You have attained mature fighting skill at last." Baldomer, his armor now lacking only a helmet, stood regarding the panting victor, the sane half of his face set in a smile of noble resignation. "It prides me to see you prevail, though my heart is saddened by your bloody rebellion."

"I am not your son," Conan told him, breathing heavily as he rose to his feet. "Favian is dead, slain by the bride he brought to his chamber to ravish."

The baron shook his head, smiling grimly. "Nay, boy, do not tease; that was the northern savage I sent to wait in your place. Now see you the timely unfolding of your father's wisdom? And yet you shake your head. If you wouldst forfeit your noble name and deny your lineage"—Baldomer reached to his belt, drawing his long straightsword from its sheath with surprising smoothness and ease—"then we must fight, resolutely and to the death! Yet be assured, son"—his eyes gleamed madly on his false child—"that whichever one of us pours out his blood on these ancient tiles, it will be noble blood!"

So saying, the baron opened combat with a sideways slash of his blade. It was no great challenge to avoid, yet when Conan replied with a downward stroke, the straightsword was suddenly before him again, turning aside his saber and boring perilously through his defenses. Only an urgent expenditure of his strength blocked the thrust, breaking apart the combatants. Conan realized that he faced a subtle foe, strong with madness and seasoned by countless campaigns. Deliberately he set about stalking the elder man so as to wear down his strength, darting at him only occasionally with swift, forceful strokes.

"Not so easy, stripling, is it, this killing game?" Baldomer gave ground smoothly before Conan's greater exertions, parrying and sidestepping watchfully. His economy of motion left him ample breath for speech as he kept eye and blade trained on his foe. "My sword would far better have been raised in your behalf, son. Yet I knew that someday you would turn on me, however much I tried to set you on the right path." The old warlord let a powerful overhand blow of Conan's slide off his sword and his armor, seeming to stagger under its force, before his blade lashed menacingly close to the younger man's throat.

"In the Einharson blood there courses a turbulent strain," the baron proclaimed, backing away again, "that distills forth every few generations in the darkest crimes—parricide, fratricide, suicide! So it must be, perhaps; a sanguine recklessness is needed for efficient rule. I prayed against it to our holy forebears . . . and yet, since your childhood, Favian, I have sensed an overlarge share of that evil ferment in you!"

The residential corridor was left behind them now, their contest having carried them onto the wide, balustraded mezzanine overlooking the Manse's entry hall. Here the combat was exposed to others' view. The stairhead was held by Iron Guardsmen wielding pikes and sabers, and the lower stairs were crowded with rebels fighting their way upward across scattered corpses. Unsure, perhaps, of which of the aristocratic-seeming duelists to support, none of the nearby defenders came to Baldomer's aid. Yet both sides paused in their fighting to watch the noble passage of arms.

Conan spoke for the first time. "You accuse others of fratricide and black crimes," he said, whirling his blade through air as he edged closer. "But what deed could be viler, old baron, than the murder of your own wife out of the north, your Lady Heldra?"

"Aye, boy, the death of your mother! A great crime indeed." Baldomer glanced swiftly around at the watchers, his voice beginning to rasp with effort or emotion. "Done by the rebels you league with even now in your unnatural treason! But why broach the matter here?"

"Because you lie!" Conan punctuated his words with a saber swipe at the baron's head, stiff-necked and slow to bend, so that the old man's long gray hairs were disarranged by the passing stroke. "After your battle-wounds unmanned you, you had no more use for a wife. You grew to hate her," Conan grated between heavy breaths, "and so you ordered her death. Svoretta carried it out, poisoning her as he tried to poison me. Together you blamed it on rebels!"

"Nay, a calumny! She was unfaithful!" Baldomer's voice spat out the words, his good eye flaring as wildly as his wounded. "I loved her still, but she betrayed me, so the spymaster said. How could I let it be known?" His face, suffused by emotion, clenched so fiercely that for once its battle-wound was invisible.

"She betrayed me! Even as you do now, treacherous boy!"

For the first time, the baron lunged onto the offensive, his sword hacking at Conan's flitting shape with lusty abandon. This voided all of the nobleman's crafty webs of defense, and in time, even as he gave back before the relentless assault, Conan saw a chance. As a wild stroke clanged off the railing beside him, the Cimmerian clenched both hands on the hilt of his saber, driving it straight forward and up. The curving blade, which would in less strong, sure hands have been turned aside or broken, pierced through the black steel of the finely turned breastplate. Before its momentum was spent, it traveled half of its slim length into flesh and bone.

The baron's sword, relinquished in mid-stroke, bounded off Conan's backplate to crash to the floor beside him. Meanwhile, the old man's gauntleted hands gripped the blade standing out from his chest. Hanging on to it as if to a lifeline, the baron eased his transfixed body to a kneeling position.

"So it ends." Baldomer's voice, lacking its accustomed timbre, ground onward with bitter strength. "The Einharson line continues after all. Good! May this murder harden you to rulership, son." Still clutching the downturned sword with one gauntleted hand, he fumbled at his neck with the other, withdrawing a gleaming pendant on a heavy chain from inside his pierced armor. It was the gold six-bladed starburst Conan had seen him wear during his necromantic devotions at the nether shrine. "This passes to you . . . and with it, the rule of Dinander and all of our family's divine rights and protections. Be harsh,

boy. . . ." As small torrents of blood issued from his
nostrils, the elder man relaxed his grip on the sword
and settled backward to the floor. His craggy face,
though pale and crimson-stained, seemed eerily composed, its features in balance at last.

With Baldomer's gold amulet dangling from one
hand, Conan felt a sudden, squeamish reluctance to
wrench his saber out of the baron's chest. Instead, he
let go of the upstanding hilt and stooped to take up
the baron's longer, straighter sword. Hanging the
pendant around his own neck for safekeeping, he
stood and turned to meet the stares of the fighters
who, all around the gallery, had halted their combats.

The scene of the interrupted battle was not only
bloody, but chaotic. The high, porched entry hall had
been designed for the defense of the main doorway by
means of arrow-fire, in case the great door was ever
breached. Yet the outbreak of the rebellion within the
Manse itself had foiled that purpose. Now the doors
stood wide, a throng of attackers visible without. The
Iron Guard controlled only the head of the stairs and
the corridors flanking the baron's suite, standing off
the host of motley-clad rebels who held the gallery
below and both wings of the mezzanine. The battle
lines were frozen as the fighters watched Conan
—most of them thinking him Favian, he reminded
himself. They were waiting to see which side he would
champion.

Beyond the stair waited Durwald and a handful of
nobles, including the silver-haired tutor, Lothian;
they looked on in silence, as uncertain as anyone else.
Abruptly then, from the corridor at their side, hurried
a distraught, disheveled Calissa, flanked by two

guardsmen. Taking in the scene at a glance, she rushed to her father's counselors, darting an accusing finger at Conan and breaking the silence with her cries.

"There he is, the traitor! One murder was not enough for him; now he stands over the butchered body of my father! Take him quickly, strap him in irons! No torment is too great. . . ." The rest of her diatribe was lost in a general clatter around the chamber. The waiting combatants, inflamed or alarmed by her words, braced their weapons in new readiness; a few even flung themselves back into battle, mouthing curses.

Seeing the guards at the stairhead shift their pikes toward him, Conan finally made up his mind. There was no place for him among Dinander's pompous overlords. He strode straightaway from them toward the wing of the mezzanine where the black-armored men stood thinnest, opposed by a dense gang of rebels. At his approach from their rear, his sword raised in undisguised menace, the Iron Guards' cordon broke and scattered apart. The rebels were quick to take advantage of their disarray, pressing forward to seize new ground. Weapons clashed on either hand as Conan, crossing swords briefly with two guardsmen, found himself among the insurgents.

They welcomed him with cheers, clapping hands on his black-mailed shoulders. To his surprise, he found the warrior-woman before him again—the one called Evadne, now wearing a man's kilt and chain vest over her yellow robe. At Conan's stare she only blinked, unsmiling, and addressed him in level, terse accents: "Noble or savage, if you join us, you are one among equals, no more, no less. Remember that." Then she turned and vanished into the press.

The battlefronts were moving now, because the guardsmen, at the death of their baron and the desertion of his apparent successor, fought with flagging spirit. Conan turned to join the attack, yet the defenders gave ground so fast that he stalked back almost to the head of the stair before he reached the skirmishing. Then, ere he could elbow his way among the battling rebels, his attention was drawn by fresh shouts and screams from below, down in the gallery.

He forced his way to the rail and looked over, seeing townsmen scattering back from the inner doors in panic. At the fringes of the crowd, weapons were flailing, swung by armored warriors not yet plainly in view. Conan leaned far out to see who they were. Reinforcements from the municipal barracks, perhaps?

"Flee, they have come!" From the panicking throng below, the cries drifted up to him. "It is the Einharsons! The dead barons are risen to fulfill their curse!"

CHAPTER 11
The Warlords

Staring down from the balcony, Conan felt his scalp tighten with certainty that the frightened shouts were true. Beneath him there stalked, amid the flying shapes of the rebels, gigantic warriors in weird-looking armor, antique fighters whose swords appeared rusted and evil and whose ancient copperplate-and-scale mail blazed leprous green with tarnish: the dead Einharson warlords! With a chill, Conan remembered the ancestral armor laid out on the stone coffins in the crypt beneath the Manse, and the mystical hints that its owners would someday arise to sway the fate of the province.

The attackers were fully suited and helmed, so there was no knowing what lurked inside the decrepit armor. Some of the fighters appeared to be damaged, or oddly incomplete. Yet all swung swords and battle-axes relentlessly, their grim efficiency evinced by the hacked corpses strewn behind them on the patterned floor.

No sooner had the Cimmerian comprehended the threat than it erupted close at hand. Astonished shouts were raised behind him, and he turned to see three of the hoary, sinister warriors issuing from a nearby corridor. In a dreamlike glimpse, he remembered the long stairway leading from the vicinity of Baldomer's apartment directly to the cellar; thence, doubtless, these marauders had crawled. Spitting out a bitter oath, Conan shoved past the scattering rebels to confront the nemesis.

The tall, menacing shape that first came before him was certainly the product of sorcery. Its bronze-sheathed limbs moved with the noiseless, supple ease of an insect's jointed carapace, while the eye-slits of its crested helm revealed only fluid darkness lurking within. The creature's long, notched sword plied air with a swift surety that Conan took diligent care to avoid; and yet the vacancies of the shriveled leathern bindings at the strange warrior's elbows and ankles did not appear to contain any form, not even bones.

Lunging in the wake of one of its long sword-sweeps, Conan struck a blow at its green-mottled breastplate. He hoped to knock it over, but instead heard his blade gong hollowly on empty metal. The stabbing force of his stroke did nothing to unbalance his attacker; rather, it left Conan exposed to a recoiling blow that stung his shoulder, buffeting him aside with its casual force.

Angered, he stalked his foe afresh, waiting his turn to feint and strike; this time, though his blade-tip passed between the upper and lower arm-pieces of the ghostly warrior's suit and scattered bits of rotten strapping through the air, the being's sword-slashed arm swung on unimpaired. Its weapon grazed his ear and dented his armored shoulder with a smarting impact.

So, Conan learned, it scarcely mattered what was done to the beings' nonexistent bodies. The power of these phantom Einharsons was in their swords, which clove onward in ravaging arcs, empowered with their own mystic energy. The armor suits seemed to march behind the weapons as mere decorations, with no vital functions within, nothing in need of protection. Conan fought on doggedly, seeking some means with which to halt his phantom adversary; whether the haunted blades could be broken, or even parried, his best fencing could not discover.

As he fell back before the mailed specter's on-slaught, a calm, fatalistic part of his mind took in the deteriorating situation around him. A few of the rebels on the balcony were halfheartedly battling the Einharsons, but none managed to hold their ground, and some had already fallen before the tireless thresh-ing of the ancient swords. At first the Iron Guard moved in to exploit the vacancy left by the rebels, assuming to fight alongside the undead warriors—but apparently the weirdlings knew no allies. Conan saw one of the guardsmen stabbed through the groin by a rusty, cobwebbed sword before his black-mailed com-rades had the sense to fall back from the monsters.

Whatever the mystical provisions of the animating curse, they did not seem to apply to the unblest, unburied Baldomer, whose transfixed body lay mo-tionless on the balcony a few paces away. Nor did the ancient spell command the baron's fine sword, for the stolen weapon had not sprung to unearthly life in Conan's hand—or not yet, at least.

These minor boons scarcely mattered, for the Einharsons already under arms were more than adequately murderous to clear the entire Manse of living humans. Cut off from the corridors along with a dozen or more of the rebels, Conan gave ground with them, eyeing the central stairway as an escape route.

"See thou, traitor!" A shrill, hysterical voice abruptly sounded close behind Conan. "Learn how the undying spite of my fathers punishes you!" A swift backward glance told him that the taunts came from Calissa, who had crept away from the broken phalanx of loyal guardsmen to advance along the front of the balcony. Clinging to the heavy wooden rail, she watched the one-sided battle with venomous, exultant eyes. "Fight your savage best, Cimmerian, and endure long, for if you do, my kin will hound you all the way back to your northern wastes! Nay, you will not escape them! Nevermore can they be laid to rest, now that you have murdered the last Einharson heir!"

She was mad, Conan knew, totally unhinged by the night's bloody events. How unlike the noble girl who had caressed him mere hours past! His heart flinched even as his body shrank before the blade of his attacker.

And yet, at her ravings, a new thought awakened in his brain. Breaking clear of his undead foe's tireless sword-play, he turned to dart after the noble girl. She sought to flee, but he caught her tightly by the wrist.

"What? Away from me, villain! Do you mean to add me to the list of your murders?" As she writhed in

170

his clutch, Conan sheathed his weapon and reached to his throat. He took the chain with its heavy amulet, removed it and drew it over Calissa's head of tangled red hair. She spat at him in fury, her struggles causing the six-pointed talisman to flail in his face like a chain-mace. But he caught hold of her shoulders and held her fast, letting the pendant settle between her unruly lace-gowned breasts.

In an instant a transformation was evident in the gallery around them. The phantom Einharson warrior that had been stalking Conan promptly ceased its sword-slashing. Exhibiting the proud, erect bearing of a victorious duelist, it pivoted away in the direction of the cellar stair. Its fellow ghosts on the terrace did the same within moments, their weapons held low at their sides. A glance over the rail showed that the combat on the ground floor had likewise ceased.

"What trickery is this?" Calissa demanded shrilly of the room at large. "Who ever said that a woman could wear the baron's sigil? Off with it, I say!" She grasped the gleaming amulet and tried to tear it from her throat, but Conan's fist knotted in its stout chain, drawing it up so snugly that a twist of his arm could easily have throttled her. "Come back, you musty tomb-haunts! Keep on fighting, I say!" But the undead warriors mechanically continued their retreat, disregarding her frantic, half-choked cries.

The surviving rebels, no longer beset, were quick to surround Conan and help him restrain Calissa. Meanwhile, they faced down the Iron Guards, who looked as if they might move to rescue her. The Cimmerian rapped instructions to those motley fighters near him.

"Keep her quiet, and keep this trinket secured

171

around her neck." He knotted the chain at her creamy nape, beneath her wildly lashing tresses. "This is the power that staves off the marching ghosts. Belike their curse requires only that a living Einharson wear the sigil, not that she rule the city grandly. Here, hold her fast, but do not harm her, at your peril! Dru, the blacksmith, can set a rivet through this chain at the first opportunity."

The last of the Einharson forebears shambled out of sight, and rejoicing cries began to sound from the gallery below. Most of the watchers audibly mistook Conan for Favian; they praised the young lord for joining the rebels and turning back his father's curse, where moments before they had sought to wipe out his line. Many who had fled now found their way back into the Manse, and the press in the lower gallery deepened once again.

The rebel force remained scattered and weakened, seemingly easy prey for the close-knit Iron Guard. And yet moments later, to Conan's surprise, a party of nobles came forth from the loyalist line, their weapons sheathed and their empty palms raised to signify a truce.

"Hold your steel, for we would parley!" came the cry. "Whoever claims to lead this uprising, come and treat with us now."

Prominent in the delegation were Marshal Durwald and the elderly chief of protocol, Lothian. Flanked by lesser nobles, they came straight toward Conan's place in the crowd, halting a few paces away for the sake of their dignity and safety. Rebel officers, including the woman Evadne, had gathered on the scene, and now the Cimmerian moved with them as a body to confront the emissaries.

"Before you wear out your tongues with lies and threats, noble rogues, be assured that we will accept nothing but your absolute surrender!" The speaker was a lean rebel youth with short-cropped yellow hair, having more the look of a Temple School acolyte than of a fighter. "The Manse is practically ours, and our followers have risen up throughout the province." Several of his companions nodded in earnest assent, though none spoke to second him.

Durwald, standing at the center of the royalist faction, his helmet laid in the crook of one arm, smoothed his rumpled black hair with his free hand as he gazed on the youth. Finally he answered.

"And so you think you can do without us? You have been pledged the support of the town's leading families and the squires, perhaps? Can you muster an army fit to police and defend this city?" His jet mustache arched in aristocratic disdain. "Or will you merely import priests of Set out of Stygia to run your stolen fiefdom?"

"Set-priests? We have no truck with the snake-cult!" This came from a male rebel, gray at the temples and wearing the brown robe of a disciple of Ulla, cinched now at the waist with an unpriestly sword-belt. "Our party is loyal to the true church of Nemedia. I have heard of the snake-frenzy sweeping the east, but our cause here is a pious one."

"Aye, and our Reform Council includes the best families," Evadne declared from the crowd, her stern demeanor silencing others who clamored to speak.

"Not the noblest, but the best." She regarded the royalists with a challenging look. "In our council, the voice of the craftsman is heard along with that of the knight, the farmer's as freely as the squire's. We claim this barony for the benefit of all, putting an end to the cruelties and inequities that have worsened daily under Baldomer's rule!"

At her speech, a murmur of assent sounded from the other rebels. She did not acknowledge it, giving attention instead to Durwald's reply.

"Fine-sounding sentiments, Evadne. And fresh ones for this tight-laced, regimented part of Nemedia. I wonder what our neighboring barons will think of them . . . especially the gentle lords Sigmarck and Ottislav?" This time Durwald's mustaches canted upward in amusement. "How long will it be, do you suppose, before they turn on Dinander with sharp swords and sharper pens, to redraw the maps of their baronies and write an end to your little political experiment?"

"But you fail to take account of King Laslo, who owns all the lands," a black-bearded rebel protested. "He holds the barons in check, and he has championed us in the past against unfair decrees and taxes. His armies in Numalia far exceed those that any local lord might muster!"

Durwald laughed. "So that is the fate you would call down on our heads: to be invested and garrisoned by royal legions! Think you that such shame would improve your lot, or that rough mercenaries from the south of the empire would be more sympathetic to your woes than our native guardsmen?" He shook his head broadly. "Be assured that they will strut and steal as ruthlessly as any invaders! Likely as not, King Laslo will appoint some petty officer as satrap over us, with unbridled powers."

The rebels, muttering and expostulating in angry dismay, fell silent as Conan spoke abruptly. "What do you propose, Durwald?"

Before the marshal could answer, frail old Lothian leaned forward at his side to speak with surprising firmness and resonance. "I can, I think, suggest a course of action that will benefit both sides. If you insurgents will decide who among you are leaders, you can withdraw with us to more private surroundings to discuss the matter."

At this the rebels fell back to confer for a moment. Though they muttered suspiciously, they were able to select delegates with a speed and unanimity that surprised Conan. Evadne and the sword-bearing priest were chosen, as well as the black-bearded man and two others. The Cimmerian found himself included without question among the elect party.

The two groups walked to one of the doors adjoining Baldomer's apartment. The rebels went in first, cautiously, to beat the hangings with their swords; then followed the half-dozen nobles. A guard of each faction stayed just outside the door, waiting in a standoff along with the battle lines nearby.

"Well, nobles and rebel . . . officers." Walking slowly across the room, old Lothian seated himself with his back to a dining table opposite the door, although the others continued to stand with hands ready at sword-hilts. "'Tis clear, I think, that some form of compromise would be in the best interests of all. As you may know, I differed with the late baron over his more draconian decrees; in fact, I frequently warned him of just such an eventuality as this." The sage adjusted his slender shanks primly in the cushioned chair. "On the other hand, of course I have firm belief in the virtue of aristocratic rule. Speaking as one of the originators of the science of noble precedence—"

"Get on with it, Counselor!" Evadne interrupted him. "If you palaver too long, your troops and municipals all across the city will be whittled away by our armed followers and you will have nothing left to bargain with. Just tell us"—her eyes flashed at Durwald as she spoke—"what interest the people of Dinander can possibly find in common with our recent tormentors."

"Here now," Durwald protested, "I, too, warned Baldomer against his excesses too. There is none here who despises needless cruelty more than I."

"There, you see," Lothian put in good-naturedly. "We are not so far apart as all that. Now if we can just settle on a suitable division of power—"

"Old fool!" interposed the slim, yellow-haired youth. "When has power ever been divided in Dinander, except by the cutting edge of a sword?"

Evadne firmly overruled her fellow rebel. "Rather, when has it not been divided? Tell me, Counselor, who is next in the line of baronial succession after Favian?"

"Why, 'twould be old Eggar, Baldomer's cousin, squire of the Forest Lakes."

"As I thought; a drunken trifler, already infamous for the misrule of his own petty domain. Our folk would never accept such a contemptible tyrant." The strong-featured girl stared challengingly around the company. "He was not in attendance at the Manse tonight?"

"If he was here, he is dead or fled," Durwald replied. "And no great loss. If you are thinking of a puppet, I agree, we need a more attractive palatable than that."

The sword-bearing priest shook his gray-sprinkled head in regret. "A shame that Lady Calissa is a woman . . . and mad, to boot. She was once a voice of moderation in the court. But then, none could expect her to countenance the murder of her kin. Now, methinks, she cannot even safely be put to death." He looked around at the others, who showed melancholy interest. "She will have to be kept under close guard all her days, or at least until our holy exorcists can deal with the Einharson curse."

In the somber silence that followed, the black-bearded rebel spoke up. "If we mean to create a baron, 'twould be best to use some youthful heir, who could easily be controlled. Or else one so old and feeble that he has no ambition left."

"But don't you see, there is no need to look so far!" Lothian rose from his chair impatiently. "We have here the perfect heir. We have Lord Favian himself!"

"Favian is dead, Counselor," black-beard said, "in case your eyesight has failed you. He lies glued to the floor of his chamber in his own clotting blood. As for this look-alike you have rigged out . . . well, he has shown himself a right-hearted sort by killing Baldomer and throwing in with us. But we of the Reform Council saw through your ruse long ago."

"Aye, to your credit." Lothian stroked his gray beard, his eyes twinkling. "And yet Conan is perfect for our shared purpose. Those who know of his imposture could, perhaps, be sworn to silence. It can be held forth that the bodyguard died instead of the noble. The outlander would then command the loyalty of the majority of subjects, those who blindly follow their traditional leader. He is a good lad at heart, and has had the benefit of my tutorship."

"But would the people of Dinander kneel to Favian as a patricide?" The rebel priest's brows were knit in earnest moral concern. "One of our goals in seizing power was to put behind us the bloody irregularities of the Einharson lineage."

"So you see, it is little more than traditional," Durwald assured him with a courtly flourish of his gauntleted hand. "Likely this slaying is the one break with the past that will allow the people to tolerate another Einharson warlord."

"Yes, truly, it might not be hard to pass him off as baron!" The yellow-haired youth stepped forward, rattling his sheathed sword in enthusiasm. "There would be no danger of the barbarian gaining real power. Just parade him now and again before the mob and keep him from blurting out anything in his pebble-mouthed northern accent. He will be baron to them, lackey to us!"

"Watch your jabbering mouth, dog!" Conan squared off on the rebel, who grew abruptly pale and still. "I am no one's lackey, and I like not the notion of playing puppet to such as you." He glared around the company. "If I continue this mummery, it will be on my own terms!"

"Of course, Conan, of course." Durwald laid a hand on the northerner's shoulder, smiling to counter his ill-humored gaze. "We shall see to it that you are paid handsomely and furnished with a comfortable style of living. There may even be a few petty military functions you can direct, to keep up a believable front. You need not worry about matters of state; we court counselors will bear the full burden of those."

"Under the direction of the Reform Council, you mean," the black-bearded rebel said warningly, echoed by murmurs from his fellows.

"Yes, yes, we can work all that out." Durwald breezily waved him to silence. "Believe me, we of the court are as glad to be free of Baldomer and his vile monkey, Svoretta, as you are. His unmanageable offspring, too! As long as the legitimate interests of the noble houses are recognized, lords and commoners can flourish together from this moment, and Dinander can look to a happy future."

CHAPTER 12
Milord Barbarian

A lance of sunlight fell through a gap in the curtains, causing stray dust motes to sparkle in the gloom of the chamber. Blazoning the great bed's rumpled satin covers, the narrow ray angled across Conan's face like a saber-slash, its brightness smiting his groggy brain with all the pain of a sword-stroke.

The sleeper, muttering faintly, stirred and tried to turn aside out of the light. When he rolled the wrong way, his legs slipped down the side of the spongy mattress, entangling with his bedclothes and the sheathed sword, which lay beside him as intimately as a wife. Groping blindly for balance, he flung out a heavy arm and toppled a low bedside table, sending its array of half-drained cups and flasks clattering to the floor.

Moaning in fresh discomfort at the piercing sounds, Conan hauled himself upright on the edge of the bed.

He blinked into the sunshot dimness around him, slowly coming to recognize his surroundings.

The room was the bedchamber of the late Baron Baldomer. High and broad, it was well-befitting to lordly dignity, although Conan foresaw that it would prove drafty and chill in winter. Having turned and beaten the great mattress himself, he had ordered the bed's heavy canopies hauled out and burned in hopes of ridding the place of any lingering sour humors. Even so, in spite of all his efforts, the lavish apartment exerted a baleful influence on Conan's nature.

Suddenly there came a brisk rapping at the door. Staggering to his feet, naked but for his cotton underkilt, Conan hastened across the stained parquetry to undo the bolt. When the portal swung wide, a harsh but good-natured bellow greeted him.

"Well, young baron, how goes it?" A burly, broken-nosed man strode into the room carrying a tray of fruit and bread under one arm. "I could tell by the clamor that you were awake—and about time, too, with the sun scraping the roof peaks! How are you feeling this morning?"

"Speak softer, Rudo; I am unwell. I think I have been poisoned." Conan shuffled back to sit on his bed. "That wine last night. . . ."

"The wine, yes." Rudo bent over the reeking pool outspread amid the tumbled flasks. "Poisoned, indeed! And by the same decoctions that send half the folk of this city staggering to bed on a feast night!" He righted the table so as to set his burden on it. Then he knelt, seizing a discarded shirt with which to mop up the mess. "Any one of these liquors would lay a healthy man low, but to mingle them in one night's carouse! You tempt the fates rashly, Conan—I mean, Milord Baron.''

As Rudo swabbed the floor, he raised a crystal decanter to his lips and swigged deeply from it. "Ah yes, truly," he said in a confidential voice, "when we gnawed bread crusts together in the town dungeon, who would have thought that we would ever again be sipping such nectar as this? I credit your success in worldly affairs, Lord Baron, as well as your faithfulness in remembering old friends!"

Sitting on the bed massaging his aching temples, Conan merely growled in answer. He pretended not to notice as his attendant crushed a goblet of soft gold against the floor with the pressure of one thick hand, to slip it discreetly into the sash of his silken pantaloons.

In a while Rudo had gone, and returned, and gone again, and Conan sat cross-legged on the bed, gingerly chewing his breakfast and drinking from the pitcher of fresh warm milk his valet had brought. The simple fare satisfied him, as had the selfsame food when he was a kitchen drudge; in spite of his earlier complaints, he still trusted his recent associates downstairs not to poison him. But now the day stretched ahead, vacant and uninviting. His duties as mock baron were laughably slight and few, consisting mainly of parading the battlements at sunset in full armor and holding brief "audiences" with the handful of courtiers and rebel officers who really ruled Dinander these days.

Not that he imagined he could run the city any better; things seemed well under control for the nonce. After that first charnel night, the insurrection

had taken hold almost bloodlessly by virtue of
Baldomer's death and the uneasy accommodation
between rebels and nobles. A few lesser officers and
functionaries, such as Fletta, the interrogator and
executioner, had been dragged before civil tribunals,
condemned, and broken on the wheel to appease the
vengeful townsfolk; and a few unpopular nobles quit
their homes and vanished, either sent into hiding by
their fellows at court, or murdered by them. The
noble party allowed none of its number to be tried,
fearing that the public execution of aristocrats might
set a bad precedent.

The nearest thing to a falling-out between the two
factions had involved the proposed abolition of the
Iron Guard; Conan had dozed through a long meeting
where debate on the subject raged hotly between
Durwald and Evadne. The proposal had finally been
agreed to, but with little impact, since the change of
the elite guard's designation to the "Red Dragons"
was a token display, after all. It meant the promotion
of a few officers, and much labor for Dru, the armorer,
who in the coming months would have to change the
outfit's armor trappings to the new motif. The troops
would still click their heels as smartly, Conan guessed,
and obey orders as unquestioningly.

He saw little place for his own efforts in the new
Dinander, except to wine, dine and wench like a
baron, and fill a suit of armor handsomely, be it of red
or black hue. His success in finding a few of his old
cronies, those who stood with him during the rebel
purge of the prisons, was gratifying; yet his message
summoning the serving-maid, Ludya, back to the
capital had never been answered. Conan suspected

that his employers, none too eager that he find a mate and sire a counterfeit noble line, might have intercepted his courier. He was of half a mind to ride in search of the girl himself.

His musings were interrupted by another opening of the chamber door. He looked up to see a figure more comely than that of the crook-nosed Rudo: the stately Evadne on her daily visit, clad in sandals and a plain, belted tunic. His sudden upward glance sent reverberations throbbing through his still-tender skull, so he only grunted irritably as she entered.

"Good morning, Your Lordship." She scarcely blinked at his state of undress, but her shapely nose wrinkled at the scent of wine-dipped bedclothes. "Recovering from another nightlong debauch, I see. Will you never tire of . . . the prerogatives of rank?" She settled herself on a lacquered stool a decorous distance away.

"In truth," he grumbled, "I am already weary of these pointless pursuits—as I long ago grew bored with the aged, motherly trollops you send me from the local ale houses. I crave more of life than this musty apartment can provide."

Evadne covered any embarrassment with a shrug of unconcern. "If you are restless, ride to the hunt again. You can decree it for tomorrow, if you like."

"What, and have the gamekeepers loose more tame deer from their cages for me to slaughter, in the company of a dozen sour-faced men-at-arms? Nay, Evadne." Conan gently cradled his forehead on an outspread hand. "In my youth in Cimmeria, hunting had a purpose, a meaning. Here, like everything else, it is hollow."

184

"Then call for fencing practice in the private court-yard. Fight three or four guardsmen at once, if you must place your life at risk in order to enjoy it." She waved a hand in exasperation, preparing to arise. "There is plenty to do here. Any ordinary citizen would give his nose and ears to be in your place. I must confess, I find it a trial to keep your savage soul entertained!"

"Then why trouble yourself, Evadne?" Conan propped his chin on one hand as he regarded her. "Why do you even bother? Is it true that you have been assigned as my nursemaid, to make sure I keep up lordly appearances?"

"No need for worry on that account; you play the degenerate aristocrat most convincingly." The rebel shook her blond locks reprovingly, sitting poised on the edge of her stool. "But remember, ours is a young, untested provincial government with ma-ny . . . ill-assorted elements. Our two shakiest props are you and the poor, mad Lady Calissa. It is neces-sary that someone take the responsibility for your welfare."

"And how fares Calissa?" Conan let his gaze fall away from Evadne with a surge of melancholy. "Does she still rail and struggle at her restraints?"

"Nay, her chafes are healing, and she no longer tugs and worries at the charm fastened around her neck. She is unbound, allowed to rove free in her room, as long as someone stays to see that she does not hang herself by the chain. She no longer raves"—Evadne smiled wanly—"or even speaks. To anyone."

"Hmm. A convenient circumstance for you and me, but an ill one for Calissa." He shook his head miserably. "And yet I wonder, am I less a prisoner than she is?"

"Nonsense." Evadne visibly ruffled, watched Conan warily. "If you decided to leave Dinander to its fate, and to forfeit the golden drams that are daily added to your account, we would have a hard time stopping you."

"But you would try, would you not?" Conan smiled grimly, trading gaze for gaze. "Is that why you venture so boldly into my room? And is that, perchance, what the dagger concealed at your thigh is for?" He let his feet slip to the floor, moving to arise. "Is it the same weapon, I wonder, that you carried for Favian?"

"Stop! I would never wish such a thing!" She stood bolt upright, her proud face pale. "But be warned, if it were for the sake of our province, I would do whatever was necessary. Your fair dealing thus far has earned you a certain indulgence. But a limited one."

"I thought so." He rose smoothly to his feet, no longer showing signs of malaise, and moved toward her. "I understand you, then; we are slayers of a kind! So our time here need not be so glum and joyless after all. Come, Evadne, I am told your recent wedding was a sham." He moved toward her, extending an arm.

"No!" She moved back a step from him, toward the door. "I am no tavern trull to lighten your leisure! Nor am I the next in your chain of conquests at the Manse. I have dealings here that are more important than that." She glared at him. "As for my wedding, it may have been only a formality. I will never know, since my husband was the first one killed by Baldomer's guards in our rising." She strode to the door, bowing

186

curtly before she opened it, and passed through. "Good day to you, Milord Baron!"

Wordlessly, listless once again, Conan shuffled back to the mattress and sat down heavily. His hand roved indecisively for a moment over the array of food and spirit decanters at the bedside; then, with an idle gesture, he tipped the ivory table onto the floor. Amidst the crashing, he sank down onto the blankets and closed his eyes.

It may have been moments or hours later that the chamber door scraped open again. Less bleary this time, Conan rolled onto one elbow. His hand clutched his sword-hilt beneath the coverlet as he watched Durwald enter, flanked by Evadne.

"Well, Lord Favian—as you must persevere in being! I am glad to see you living the part so well. Your hair grows a bit shaggy . . . but then, what does it matter, since there is no longer a living counterpart to compare you with?" The leather-kilted noble spoke with brusque humor, pausing a few steps short of the litter surrounding the bed. "But I hope you have fully recovered from your night's merriment. A challenge awaits us that will require our best wit and readiness."

"A fresh basin is being drawn," Evadne added. "We expect you to be washed and dressed soon."

"And what is the occasion?" Conan ran a hand across his forehead, sweeping his black mane out of his eyes. "Is some young bride taking her vows and awaiting a tryst with the lord of the Manse?"

Evadne stiffened at this remark, but Durwald only smiled. "Advance couriers have just arrived, from an armed force of our neighboring barons. The lords are sending a punitive expedition westward against the snake-cultists, and they expect us to join them."

"Against the cultists, you say? A ruse!" Conan bolted up from the bed, dragging his longsword out from beneath the linen. "More likely the warlords are marching against us in our time of weakness, as you foresaw. Will we ready the town for a siege, or meet them on the plain?"

"Nay, fellow, be not so eager to enter the fray!" Durwald shook his head patiently. "To be sure, the barons have heard of our recent change of rulership; doubtless they wish to test our strengths and spy out whether Dinander can still hold her territories. But I would wager that their purported mission is genuine."

The marshal seated himself on the edge of the broad writing table, folding his arms on his chest as he expounded. "The western cults are an intolerable nuisance to them; they raided southward into Baron Ottislav's domain, and he went first to his friend, Sigmarck, for aid. Now the two come here. This is our chance to show them, first, that we have no ties with the snake-cult and, second, that we have a firm grip on our province and a good resolve to defend it."

A washbasin and fresh linen had been set out by Rudo as Durwald spoke. Conan submerged his face in it for a long moment, then shook his dripping head like a terrier, spattering water on his unprotected guests. "Mayhap we should join forces with these cultists instead, if the barons are as greedy as you say."

"Take sides with Set-worshipers? Co . . . Lord

Favian, that would scarcely be politic." Evadne glared at him with distaste.

"And how like a rebel you are! Once in power, you take up arms against all your fellow rebels and crush them." Conan splashed water vigorously onto his chest and mopped it with a towel. "If these neighbor barons can set you against your own populace, the scoundrels have won half their fight."

"No, truly, Lord Baron, these cultists are less than savory." Durwald exaggerated Conan's false title archly. "Hardly human, if you ask me. You saw the specimen we interrogated at Squire Ulf's keep."

"That is so, believe me," Evadne seconded. "When we rode east to ambush Baldomer's train, we passed through a valley denuded by their sweep. There have been outbreaks before in these regions. It is not really a faith—more a plague that spreads and spreads, unless it is finally stopped by force of arms." Evadne averted her eyes, either out of emotion or because Conan had set to scrubbing his nether parts.

"Well, if the two of you finally agree on something, it must be true." Conan began toweling himself furiously. "So what must I do to appease these barons? Will they know me by sight?"

Durwald shook his head. "Diplomatic relations have been cool; I would guess that none in their party will have seen Favian in the past dozen years. You can doff your helmet in their presence." The marshal sat easy, exuding confidence for Conan's benefit. "They will surely have heard conflicting rumors. If you keep your peace and appear determined, we should be able to pass you off without question."

"Use the salutes and protocols you have been shown," Evadne added. "You will be well-protected by guards."

"Yes. We, as your counselors, will do the talking," Durwald emphasized. "They will expect no great statesmanship from such a youthful heir."

"The inner hall is being readied," Evadne finished. "The troops will camp downriver, and their officers are expected here by nightfall. We must go and assemble the counselors, for there is much to be discussed."

Lamps flared yellow in the Manse's Hall of State as lords and warriors took their places at tables spread with loaves, salt meats and ale puncheons. Here was not the gala extravagance of one of Baldomer's gatherings; the feast was Spartan by comparison, with shadows brooding in the sparsely lit upper vaultings of the gallery. The intended effect was one of strength and resolve; to this end the crowd of townsfolk filling the courtyard saluted the guests with lusty shouts; the counselors, even old Lothian, wore military costume, and the Manse's guards deployed along the walls of the chamber with extra quickness and precision.

The visiting lords gave no hint of being impressed by the display. Baron Sigmarck, a short, slender man with cruelly handsome features, arched his aquiline nose over his food in distaste and spent the rest of the night regarding the company around him with cynical, dark eyes. Ottislav, a bald, mustached warlord decked in gold chains and bristling with furs, served himself profusely and impartially from all the nearby plates and beakers; but it seemed to his hosts that whenever they sought to address him on any subject, his sole, invariable reply was the word "Haw!" —spoken sharply, with a twitch of his greasy whiskers and an unpleasant leer.

Noting the behavior of these two, Conan took comfort that none would expect him to be very mannerly or forthcoming. Flanked at the table by Durwald and Evadne, with the other counselors seated between him and the noble visitors, he was well-nigh immune to questions. He feigned great interest in his food and drink, then sat taciturn through the interminable program of Nemedian peasant dances that the rebel leaders had furnished as entertainment.

When the milling peasants were finally cleared from the room, discussion of the eastern campaign commenced. In terse, barking statements, the barons' tight-faced, armored marshals decreed their objectives, amounting to nothing less than total extermination of the eastern insurgents, and withdrawal westward before the first fall sleets turned the roads to mud.

Curtly then, the visiting officers answered questions put to them by Dinander's counselors. At first these delegates' remarks were full of gruff hints and insinuations that the snake-cult raiders were supported by the new rulers of Dinander. When their hosts protested otherwise, the visitors deftly changed their tune, demanding military support for their own venture.

During the negotiation, Durwald, Evadne and Lothian feigned earnest consultations with their baron. These were actually heated exchanges between the three of them, which Conan could barely follow,

191

though he remembered to mumble and nod occasionally to keep up appearances.

The diplomacy grew tense, with both counselors hurrying down the length of the table to address the foreign barons themselves. At one point there came a bellow that caused the Cimmerian to raise wary eyes to the end of the board: Evadne clutched Ottislav's thumb, bending it back ruthlessly as she detached his hand from her midsection, where it had groped too freely. The bald noble, once she had released him, flared and blustered at her, and his aides gathered close about him. But his display of temper was cut short by a wicked laugh from across the table, where Lord Sigmarck sat stroking his sharp chin.

The diminutive baron was obviously scornful of conducting business through so many intermediaries, with no single one of them clearly in charge; now he leaned across the table toward Conan. "I say, Favian! Enough of this nattering. You provide ten companies —no more, no less. After all, this rebel nuisance arises from your own unruly hinterlands. Ten full companies"—he glanced contemptuously to the aides who crowded anxiously nearby—"that is, if your privy counselors will permit it!"

Before the others could speak, Conan found himself nodding decisively. "Done!" He raised his ale-jack in salute, ignoring the nervous whispers behind him.

"Good, then!" Sigmarck likewise sloshed his cup high and drank on the bargain. "That will enable us to sweep this pestilence all the way to the edge of the Varakiel. 'Twill be a jolly hunt!" He set down his flagon, smiling slyly across at Conan. "Tell me, Baron, will you be accompanying us?"

This time Evadne was quickest to reply. "Nay, Baron Sigmarck, our liege regrets that he must remain in Dinander at this critical time. Marshal Durwald will command the force on his behalf."

But Conan had heard Sigmarck utter an eerily familiar word: Varakiel, the name of Ludya's home district. "Indeed I'll come!" he thundered over Evadne's equivocations. Banging down his ale-cup, he turned to his startled guard officers. "Pass the word all down the ranks. We ride on the morrow!"

CHAPTER 13
The March into Hell

Like rotting fangs, stark in burning daylight, rose the soot-blackened walls and ruined towers of Edram Castle. The collapsed interior of the keep was a pit of jumbled darkness, gaping all the blacker because it lay open to brilliant blue sky. The devastation was days old, and no smoke or flame lingered, but the musty stench of damp charcoal filled the outlander's nostrils as he turned from the broken archway.

"So they burned Squire Ulf's castle, as he burned the wretched town upriver," he muttered to Evadne. "I cannot blame them; I longed to do it myself . . . and yet, 'tis strange. I would expect any band of rebels to seize this place and use it to gain control of the valley." Pausing on the stone entry ramp, he gazed along the breached wall, half-tumbled now into reedy swamp. "They could have held off a force like ours for days."

Evadne continued down the walk, answering him over her chain-mailed shoulder: "As I told you, we face not a rebellion here, but a plague! The snake-worshipers spread havoc wherever they go. 'Tis lucky for us that they destroyed only one span of the river bridge."

Conan turned his gaze up the road to where the last of their party was crossing the broken causeway, via an unsteady ropeway floored with charred planking salvaged from the castle. While the rest of the column stood waiting in road order, a few men at a time walked horses and carts across the ragged gap in the bridge, moving slowly and cautiously above the swirling river.

At the road junction just outside the castle's tumbled gate, the diminutive Baron Sigmarck stood with a drawing board at the road's junction, sketching a map; his fellow noble, Ottislav, hulked over a nervous-looking cavalry officer at the base of a nearby wall, cursing lengthily and obscenely over a cast of knucklebones. As Conan walked past the barons, the shorter one looked up to him with a bleak smile. "I think we can move forward safely now, noble Favian. I suggest that we retain our former marching order."

Grunting his assent, Conan sprang onto his chariot, feeling Evadne's vigorous step on the platform beside him. As he took up the reins and made the sweeping arm-signal to advance, she tossed her hair impatiently over her shoulder and spoke guardedly. "As usual, your fellow barons are none too eager to ride in the fore."

"Aye." He waited for the dozen cavalry of the vanguard to get under way. "'Tis a relief not to have to keep company with them, and play an impossible charade. But an honor, no doubt, to lead the column." Working the reins smartly, he wheeled the chariot onto the road in front of the loitering body of Dinander infantry; led by Rudo and others of his cronies, they hailed him in Favian's name with a scattered cheer.

"An honor indeed!" Evadne laughed cynically. "The question is, can we trust the scoundrels at our backs? When the forequarter of our column meets the enemy, how prompt will its hindquarter be in joining the fight? And whom will their swords and barbs strike down, our common foe or ourselves?" She shook her head bitterly. "This military junket is a fine pretext for the barons to cripple Dinander's strength!"

"As I said before," Conan growled, adjusting the hilt at his waist. "But fear not; should the knaves try any treachery with me, I'll skewer them both with a single sword-thrust!"

Ignoring his boast, Evadne spoke on. "More vexing to me are our affairs at home. I worry for our party's shaky alliance with the nobles." She adjusted her grip on the rail as the chariot gained speed. "Durwald controls enough of his former Iron Guard to seize the Manse and declare himself baron, should he take the notion. I only pray that my comrades are strong enough to curb his ambition, and keep him from undoing all our reforms."

"Then I ask you this, Evadne: why did you choose to leave Dinander and ride with me?" Conan glanced aside from the road to look at her, watching as the longest strands of her blond hair stirred with the wind of the chariot's rumbling motion. "The marshal was eager enough to come and oversee my command, until you warned him off."

The mailed woman turned her unflinching blue eyes on Conan. "Do you really think that I would let the two of you consort alone with these sneaking barons? That would be putting too much at risk: our city's security, our troops and our counterfeit heir, all at once!" She set her chin firmly. "If the gods allow it, I must see that you and these troopers return safe to Dinander." She swung her gaze back along the roadway. "You in particular, for the sake of the realm.

"Besides, Conan, one might as well ask what made you insist on coming." It was her turn to watch him from the corner of her eye. "Oh, I know that Cimmerians love a battle better than a currant cake . . . but I sense in you some other, hidden purpose. Ambition of your own, perhaps?"

If the northerner's shrug was a little too casual, Evadne did not seem to detect it. "Why, woman," he told her lightly, "another day of languishing in that worm-eaten Manse would have driven me mad as poor Calissa! Better to face grinning death out here. Better to shiver and perish in the Varakiel marshes."

"I see." Evadne eyed him skeptically. "Perhaps, in your rough, barbaric way, you guessed how much more respect and obedience your uncouth grunts and grimaces would command on a battlefield!" She settled back against the seat-plank, her gaze abandoning him once more.

"Well, Conan," she continued at length, "you usurp baronial power too lightly! However bold you may be, however handsomely you pose at the head of this column, you lack the skills of a trained commander. You will do best to remain silent and heed my advice. As here ahead, where the trees come down close to the track." She gestured toward a hill that rose on one hand, forcing the road to ascend out of the low plain and wind through stands of woodland.

"Aye, Evadne, I know. Having once played hare-and-hound with your rebels in such a place, I would not wish to repeat the experience."

Giving a whistle and a broad wave, Conan slowed his team to a halt, while the officers of the van and the infantry passed his signal back down the line. Then, instead of waiting for his counselor to give the order, Conan addressed the cavalry officer in his own rough accents: "Send two scouts forward through the woods at each side of the road, and two up the center. Tell them to trumpet an alarm if they find the enemy."

As the officer dispatched the riders, Evadne shook her blond head in astonishment, rebuking him with a whisper. "You are too bold! Your foreign speech will add credence to the rumors of your imposture, which already undermine our troops' morale!"

Conan shrugged. "Better that they come to believe the rumors now than in the midst of battle."

Waiting for the scouts to draw well ahead of the formation, they heard horsemen approaching from the rear. They turned to see Sigmarck and Ottislav cantering up, each followed by a pair of well-armed retainers.

"Well, Baron, what is this new delay?" Sigmarck spoke haughtily from his saddle, able for once to stare down his thin nose at Conan standing in his chariot, though only by a slight margin. "Did we not lose time enough crossing the river?"

Evadne was quick to reply. "We might lose all the time that remains to us on earth if we ride into an ambush in yon woods."

"Haw!" Ottislav, hulking on his large horse behind the lesser baron, brayed forth his opinion. "One should not give too much rein to one's fears, blond-hair!" His mustaches twitched with insinuation. "We have to face the enemy sooner or later at all events! Why not just instruct your young master to press on—"

"I ordered a halt," Conan interrupted with gruff restraint, "as is the lead officer's right. If my pace doesn't suit you, you are free to take your troops past me into the van."

"Nay, Baron—or whatever you are." Sigmarck gazed down at him keenly, almost as if seeing him for the first time. "No sense in disrupting the entire column. We leave the matter to you and your lovely . . . advisor. But remember, as senior lords, we claim precedence in all battle decisions." The aristocrat sat gracefully upright in his saddle, turning an insolent charm on Evadne as he continued. "Your regime in Dinander may be new and somewhat . . . informal in its practices; still, it is bound by the traditions that regulate our Nemedian Empire and keep all its parts working together in harmony."

"Not always in harmony," Evadne corrected him. "As when your father's armies mobilized across the Sharken Hills to seize my city's western lands, and had to be driven back by force of arms. Or when your own provincial troops sought to invest Ruthalia, until banned by King Laslo's decree—"

"Now, now, Milady . . ." but Sigmarck's protest was cut short as Conan signaled the column to advance, lashing his team to join them. As the chariot jolted forward, the nobleman spurred his mount to keep pace alongside.

"If you would read to us from the annals of baronial strife," Sigmarck went on smoothly, "there are faults and injustices I could lay at your own province's door. So, doubtless, could my noble friend here." Sigmarck gestured at Ottislav, whose heavy mount clopped close behind. "There are things to be said on both sides in such affairs. Though I would not judge it in the best interest of a government so young and . . . vulnerable as yours to prosecute these ancient feuds."

"No, indeed, Baron Sigmarck." Evadne spoke coldly, yet forcefully enough to be sure the horseman heard her. "We mean to be steady, unquarrelsome neighbors—speaking for my liege lord, of course." She made a stiff-necked bow to Conan, who stood handling the team as if oblivious to the conversation. "Our Baron Favian is a forward-looking ruler; he does not cherish these old grudges."

"Aye, I can tell." Sigmarck nodded slyly to her. "He would seem to have little concern for your city's past; indeed, little link with it. But say"—the suave baron, showing deft horsemanship, reined his steed as close as possible to the chariot's trundling, jolting wheel —"'tis perhaps because of this very newness that your court, as my confidants tell me, is troubled by factions and petty disputes. Ottislav and I want to suggest, should these internal matters ever become

200

too vexing, that you look to us for military support. Our voices have influence beyond the bounds of our own provinces, you know, and our troops stand ready to aid beleaguered friends and fellow nobles where the need is great and . . . heartfelt."

"A thousand thanks, on behalf of my Lord Favian." Evadne nodded curtly to the horseman. "But I think it safe to say, 'twill be a long time before such aid is needed or requested in Dinander. Just now the main threat to us, as to you, is the snake-cult. Hence our support of your present cause; our land has ever been averse to the wiles of the serpent." Her lips flashed a tight, wry smile at the baron. "Once that menace is disposed of, we shall return home to carve out a strong, independent Dinander."

"Haw! For one of your frail sex, you speak with great authority," Ottislav put in with mock approval. "Your baron is lucky to have your protection."

"Aye, though I am a mere woman." Evadne's sarcasm matched the foreigner's. "'Tis a mistake my enemies have made in the past, to forget that the crucible which smelts cook pots can pour out sword-hilts, and that the hand which plucks a loom can also draw a bowstring."

So it went for further leagues through the broadening expanse of the Urlaub Valley, the chain-mailed woman skillfully fending off the threats and blandishments of Baron Sigmarck and his larger, cruder accomplice. When the two nobles finally tired of the pursuit and fell back toward the middle of the column, Conan vented a gusting belly laugh at their thwarted efforts. But Evadne turned on him with a savagery she had spared the foreign nobles.

"Barbaric fool, why must you open your mouth in front of them? You think it a jest, perhaps, to reveal yourself to those schemers? Do you not see that they are subtle foes, whose wiles may yet take a dozen years to unfold to our sorrow?" She grasped the edge of his hauberk with a gloved hand, shoving at his unyielding shoulder in reckless wrath. "I should have known that you were too dangerous, from your stubbornness! And from your habit of promoting your old prison mates, and of arrogating unrighteous authority to yourself!" Her eyes, he was surprised to note, glinted with angry tears. "Well, Lord Conan, I hope your barbaric pride is vindicated. You may have dealt my city her deathblow!"

They rode on in silence, not only because of her smoldering ill-temper, but also because the prospect before them had gradually changed. As the valley broadened, leveling out onto the lush plain where a score of rivers converged to water the Varakiel marshes, the sky ahead had darkened to an eerie grayish-brown.

A pall of smoke, it clearly was, so vast of extent and dark of hue as to signal great devastation in the country ahead. The ominous curtain lay across the eastern sky from pole to pole, scarcely blown before the day's damp, listless breeze. Its crest was formed by towering thunderheads, copper-colored monsters that Conan surmised had flown hither to rut and mate with the dusky, dark billows the earth had spawned. In places the cloud's underside was whorled by darker puffs coiling up from distant conflagrations—the pyres of whole villages and forests, by their size. If this was the work of the snake-cult, the sect was indeed a great sower of havoc.

The unfolding evil was equally evident in the country alongside the arrow-straight, deeply rutted road ahead. Before crossing the Urlaub River, they had passed many inhabited farmsteads and cottages. If the dwellers in those crofts were rough and ragged, their crops sparse and their livestock lame and stunted, at least they hinted at the existence of greater wealth lurking in the thickets, concealed along with the womenfolk well back from the foraging army. But here in this lower, richer land were seen only gutted ruins, flame-blackened coppices and orchards, and crops systematically uprooted in trampled fields. The desolation lay heavy in the troopers' hearts, along with the knowledge that they must rely henceforth on the sparse provisions they carted with them.

"Where in Crom's kingdoms are the bodies?" Conan finally demanded of Evadne, breaking the somber silence between them. "Back at Edram Castle I assumed they had been tossed into the river. But here there are no graves, no human bones, only the rotting carcasses of slaughtered animals!"

The warrior-woman shrugged under her glinting mail. "It is said that in past outbreaks of this madness, all were converted to the new faith, even infants and the very old, and led forth from their homes at the beck of a great prophet. Rare indeed, it is said, is the woman or man who can resist the inducements the great Lord Set offers his disciples." Her weary, unemotional voice stayed level as she scanned the ominous horizon to southward. "Whether they lay waste the earth to deny us forage or to prevent desertions from their own ranks, I know not. The tactic is remembered of old, but I never fully believed the stories until now.

"In view of this chaos, you can well imagine what we shall face." Her words clanked flat and gloomy in the artificial dusk. "No ragtag band of heretics, these! Rather, the entire populace of this district, united in arms and consumed by fanaticism, with nothing left on earth to lose. How, I wonder, can we ever hope to prevail against them?"

"How can we dare fail?" Conan lashed the reins to speed the team along, tossing a discreet glance behind; the yellow-lit faces of the foot soldiers following the chariot appeared sour with the acrid wash of smoke, and deep-shadowed by dread. The Cimmerian told Evadne, "Surely this menace threatens the whole province, by an indirect path around the southern hills. As it may peril other Hybonian lands. Even if it ravages whole empires first, it would be our fight too in the end, methinks. This is our best chance to stop it, perhaps the only chance."

The light was sinking low behind them, splashing lurid reds and yellows onto the tainted sky ahead. A courier rode up from the barons at the rear to inquire about making camp; after conferring, Conan and Evadne sent back word that they would march until nightfall to reduce the threat of desertion.

They pressed on through scorched, desolated croplands, halting only when the sun had finally quenched itself in a bloody, smoking cauldron to westward. By torchlight they built a camp hedged with muddy ditches and clumps of briar, since there was no unburned timber remaining with which to form a proper palisade. In the smoky gloom of night, Conan and the barons ordered doubled sentries, as much to keep their troops within as to fend off what might lurk outside.

CHAPTER 14
Dawn of Blood

"Soldiers, loyal retainers! I called you here tonight to remind you of the duty that carries you so far from your homes. You have come these many leagues, across this ravaged country, to serve your barons; never forget that. I, Sigmarck, have sworn a sacred pledge, as has each and every one of you. My oath binds me to a purpose, just as irrevocably as yours binds you to me and to the other lords here assembled.

"Since passing the village of Kletsk this noon, you have been traversing the domains of Baron Ottislav, my noble ally. The village was destroyed, of course, as are the farms and forests around you. The baron's crops are ruined, his serfs and livestock slain or taken in unrighteous bondage. Thus has the harmony of my friend's rule been interrupted, his rulership insulted!

"It is not in the nature of a baron to tolerate an

insult, be it to himself or to a fellow baron. Therefore, I have sworn to aid Lord Ottislav in avenging this wrong . . . avenging it to the last drop of blood in my body, to the last inch of steel under my command! That, loyal troopers, is why you are here.

"A hard service it has been, I know; harder still it may be on the morrow. But the harshness of the service is matched by the richness of the reward, both in honor and in your lord's esteem. As you go into battle, remember that! Once we are victorious, glory in it! For victorious we shall be!

"I now make way for my gracious friend himself, Baron Ottislav, who wouldst address you. Afterward, we drink a toast to tomorrow's victory!"

Yellow-lit by the torches raised nearby, Sigmarck was careful to leap down from the seat of the two-wheeled cart before its angle was skewed by the weight of the heavily armored baron heaving himself aboard. Ottislav loomed taller against the sky than his predecessor, even though he stood in the plank bed of the cart and cocked one boot against its seat. He turned his habitual sneer for a long moment around the upturned, dutiful faces of the soldiers crowded near the fires. Then he spoke.

"Haw! Men of the eastlands! Nemedians all! You have seen the wrack of our homeland, the rape of our farms and holdings. A dreadful thing, you say to yourselves. What terrible foe, you ask, could have done this to our fine land?

"Well, Nemedians, I tell you, you are wrong! Put aside such unmanly thoughts. There is no terror here, nothing at all to fear—at least not yet. For nothing can compare with the terror of a Nemedian army on the track of vengeance. You are the menace, my ravening hell-hounds, you the terror!

"This havoc is small compared to that we mean to inflict on the enemy. From this moment onward, their lands and possessions are forfeit, their women our cattle, their lives our playthings. We shall scythe them like new grass and thresh them to pieces like brittle grain. Their guts will grease the points of our sabers, their heads dandle from our saddle-posts like green gourds!

"For know you, the carnage of war is a healthy, natural thing. It purges the blood and strengthens the stomach. Bloodletting reminds a man of what a man is made of. A few of you will die, to be sure; and some will suffer grave wounds. But no true Nemedian would let that stand in his way. I bid you go forth to the slaughter in a spirit of honest sport!

"And now I give you—unless the raw lad is tongue-tied—young Favian, Baron of Dinander! Will you let your subjects hear you, sire? Here, come on up." Ottislav tramped down the length of the groaning wagon and dropped to the ground, leering at the object of his challenge.

Conan, seated on a cask at the fringe of the torch-light, looked up blankly as Evadne leaped to her feet by his side. "I should have known this was their plan!" she whispered fiercely to him. "Here, stay, I'll speak for you." In a trice she clambered up the wagon to stand before the troopers, whose ranks rustled and twittered with expressions of admiration for the trim figure silhouetted against the dark sky.

"Fellow Nemedians, I address you on behalf of my liege, Lord Favian, heir of Dinander. He does not style himself a fancy orator. But he wishes me to remind you that when you fight for him on the morrow, you will be fighting for yourselves as well, for your homelands and for the loved ones biding there. . . ."

Evadne's speech was interrupted by a bulkier shape looming at her side: that of Conan, effortlessly mounting the wheel-spokes and stepping into the cart. As he placed an arm across her shoulders to steady her, whispers flew among the troops at the sight of this handsome couple standing limned in torchlight.

"Troopers," Conan's timbrous voice carried out over the throng, "I come before you not as a baron . . ."

At this a buzz of bemused assent issued from his listeners, since rumor held that, indeed, he was not one.

". . . or even as a Nemedian."

Again, at Conan's hesitancy, there sounded earnest agreement from the throng, for the accents of his speech corroborated his words.

"I stand before you as a man."

Although murmurs still coursed through the crowd, there was none who could gainsay this, so the troops stood patiently awaiting his next pronouncement.

"As a man, I know good from evil. Or I try to know it. I surely can recognize a great and growing evil when it tweaks me in the face." He paused uncertainly again as his listeners nodded and murmured, affirming the wisdom of his words.

"I have marched with you in these past days. I know, as you know, that what we face here is wholly, utterly evil. It is the way of the serpent." The muttering of the troopers grew heartfelt, with occasional strident yells of agreement. Conan's next words had to be shouted to be heard.

"As a man, I know enough to set my boot heel on the head of a viper!"

Without further oration, he turned and was gone, helping Evadne down from the bed of the wagon. He left the troops in a turmoil, cheering, jostling and waving fists in the air. A chant of "Favian" was set up somewhere, to die away just as quickly in disputes over the truth of the name.

Whether the soldiers had enjoyed his speech for its sentiment or for its brevity was unclear, even to those who liked it best. The hubbub was due in part, certainly, to the eve-of-battle toasting; tots of rum were promptly dispensed from heavily guarded casks around the camp. The northerner tossed off the one that was handed to him and sat down again in the torchlight, disregarding the thoughtful, resentful stares and whispers of Sigmarck and Ottislav. Evadne, saying nothing, settled down close by his side.

Conan was pensive, pondering recent events. After passing the ruin of Edram Castle and making their first night's camp in the wasted lands, it had taken another day's brisk march to draw near the creeping edge of the devastation. The ashes of cottage and barn had grown gradually warmer, the air darker and fouler with smoke, and then, toward dusk, their scouts had reported finding the enemy. No refugees, no trailing supply lines, just swarms of footborne ravagers bearing crude weapons, torches and firepots through the fields. Even now, by night, distant red-lit underbellies of cloud could be glimpsed where fires flared to southward and eastward.

Conan still hoped to find Ludya, or to send word for her. Yet he was forming the eerie conviction that no living human remained between himself and the Varakiel, long leagues to northward. Nor were there yet any bodies. In the chapel-yard of the ravaged village of Kletsk, even the new graves had been ruptured, their soil upturned and their tenants vanished with the rest of the townsfolk.

At these odd circumstances, superstitious fears beset the troops. Worst was their dread of the vipers that seemed so strangely prevalent in these damp lowlands; fortunately, none of the men had yet been bitten. Desertions had been surprisingly few, and were less likely this deep in enemy territory. The troops seemed ready to fight—more so, possibly, than were their leaders.

Now they awaited the dawn to face a foe they knew nothing about. The barons, confident of victory, had formed only the vaguest battle plan: march forth at first light, attack from the flank and the rear, and rely on the snake-cultists' relative lack of weapons, armor and training to defeat them. Conan himself knew no better approach. If the Nemedian companies kept their formations tight and mobile amidst a scattered enemy, there was no reason why their few hundred troops could not vanquish ten thousand and more.

And so the Cimmerian sat brooding late into the night, pondering the turbulent events in Dinander and the strange turn of fortune that had brought him to his present station. Of course, he reminded himself, he could still make his escape. Never would it be easier than now; he need merely stray beyond the torchlight on an errand of nature, and fail to return.

But he knew he would stay; he had spoken truth to the soldiers earlier. He found himself confronted with an evil well worth the battling; also, there was the dwindling hope of finding his old love. But even more, he sensed a dawning of unknown potentials; if he survived this battle, where would it leave him situated with the barons and thralls of Nemedia?

So he sat until long after Ottislav and Sigmarck had drunk their fill and retired to their tents, when the only lights remaining were a few dim tapers marking the sentries' routes. Evadne dozed near him, curled on the ground, a horse blanket drawn across her chilly mail; she tended to stay close to Conan and her few faithful guard officers, in this camp full of lusty foreign males. Now, as the outlander sat brooding, she stirred in the starless, smoky dimness and spoke to him.

"Perhaps you were right, Conan. I despised you yesterday, but now I understand you better." Fresh from her rest, and without the tension of public discourse, her voice sounded pleasantly soft. "This battle we face may be more important than any politics, even more important than Dinander itself."

"It will be all-important to us, if we are to die in it." As he spoke, Conan scanned the darkness for any last sign of distant fires; he saw none.

"No, do not think of death. Just lead your troops well." She sat up, hugging the blanket around herself. "You primed them well tonight; now they will follow you more loyally as Conan than they ever would as Favian. Be yourself, do not trouble to play a role."

"The role is outworn anyway." For the tenth time that night, Conan tilted his cup to his lips to make sure it was empty.

"You no longer need it. I have seen you fight fiercely, both for and against our cause. You have the prowess to be a strong leader in battle."

"Aye, if nowhere else!" Conan's gloom lay on him as black and heavy as the night shrouding the camp. "But you, Evadne . . ." he turned to her . . . "you have the wit to govern a land at peace, to steer the destinies of courts and kingdoms. Pray you, take care in battle tomorrow; stand apart with the barons and see that they don't betray us. You are too valuable to be sacrificed in the front line."

At these words Evadne stiffened beneath her blanket. "I am a warrior, remember! I did not bring an end to the Einharson tyranny with honeyed words, but with bloodied steel. My place is among our troops."

She halted abruptly in her speech as a footfall sounded nearby; when one of the officers stepped into the light and saluted, followed closely by an infantryman, her steel dirk winked back into its scabbard. Conan, likewise, laid down his sword and spoke a greeting. "Yes, Rudo. What is it?"

"Co . . . Milord Baron, we sent forth roving patrols as you ordered. Now this sentry"—Rudo pushed the footsoldier forward—"brings a report of enemy movements to eastward."

"Yes? What did you see, then? Speak, man!" Conan admonished him.

"Milord, we saw nothing. They carried no lights, and we dared not show ours. But we heard footsteps —a great many, moving steadily on both sides of us.

213

Also, a strange sound . . . it may have been just their feet sliding through tall grass, but it sounded like . . . like hissing snakes." The sentry choked to a halt, flustered. "We . . . we made our way back to camp by following a ditch. They must have seen the camp lights earlier; I think they mean to strike at dawn."

"Crom! I told Sigmarck his torchlight ceremony was a mistake!" Conan reached out to extinguish the flickering taper, then thought better of it. "Rudo, what about the other approaches to the camp?"

"No word yet. The last patrol we dispatched to westward is overdue."

"Hell's gnawing fiends! Rudo, alert the barons! And you, man, make the rounds of the officers' tents. Have them bid the troopers ready themselves quietly, without lights. Full armor. And tell them to lace their buskins up high against serpents!"

Conan strode to his tent, followed closely by Evadne—for they shared the same pavilion, a chaste curtain strung between their cots. As he fumbled for greaves and bassinet with which to complete his armor, her whisper came to him through the cloth: "There is little in this fight for a crack Nemedian legion to fear. The snake-worshipers can scarcely have mastered military tactics and drill."

"Only enough to raze Edram Castle." Feeling for the tent post, he clutched his steel buckler to prevent it from clattering to the floor.

"Well, at least they have lost the advantage of surprise." He heard the soft clink of her chain-mail being arranged.

"Aye. But if they are not utter fools, they have surrounded us by now."

"Conan, do you remember what you once said at the Manse? About us being two of a kind?" Her whisper in the darkness was made even softer by a faint huskiness in her voice. "Tonight I saw that like me, you have a knack for leadership. I know you better now. Perhaps there could be profit in a union between us. . . ."

"By Ishtar! You women are seized by lust at the strangest times!" Conan's ill-restrained astonishment gusted through the tent. "I would oblige you, Evadne, but it could scarcely be managed in this armor."

"I didn't mean that!" Her momentary closeness vanished in a long, unmoving silence. "Although," she finally added, "once this battle is past, you could ask me again."

"I shall, depend on it!" The brisk rattling of his armor-stays revealed his exhilaration at the thought.

In another moment both Sigmarck and Ottislav were before the tent, gruffly demanding Conan's presence. With a last click of his sword-buckle, he strode out to meet them. "Hush, you two," he rasped, "or the enemy will be no more surprised than we are."

"So? What does it matter?" Sigmarck's voice issued low in the night gloom. "Neither of us can do aught in this blackness anyway. We make ready, and come morning, we fight them; what more is there?"

"You intend to wait here behind our flimsy barricade and let them come at us, in all their multitudes? What will you do if they decide not to attack us, but merely stand off and throw fire and snakes into our midst? Or build defenses of their own, and starve us out?"

"Aha, I see that the young baron knows the value of

215

discretion!" Ottislav's laugh fell unpleasantly on Conan's ear. "But how do you expect to run, lad, if we are surrounded? 'Twould be disastrous to be caught by the enemy while sneaking away. . . ."

"Run? I said nothing of running. I mean to attack at first light!" Conan's voice throbbed forcefully in the darkness. "That way we can break the encirclement and hold on to the initiative. What are our cavalry for, if not to attack and keep the foe off balance?"

"But attack whom, and where?" Sigmarck demanded. "To attack outward in all directions at once is madness! It would disperse our force."

"When you fight a serpent, where do you strike? At its head! Once the head is destroyed, the body twitches and dies." Conan's words flowed out swift and sure. "So we press toward the enemy's commanders, who will be somewhere to eastward, near their center. That will be easy once dawn comes: we simply order the men to attack into the rising sun. When we've overrun their first perimeter, we can turn our strength where it will do the most good."

Evadne had come out of the tent to stand close beside Conan. "A clever plan, my baron—but remember, we have the burden of a shared command. I think it might be better to stand on the defensive at first."

"No, wait, there is something to be said for his idea." Smoothly Sigmarck took up the thread of the argument. "After all, our elite companies can certainly hold formation against an unruly mob, and the offensive will give us commanders a degree of control we would otherwise lack. If we can ready the men and horses with a minimum of noise. . . ." He muttered

orders to one of his officers, who nodded an acknowledgment and turned away.

"My salute to you, young warlord!" Ottislav
chimed in. "Your plan embodies the best Nemedian
virtues: ferocity and resourcefulness! I too will back
you!"

And so the nighted camp stirred with furtive activity, firefly wisps of tapers the only light. Conan saw to
the hitching of his chariot and the most essential of
the supply carts. By the time he was finished, a faint,
half-illusory radiance was mounting in the eastern
sky.

The silence intensified then, as troopers knelt in
readiness about the camp. Token forces were assigned
to hold the north, west and south perimeters, but only
until a breakthrough was signaled to eastward; then
they would move forth, following the wagons through
the gap made in the encirclement.

False dawn faded, and the light seemed to take
forever to return. The waiting would have been easier,
the men thought, if only they had some idea of what
lurked beyond the low barricade of shrubs and
outward-pointed snags.

Conan stood vigilant in his chariot as the dimness
spread and then deepened into a faint, muddy smear
low in the sky to eastward. Evadne waited beside him,
quietly at work in the ghost light, bending and string-
ing her long, slim bow and lashing extra quivers of
arrows to the chariot rail. The driver they had chosen
stood by the horses, murmuring softly to quiet them.

Finally sunrays pried through the dense, stale layers
of sky at the earth's rim. Smoke-tinged, the light
blossomed brighter and more luridly by the moment,

brushing orange highlights across the undersides of hanging clouds. Conan saw reflections playing redly on the metal curves of the horses' harness; he heard low grunts and scrapings ahead, as troopers toiled to drag aside movable sections of barricade. He raised his arm high, and his driver swung aboard, taking up the reins; then he lowered his hand, and barked an order. Trumpets shattered the stillness at either side as the chariot leaped forward.

CHAPTER 15
The Thousand-Tongued Serpent

At first they saw nothing in the dimness but brush-mottled meadowland spreading before the paling smudge of sunrise. Then the riders felt the muffled jolting of hooves and chariot-wheels laboring over low, unseen obstacles. At last, arising from the knee-high grass all around, a few dim shapes appeared, growing to a swarm and then a host as the camp's besiegers broke from concealment on all sides.

In a moment they loomed so thick before the straining chariot-team that they slowed the battle-car's progress. The horses whinnied with rage and fear as they plunged to obey the charioteer's lashing whip. Conan struck out fiercely with a javelin clutched in either hand, stabbing ahead and sideward at the half-seen, converging figures; the attackers pressed so near that there was no need to cast his weapons.

Beside him he heard Evadne's bow twanging steadily, plied with desperate swiftness.

From the rear, the thunder of hoofbeats continued as the cavalry erupted out of camp. Screams, curses and the clang of weapons told how quickly it was engaged. Yet those horsemen who galloped in the body-littered wake of the chariot soon overtook it, veering left and right to broaden the attack front.

Conan, straining and striking from his fighting-platform, listened behind him with a worried ear. Finally, on hearing a distant, spreading clamor born of a hundred throats, he smiled in grim satisfaction. The infantry were being ordered forward; at last the battle was fully joined. Plying javelins with remorseless vigor, piercing each dim target as it flashed by, he searched ahead in the dawning light for sign of the enemy commanders.

He saw none, but what he did see almost made him regret looking too closely. Now that the sun's full intensity broke over the plain, spearing it with violet rays and seeming to kindle the easterly grasses into a band of smoldering orange, it revealed more starkly the nature of the foes he had been striking at. Looming against the sunrise, tall-shadowed in the low, crimson light, these were beings who had long since forsaken their humanity.

He had expected to face gaunt disciples of Set, mad-eyed and tongue-slit like the pitiful youth he had seen in Ulf's tower. But here were veritable demons: hissing, grimacing things leaping at him out of the dawn, knowing no regard for their own lives or those of their comrades. Their picks and scythes were terrible enough, flashing high against the red sky to strike dartingly at men and horses. But many of the attackers also bore snakes as weapons, or wore them as adornment, looped around their necks, writhing in their filthy garments or plaited into their lank, straggling hair.

To compound the menace, the lunges and grimaces of the cultists had a supernaturally fluid, reptilian quality; and Conan swore that some of the wrathful eyes flashing past him bore vertical, slitted pupils, like those of serpents.

But the greatest horror came as one of the reckless attackers transfixed himself on the point of Conan's spear. At the fatal instant, the man's mouth opened in a rage of agony; but instead of a tongue, there darted forth from his lips a green-headed asp, a living snake rooted in the wretch's mouth, striking vainly and repeatedly with its tiny fangs at the shaft of the javelin that transfixed its writhing, gasping host. Conan quickly relinquished the spear and its horrid burden, groping behind him with an unsteady hand for a fresh weapon as more attackers loomed beyond the fallen thing.

Gazing around the wheeling, converging horde of enemies, he glimpsed a new wave of serpent-tongued fighters, and he could tell from Evadne's gasps of consternation that the lurid daylight was revealing hideous sights to her as well. The effect was most telling on the horses, who tended to balk or shy at the sight of snakes. Fortunately, all four of the chariot-team were armor-masked and narrowly blinkered. Herd instinct, or sheer momentum, augmented by their driver's deft handling, kept them moving through the press of battle, if unsteadily. The passengers saw several nearby cavalrymen stopped in their tracks, thrown from their saddles or dragged down by mobs of snake-teeming foes.

The Nemedian infantry, slower in overtaking the main attack front, must needs meet the demonic horde face-to-snarling-face; consequently its ranks suffered the worst from the cultists' jabbing blades and fangs. A favorite tactic of the snake-tongued fighters was to parry or clutch their adversary's weapon with one hand, heedless of injury from its edge, while wresting aside the swordsman's shield or buckler with the other hand. Then, leering hideously and pressing intimately close in the thick of battle, they would open their lips in a venomous kiss. The agile tongue-vipers, long and sufficiently slender to penetrate a breathing-slit or an eyehole, found a tightly visored helm no obstacle. Their bite, to all appearances, was agonizingly fatal.

Conan cursed himself for failing in his battle plan to foresee the extent of the enemy's sorcery. Besides enhancing their deadliness and threatening to devastate his side's morale, their utter inhumanity seemed to exempt the snake-worshipers from the ordinary requirements of command. Even now, having broken through the main ring of besiegers circling the camp, he could see no sign of a central leader—or of generals or reserves, or even of petty officers to marshal the attack. The cultists seemed to throw themselves forward, sustaining their effort with a tireless, unquestioning unanimity; possibly they harked to the voice of immortal Set himself, hissing assurances ceaselessly in their ears.

Whatever their mystical unity, it appeared to leave

the counterfeit warlord no place wherein to strike a fatal blow. Ordering his charioteer to wheel back through the thinning straggle of enemies, he reconnoitered toward camp. There he saw the escape corridor widened and the supply train and rear guard finally moving forward—an army intact and mobile, but lacking an objective! Rasping with ill temper, he ordered his charioteer to turn eastward again.

"At least we broke free of the camp," Evadne remarked to him. "With these thousands pressing us, it could have been a death-trap." Her archery had long since diminished to occasional stray shots; now she stooped over her bow to fit a new string to it, using a razored arrow-tip to slice away the loops of the old frayed one.

"Aye. 'Tis best to keep our army on the move, if it prevents the bulk of the enemy from converging on us at once." Conan gazed past the wheeling, skirmishing cavalry toward the southern flank of the army, where cultists still threw themselves against the Nemedians' close-knit line. "But we must find a target worth attacking. We spend our strength too freely against these unending hordes." He stepped up onto the grillwork of the chariot, steadying himself by grasping a harness rope as he scanned the field. "Ah, there, driver! Forward quickly, past those stunted trees. I want that man!"

The momentary splendor of sunrise had faded to a smoky radiance in the east, yellow-brown where the orb's light trickled through a dark, formless ceiling of mist and smoke. The sky's sooty translucence made it seem likely that before another hour had passed, they would no longer be able to tell direction by means of the sun. Yet the jaundiced day permitted visibility a good way across the plain. By its light to eastward, a crowd of figures could be seen straggling through the tall grass. The foremost of them, a stout warrior, moved to meet the chariot with the same numb steadiness the other cultists showed, but his silver-bright armor drew attention.

Evadne stared his way, exclaiming to Conan, "Why, that is Ulf, late the squire of Edram Castle! The old scalawag!" Smoothly she nocked a hard-pointed shaft to her bow, sighting on the breastplate of the distant, shambling figure.

"No, feather him not!" Conan clutched her shoulder to spoil her aim. "We need a captive to guide us to these hell-fiends' leader. Ulf is a recent convert to their cause, and he may not yet be so far gone as the rest. Swing near him, driver—take care not to trample him."

The fat warrior, tardy for the camp siege, plodded doggedly forward, dragging his long-bladed sword along the ground. As the chariot bore down on him, he perked up, his gait changing to a lumbering trot, his weapon lifted two-handed in readiness. Then the horses thundered by, blowing the nearby grass blades flat with the wind of their passing. As the chariot followed around on one wheel, Conan launched himself from the platform to strike the man full on, body to body, forearm to throat. The squire's raised sword sailed off into a bush as the two armored bodies rolled on the turf, grunting and clanking.

"Ulf! Yield, old tyrant!" Growling with effort, Conan forced his weight atop the struggling squire. "You are my captive, and we will have speech together

224

if you value your nose!" With a convulsive movement, he drew his dagger and held it poised before the supine man's face.

"*Sa setha Efanissa*!" Ulf spat out the ritual syllables at Conan, his slitted tongue lashing and sibilating against dry, cracked lips. "*Hathassa fa Sathan*!"

"Enough!" Forcing down a spasm of revulsion at the sight, Conan smote the butt of his dagger against the temple of his enemy's helm, causing the stubble-jowled head to rattle within. "You are Squire Ulf, late of Edram Castle! You may have been a black-hearted rogue, but you were a man! And a man you still are, or shall be—if I have to sew up that forked tongue of yours myself! Now answer me, who is the leader of the snake-cult?"

"Laa . . . larthhh! Larrrhhhh!" The eyes of the haggard man seemed to focus somewhat, and his struggles ceased, but his tongue had difficulty in forming its accustomed sounds. Occasionally, between his efforts, it escaped his mouth to lash crazily against his bleeding lips. "Larrrhh isss priessssst!"

"Good, man, that's better." Leaning closer, Conan braced his knife-holding fist against his captive's chin. "And where can I find this priest Larth of yours? Which way do I ride?"

"Eassssttt!" Ulf worked an arm free to wave it behind him, indicating the grassland. "Larrrrhh is eassst. Eassssssttt . . . ahh! Aieee!"

Startled at his prisoner's convulsive shrieks, Conan glanced down to see with a shock that a small purple viper had wormed its way from beneath Ulf's breast-plate and was sinking its fangs into the unwilling informant's neck. He reached down to flick the serpent aside with his dagger blade, only to discover a second snake's emerald body threading up out of the grass. Its fangs went deep into the hapless squire's cheek.

With a spasm of uncontrollable dread, Conan leaped to his feet, spying more serpentine flickers in the grass all around him. Sheathing his knife, he drew his sword to hack fiercely at those nearest. Then, standing over the gasping, blue-faced Ulf, he raised his weapon high and brought it slashing down. The stroke ended the squire's writhing agonies by severing his head.

"Conan! Beware!" He turned to see an ax-wielding cultist rushing at him through the grass; but before he could raise his sword to meet the charge, the form staggered two steps and collapsed, an arrow jutting from its armpit.

"Why bother to warn me at all, Evadne, if you insist on taking the mark every time . . . Crom!" His grim good nature turned to alarm as he swung around to see that the chariot moved at a near stop a few dozen paces away, suddenly beset by attackers. The driver lay thrashing helplessly a dozen paces in its wake, his neck seized in the jaws of a large serpent that had been hurled onto him as he drove. The chariot-team was rendered nearly immobile by the loss of the reins, and by a cultist who had thrown himself onto the starboard horse, clambering back along its harness toward the fighting-platform. Evadne was preparing to launch an arrow into him, but even as she raised her bow, three more attackers overtook the slow-moving chariot.

"Mannannan's black blood!" Pelting through the

226

grass, Conan roared the war-cry to distract the enemy; but the cultists did not trouble to look back. As the arrow-pierced snake-worshiper slipped from the shying horse's trappings to bump briefly under the chariot's rolling wheel, the foremost of the pursuers vaulted onto the platform. Evadne turned and slashed with her bow to club him off, but he ignored the blow, hacking low and viciously at her with his long-handled scythe.

"Bite steel, dog of Set!" Conan's sword-slash laid open the rearmost harrier's back from nape to kidney, driving him to earth. The Cimmerian trod the writhing corpse underfoot without a glance, dashing for the chariot, where Evadne had no chance to avoid her attacker's sickle-strokes.

"Die, worm-spawn!" The second cultist left one arm clutching the chariot-rail, the rest of his body shorn away bleeding as Conan boarded the car. He was too close behind Evadne's attacker to swing his sword. "Wretch! Go find your father in hell!" The man was already choking on one of Evadne's arrow stabbed shallowly into his throat; now Conan jabbed it deeper, twisting it cruelly as he hurled the creature away behind.

"Conan . . . please . . . " Evadne slumped to the floor, clasping reddened hands beneath her heart. "I am slain."

"No, girl, lie still." Searching in vain for a whip or the reins, he used the flat of his gory sword to slap the horses' skittish rumps into a trot. Once the chariot was trundling faster than the pace of the converging scatter of enemies, he knelt beside Evadne. "Here, let me bind your wound." His throat clenched to see how much blood washed the chariot floor. "I'll take you back—"

"Conan, listen. . . ." The rebel woman's voice was weak, her face waning paler than her blond tresses. "If you survive, you will return to Dinander. Promise me!"

"Yes, Evadne." He reached underneath her to prop her sagging back. "So shall you; we will ride there in triumph. . . ." But it was too late; her head tilted away sightlessly toward the murky sky.

He knelt with her for a long moment, cradling her slack, almost weightless body against the jolting of the cart. Finally he lay her down gently and climbed to his feet, taking up his sword in blood-grimed hands.

He stood numb in the chariot, scarcely aware of the hissing, grimacing snake-worshipers who jogged after him in pursuit. Far to eastward, a column of smoke rose into the murky sky. Glancing back toward the camp, he saw a few cavalry, all of them black-mailed troops of Dinander, riding down stray enemies. Farther beyond, he could hear trumpets skirling, calling masses of troops together under the raised banners, hanging slack in the airless morning, of Sigmarck and Ottislav.

How like the swinish barons to stop and look after their own interests at the first opportunity, instead of pressing onward as agreed! Perhaps, had they not lagged so far behind, Evadne might yet be alive; he shook his head bitterly, blaming himself nevertheless for her death. At all events, her dying wish still whispered in his brain. He must now turn back to protect the interests of his troops, lest the warriors of

Dinander be callously scattered and sacrificed to the enemy.

But as he turned to the front, his chariot suddenly pitched and stopped short, hurling him sharply against the rail. The horses of the team reared and lunged to both sides at once, terrified by the sight of a naked, dancing warrior decked with living snakes, who had sprung out of the low sedges directly in front of them.

Struggling for footing on the blood-slick, heaving platform, Conan abruptly found his arms pinioned as two of the hissing, chattering pursuers hurled themselves simultaneously atop him. He twisted to break free, but a third snake-eyed attacker leaped aboard to straddle all three, wielding high a stone-headed hammer. It plunged swiftly downward, striking the northerner's helm with an odd, stunning silence. Again, silently, it rose and fell; then again, as if Conan's skull were the head of a spike being patiently driven into the chariot timbers. With the hammer's fourth stroke, the numb silence exploded to engulf everything.

CHAPTER 16
The Head of the Serpent

Ravening flame consumed all. It spread and flowed like a mighty cataract, writhed as exquisitely as a tortured animal and sent blazing rootlets and blossoms creeping forth with tireless, plantlike energy. From its fury and withering heat, Conan knew that the Set-cult had triumphed. It's unquenchable holocaust had engulfed not only the Nemedian plain, but the entire world of men. Mad, surging flames now danced their ultimate victory; they would continue to do so for all eternity.

And yet, perhaps not everything was destroyed, for deep within the flames there hovered a ghost. Dim and remote, at times distorted or melted entirely by shimmering heat, the face was nonetheless beautiful. Dark-shadowed, gleaming eyes like dusky wells of dream; delicately round, blush-tinted cheeks; lips stained deeply red, as from tasting the juice of pomegranates. The face gazed forth beatifically from the fire, radiating at once the complacency of total knowledge and the passion of boundless desire.

Was it lost Evadne? No, this visage was framed by black curls that gloomed as night to her day-bright tresses. Yet it was a familiar face, and a loved one. It smiled serenely from the flames as if witnessing the world's fate and accepting it utterly, blissfully.

Ludya.

The shock of the name brought Conan more fully to consciousness as he lay stuck with congealed blood to the bed of the motionless chariot. He shut his eyes, their pupils scorched dry by the heat of the campfire, and learned that even the least flick of his eyelids sent tremors of discomfort throbbing through his skull. When he tried to raise his head from its lolling, crook-necked posture at the edge of the platform, all the unfelt pain and din of the hard-swung stone sledgehammer caught up with him at once.

He lay still then, trying to fix his aching, echoing brain on one certain fact: across the fire-circle from him sat a painted, smiling girl, and that girl was Ludya.

As his misery gradually diminished, he sensed movements nearby. A languid voice drifted toward him.

"Oh, indeed, this is a fine chariot! Better by far than our rickety old haycart." It was a boyish contralto, speaking guilelessly and sweetly, though at times it cracked with the huskiness of approaching manhood. "At long last I can transport you in the fashion you deserve, Milady! We will pile it thick with cushions and soft tapestries for your comfort."

"That will be fine, Lar." The answering murmur caused Conan to stir again with recognition. Consequently he suffered a new wave of pain, though less intensely than before.

"It will have to be cleansed first," the boyish voice said. "One of its riders, a woman, spilled her life's blood into it, so I am told. A sad waste—now she can never join us." The speaker moved closer to Conan's inert form. "But life still lingers in this man. Even if he fails to recover from his wound, he can be reclaimed to our cause."

Feeling a soft, tentative prod at the unarmored skin of his arm, Conan stirred, or tried to. "Wretched scut . . . I'll drag you . . . screaming to hell first!"

His threat was scarcely audible, blurred by his gasps as he slowly heaved himself onto his side. He groped among blinding, pulsating curtains of agony for his dagger. But he found none, and the insolent, piping voice would not retreat. He realized that he was out of doors and that it was day, though the dim lowering of the sky made the fire seem bright.

"For shame, fellow! Your threats do not swerve me. Why must you Hyborians ever practice violence?" Lar shifted impatiently before the flames, his voice cracking as it grew self-righteous. "Your unprovoked attack costs many lives on both sides—taking countless souls who would have rejoiced to serve our cause." He shook his tousled head resignedly. "You will never stop us, of course, but still I mourn the loss. It would be so much easier if you would simply try to understand."

"Understand!" Grasping the chariot rail, Conan

dragged himself to a sitting position. "Talking of losses, your host moves through the countryside like a locust swarm—slaying and burning what and whom you do not steal!" He blinked hazily at the frail figure outlined by the licking flames, to see it suddenly joined by the burly silhouettes of two peasant guards.

"A common delusion." Lar cast his voice across the fire to where Ludya sat encushioned as his audience. "Like most people in these decadent times, you overvalue transient, temporal things. You have forgotten the strength of true devotion. Before it, material goods and personal obligations are as nothing."

Conan did not reply. He was occupied in holding himself upright, swallowing the deep draughts of pain that pulsed from his throbbing skull, flexing his fingers and toes to test them for sensation. Then, under the incurious eyes of Lar and his guards, he set about prying the dented, split helmet away from his skull, probing carefully at the broken steel where it was embedded in the clotted mess of hair and scalp. Finally, agonizingly, it came free, and he prodded gingerly above his ear to make certain that his brain did not lie open to the sky.

No, he decided, the wound would heal, if only Crom granted him life for another fortnight. He cast away the shattered husk of helmet and focused his slowly clearing vision on his captors.

The boy had none of the monstrousness that Conan had expected to find in the cult's prophet. He seemed strangely innocent, enough so to disarm the Cimmerian's natural impulse of mayhem toward him. He was, after all, only a child, hovering at the brink of the mystic transformation to manhood. A fine-featured, yellow-haired lad, slightly arrogant perhaps, and looking almost effeminate in his cape of gold-embroidered purple and his heavy gold chaplet. But he moved with a careless lightness of limb that bespoke an easy conscience, boding no conceivable threat to the onlooker.

His hulking guardians, one dressed as a smith and the other as a fur-trapper, appeared to be stolid, mindless types. They stood ready to obey, albeit without speed or initiative. Like their leader, they showed none of the bestial marks of Set, though for all Conan knew, their shut mouths might harbor nimble snake-tongues.

They waited with their young master before the fire, in the meadow in the midst of the trackless plain. Overhead stretched a taciturn sky whose cloudy, smoky expanse betrayed neither time nor direction. The camp's appurtenances were few: a tent painted with serpents and other mystic symbols, a battered ox-cart decked with faded pillows and tapestries, an open chest of food and wine-jugs, and Conan's own chariot.

His weary horses were tethered nearby, grazing with several other mounts along a shallow, meandering stream. Across the brushy grassland came no sign of the roving cult-hordes, no echo of battle cries or trumpets. The horrors of the morning could have been a dream, except for the blood that caked the Cimmerian's armor and stained the chariot where he sat.

Finally, tardily, Conan shifted his attention to the

other person present. He felt a reluctance to turn his gaze on her, greater even than his disinclination to stare into the blinding heart of the fire. This hesitancy, amounting almost to a fear, came not only from her stunning beauty, but from her inexplicable, evil presence here. He met her sloe eyes cautiously and found them staring back at him with some of the same blithe innocence as the young cult-leader's.

Ludya rested on a litter of pillows spread before Lar's cart. She was carefully groomed and painted, dressed in bits of finery well-calculated to accent her womanly charms without concealing them; she looked as passionately immodest as any courtesan of the king's chambers in Belverus. Her hips and breasts were bound in fringed scraps of embroidery, the tapering curves of her legs veiled by gossamer pantaloons, her feet fitted with the frailest of sandals, her ankles, waist and brow circled by glittering gold chains. Her figure was as full and supple as Conan remembered, but daily exposure to the sun had darkened her skin to a tawny color. He could not see whether the stripes of Favian's lash still marred her back, but her lithe languor made it clear that her body, if not her mind, had recovered from her ordeal in the Manse.

"I see that you appreciate my Ludya's beauty," Lar piped up beside Conan. "She is a cherished companion, my one indulgence. Go sit by her and make her acquaintance. Here, you will be more comfortable lying on these cushions." Striding to his wagon well in advance of his lumbering guards, the youth dragged forth more pillows from it and spread them on the ground beside the reclining girl. Kneeling before her, he said, "Entertain our guest well, my love. Teach him in your gentle way the wisdom of our beliefs, whilst I attend to some small chores."

After addressing his consort, Lar kissed her, administering only a swift, chaste peck to her cheek. Watching the boy's manner with Ludya, Conan realized that he did not use her as a man would. Rather, he primped her appearance and cared for her as a child dressing a toy doll, lavishing some of the doting affection on her that boys commonly reserve for a mother or an elder sister.

Striding over and tugging at Conan's arm, Lar raised him up, admonishing him, "Come, do not be shy!" Conan shook off the boy's weak grip; nevertheless he followed his lead, remaining just as dumb as the bodyguards who loomed close on either hand.

"Here are fruit and cheese and wine," Lar said, indicating the food chest that stood open nearby. "Satisfy yourselves; I do not feel like eating on this battle-day; my stomach is all astir. Now come along, you two lackeys! Help me drag this chariot down to the stream." As the three turned away, Conan stood mute over Ludya, reeling with his wounds and numb with a vague dread, expecting at any moment to see snakes squirm from the houri's scented hair or a reptile tongue issue from between her pert, painted lips.

"Conan, do not fear. I know it is you. Come sit by me!" Adjusting her veiled limbs with simple grace, Ludya arose to her knees and beckoned with supplicating hands. "When first they brought you here, I

thought you were Favian. You seemed to be dead, and
I rejoiced at it. When you stirred and answered Lar in
those coarse Cimmerian accents, I thought my heart
would burst from my chest with joy!" Smiling up at
him, she pressed her hands to her sparsely covered
bosom to emphasize her emotion. "But come and
rest, my love, and I will tend your wounds. I now see
that I have no need of this." Reaching down behind
her into a shallow fold of tapestry, she produced a
long knife, wickedly curved and razor-tipped. She laid
it on the cushion before her.

"Ah, Ludya, more than one wench has carried a
sharp dagger for Favian!" Conan could see that his
friend was her old self; grating out a painful laugh, he
stooped down to seat himself on the velvet beside her.
"'Tis no marvel that his life was short."

"What, he is dead? And you have taken his place in
Baldomer's affections?" She clutched Conan's shoulder, gazing into his face with eager, mascared eyes
while he nearly swooned at the ravishing sight and
scent of her.

"Easy, girl, back off and let me breathe!" He pushed
her to arm's length, nevertheless keeping a hand on
her warm shoulder to steady himself. "The Einharson
tyrants are both dead, overthrown by a woman much
like you. . . ." With frequent halts and backtrackings,
and carefully omitting any mention of his tumblings
with Calissa, he told Ludya of the events that had
unfolded after her exile from the Manse. While he
spoke, she fussed over him; though he would not let
her probe or bathe his wound, she bound a dry herb
compress over it by means of a thong around his head.

". . . and so Evadne died. I could gut those barons for hanging back and not supporting my advance!" He stirred restlessly, drawing her gentle hands away from his brow. "But tell me, what happened after you returned home? How did you fall in with the snake-cult?"

"Lar's coach met mine on the road. I never again saw my home or my parents." She shook her head slowly, in uncertain remembrance. "I was half-mad with hatred then, and sick with a brain fever. But Lar did not trouble me with questions or make any demands. He just kept me at his side and cared for me, like a true friend. Our talks are mainly of foolish things—the songs of birds, the waves the wind makes in the grass of the steppe. These clothes . . ." unblushing, she indicated her scanty array . . . "are treasures his followers bring him."

"But what of the marches and the sieges?" Conan prompted her. "Your young boyfriend is a formidable general!" He looked across the meadow to the bank of the stream, where Lar stood overseeing his helpers as they washed the blood and muck from the chariot in its slow waters. "He has conquered a tenth part of Nemedia; by now he must have the Brythunians worrying, too."

Ludya shrugged, dismissing the matter. "I know nothing of all that. He leaves me in the tent when he tours the front lines. He gives few orders, and has fewer officers with whom to carry them out. People follow him willingly; they would sacrifice their lives for his cause."

"Aye, because of the dark grip of his sorcery."

Conan peered gravely into her face. "Do not blind yourself, Ludya; there is something far greater than little Lar at work here—something as ancient and evil as the serpent-god himself!" He lowered his gaze from hers, frowning in distaste. "His followers become beings less than human, you know. They bear foul stigmata. . . ."

"I know something of it." Ludya nodded reluctantly, averting her eyes. "He has strange powers of transformation. Of all his disciples, I think he keeps me mortal only through a whim."

"Likely you are the only one who ever joined him freely, without being converted by a mystic snake-bite." Conan searched her face, seeking agreement. "So you see, girl, he is no bright savior. He is evil, a slave-master!"

"Well, and who is not?" Suddenly Ludya flared back at him, her eyes aflame with the consuming wrath Conan had glimpsed once before. "What leader in this great prison-pit of Nemedia does not rule over abject slaves? Or in all Hyboria, for that matter? What husband does not degrade his wife? What squire allows his serfs free will, except in choosing their own slaves?" She shook her dark ringlets, her mouth twisted in a cynical scar of a smile. "What baron, my Lord Conan, does not cozen his subjects by slicing their veins and lopping off limbs?" She clenched her red-nailed fists angrily before her. "At least Lar's followers think they are happy! At least they are beyond having their hopes thwarted, their dignity violated!"

To Conan's surprise, she threw herself on him then,

pressing her tear-streaming face against his armored breast, clutching at him with anguished fingers as great heaving sobs coursed through her.

"There, there, girl, it does not have to be that way." He held her close, watching Lar's slim figure where he stood on the stream-bank, apparently unaware of the hotter streams of tears flowing behind him. "Things have changed in Dinander," Conan murmured. "There is a chance, at least, for something better. You can return there with me."

In a few moments her sobs abated and she lifted her smudged, reddened eyes to him. "I do not know if I will go with you. I have found a place with Lar. . . ." Then she clutched his arm urgently. "But Conan, beware of him! He can kill with a touch. I have seen other captives brought before him—foul old shamans and witches, mostly. He tosses something into their faces, they tell him things, then they die . . . but take care now, here he comes!"

Conan looked across the dwindling fire. His chariot was being trundled back from the stream by the two bodyguards, with Lar riding proudly behind the now-gleaming brightwork. Ludya produced a mirrored wooden chest and busied herself in renewing her makeup, while Conan fished a dried sausage out of the nearby food box and began gnawing at it. The chewing hurt his skull; otherwise his wound no longer pained him unduly. He took up a wineskin and swigged deeply from it as the guards wheeled the car close by. To dry it more efficiently, they immediately began poking the fire and throwing on fresh brushwood.

240

"See what a splendid conveyance it will make, for myself and my entire household!" With boyish energy Lar leaped down from the platform to face his prisoner. "Oh, Sir Baron, I hope you will not mind my using it, since you will have no further need of it." He gave an impulsive laugh, revealing fine, straight teeth. "Many great cities lie ahead of us on our march; I fear that their lords and ladies might despise my ramshackle old vehicle."

Conan sat munching his sausage, watching his host warily. "You plan to continue moving southward, then?"

"Oh, indeed!" Lar nodded briskly. "To south and west lie the heaviest populations, the most fertile ground for our teachings. Although in time I anticipate sending missions eastward and northward as well, to all the corners of the earth."

"Once you have dealt with my fellow barons, you mean," Conan said guardedly. "How fares the battle, then? Do you know?"

Lar turned his gaze earnestly and slowly across the unfeatured plain, as if the combat raged mere paces away. "Your side is doomed, I fear. For every five of my followers who die, your barons lose one."

"Aye." Conan nodded, believing implicitly in the youth's pronouncement. "Their troops are staunch fighters, vastly outnumbered. But can you afford such losses, even from your huge host?"

"Fear not. If there is an imbalance, it is only temporary." The boy shrugged blithely, stretching himself before the fire. "Daily my minions grow stronger—in their devotion and in their fighting skills. Truly, I should thank you Nemedians . . ." Lar laughed impulsively again . . . "for bringing us weapons, armor and fresh converts, all of which will serve our needs later on."

Conan shifted on his cushion, dispirited by the lad's calm confidence. "And yet the army you face here is tiny, compared to those of the southern kings."

"Aye." Lar nodded thoughtfully, gazing at Conan. "You have traveled in the south, have you not? Doubtless there is much you could tell me that would be useful later." His hand reached absently into a fold of his tunic as he studied the Cimmerian's face. "But no! What could possibly lie before us that is stronger than our faith, stronger than the ancient wisdoms of our sect?" He grinned impulsively, moving away to bask nearer the fire.

"The magic you command is powerful." Taking another pull from the wineskin, Conan pressed on in his resolve to draw the youth out. "It must be very ancient."

"Oh yes, it is." Lar smiled boyishly at Conan, then at Ludya, who sat nibbling dry bread and cheese beside him. "More ancient than the cities that will soon throw open their gates to welcome us, more ancient than the human race itself! Older even than these plains, and the hills that border them, and the ancient mountains that birthed the hills!" As the youth grew excited, his voice cracked and rasped more frequently than before. "When the first creature raised itself out the primordial slime, our faith was here. Its strength remains with us to this day!"

"An elder faith indeed," Conan said, gazing at him

thoughtfully. If only he could get a blade next to the lad's throat, he could use him as a hostage with which to stand off the guards. But he must avoid the fellow's magicks. "Does your religion have many shrines and temples?"

"Temples!" Lar obviously found the question comical, for it sent him into a silent spasm of laughter lasting for long moments. Conan, disturbed and irritated by this rambunctious behavior, took a long swig of wine while the boy composed himself. "Indeed," he gasped, "the ancients reared strongholds of our religion in the southern desert: lofty fanes and tombs that grace an ancient land called Stygia. But the real temples of our faith" —here his face contorted again in a grin as he raised his fingertips to his golden chaplet and removed it, scratching his scalp—"why, the oldest temples are here, at the sides of our heads!" His words ended in a falsetto squeak as he stepped to his cart to place the golden ornament out of sight among his possessions.

"For you see, Baron, the worship of our great god lurks unbeknownst in every mortal's brain." Starting in to preach enthusiastically, Lar returned to the fireside. "You may not remember, but the old legends tell it: the serpent is father to the man! In dim past eons, the transformation was made, but the old wisdom still remains. Human hide and hair are but a flimsy integument laid over the gleaming scales of Set's children!"

"What do you mean? That men were first begotten by snakes?" Conan laid aside his wineskin, perplexed and annoyed by the precocious mouthings in the lad's quaint, cracking voice. "Why, that is sheerest folly! Wherever did you learn such rot?"

"I tell you, it is all within us! Brrr, this northern wind blows chill today." Lar stirred the fire with an iron poker as his guardians scurried to throw on more brushwood. "But don't you see, that is why it is so easy to win converts, and why our faith will inevitably triumph!" He turned to Conan, laughing once again, his face caught in the tight rictus of a grin before it smoothed back to handsome regularity. "All that we were is what we now are. The serpent-brain slumbers in us all. Bringing back the old faith is just a matter of waking it up!"

"Curse you, lad, you talk in riddles!" Primed with wine and disliking the trend of Lar's speech, Conan arose to his feet and moved cautiously near the youth as he stood facing the fire. The short bread knife was palmed invisibly in his oversized hand, yet he had not resolved certainly to use it. "Aii, boy, why do you stand so close to this inferno? You'll set your breeches ablaze! Now tell me, how can you possibly say—" His words choked off in mid-sentence as Lar pivoted back to him; for something inexplicable had occurred. The youth was grinning again, convulsively, from ear to ear, this time for no apparent reason, and his face had an odd look of having been scorched or blistered. As Conan watched, Lar's eyes filmed over whitely. His features began to shift eerily just beneath the surface of his face.

Then the youth's skin cracked and split apart, peeling back from a shiny underlying stratum. Dry and brittle, it curled away from his countenance to

244

reveal diamond-shaped, glistening scales, tender and moist like those of a newborn serpent. The strange, violent contortions and grimaces of his features continued as the inner serpent-body squirmed and struggled to free itself of its mortal husk. Reaching up spasmodically to his head, the youth plucked and tore at the ragged remnants of his human hair and scalp, groping with hands that were themselves blossoming and exfoliating into supple, blue-gray reptile appendages. Meanwhile, a thick, forked tongue flickered from his mouth, spitting out pink shreds of its former skin.

Ludya's full-throated scream vibrated in air at the hideous sight. As she paused for breath with which to renew her shrieks, Conan dropped his short, useless knife and stooped to snatch up the long iron poker, orange-tipped now from the fire's intense heat. Drawing bright curlicues against the sky, its unwieldy length rose and fell relentlessly. He struck again and again at the head of the newborn abomination, crushing and effacing the unholy thing even as it sank hissing and spluttering to earth.

An instant later one of snake-priest's bodyguards, the former hide trapper, came lumbering around the fire. Conan laid the poker across his jaw, knocking him into the flames, where he lay senseless, though his animal furs quickly began to blaze up. Hearing heavy footsteps behind him, Conan turned to see the other guard, the blacksmith, not rushing but staggering toward him.

Ludya, tear-eyed, stood by in a fighter's crouch that ill-suited her erotic raiment. She had struck at the guard with her curving dagger, and a bleeding wound creased the man's shoulder, which was unprotected by his brief leather vest. The cut was clearly not enough to disable him, yet he stumbled weakly, staring blankly ahead, with confusion and pain across his hamlike face. Faltering, he dropped to one knee, then silently flopped to his side on the trampled sod.

Conan watched the unmoving form warily. "Was that blade poisoned?" Ludya's pale, tear-stained face shook slowly in the negative. "Well then, the thrall's death must be caused by that of his master." He cast a glance out across the vacant plain. "Let us hope that Lar's lesser servants will likewise follow his example."

He turned to gaze down at the corpse of the prophet, simmering now at the edge of the fire. The ruined visage was no longer recognizable, either as reptile or as human.

Abruptly, within the ichor-stained folds of the corpse's purple tunic, something stirred, then wriggled out tadpole-like across the ground, seeking to escape. Deftly Conan speared it with the still-smoking tip of his poker and flicked it into the incandescent coals. Its wriggling grew momentarily frantic, then ceased in a hissing burst of steam.

"There may yet be dangers here." Conan moved close to the shivering Ludya and enfolded her in his arms, his eyes roving warily around the camp. "I hope Lar lied and that we are safe from old Set's power. But what has lain waiting so long to awaken can surely do so again. We must prevent the looting of this place, and make sure these remains are properly disposed of."

They set to work. Before long, while day still hung colorless over the plain, they finished hitching the chariot-team and drove the horses forward to find the battle.

CHAPTER 17
Homecoming

"As I predicted, Barons: a swift, successful campaign—and now homeward!" Sitting with one leg cocked along a broken fieldstone wall, Lord Sigmarck raised his cup to his lips. He drank deeply before looking again to his fellow warlords. "Our men acquitted themselves bravely, I think. They deserve a good carouse on their return, with wine and wenches aplenty."

"Haw! I suppose so—although the enemy proved less fierce than I was led to believe." Ottislav, bristling with furs even under the warm noon sun, cast a surly glance back along the tree-lined road where the columns of soldiers had fallen out of formation to rest and take refreshment. "Casualties were not so heavy this time out."

Conan, sitting along the wall with Ludya, shifted so abruptly at this remark that his armor clanked.

"Hell's hoary devils you say!" Scowling, he stared down at his depleted segment of the line, which took up little more than half the length of roadway it formerly covered. "I wish the deaths were shared out more evenly amongst our companies! My fighters of Dinander did not earn their victory so lightly." He turned his gaze ominously to the other warlords.

After a moment's disdainful silence, Ottislav answered up tolerantly, even soothingly. "Ah well, Baron" —neither he nor Sigmarck bothered any longer to use the name of Favian— "do not be too hard on yourself. 'Tis no surprise that a young, inexperienced commander should suffer heavy losses in the field while his seniors go unscathed. Even you will learn in time."

"Rascal!" Conan sprang to his feet, clutching his sword-hilt. "I hope time never teaches me to skulk behind the lines, shirking the enemy!"

"Now, now, Baron," Sigmarck interrupted, holding up a trim, well-manicured hand to signal restraint. "Do not forget your lordly dignity. And Ottislav, do not provoke the young warlord just now. Can you not see he is distraught over his recent losses? And rightly so." Perched on the wall, the slight, slender man regarded Conan with inscrutable calm. "In particular I offer you condolence on the death of your friend, Evadne; she was a handsome piece of woman."

Before Conan could find words scathing enough to reply, the brutish Ottislav chimed in again: "Haw! I would not mope so much about it if I were he, Sigmarck. He seems to have plenty of luck finding stray wenches along the way!"

If Conan's sword-hilt had been a human neck, it

would have snapped in the swiftly tightening grip of his fist. And yet, feeling Ludya's equally urgent grasp on his arm, and hearing her intense whisper in his ear, he checked himself.

"Stay, Conan, please! Do not start another war, for your weary army's sake!" At her tugging insistence, he shot his fellow barons a last withering glance and stalked away, his lover holding firmly to his arm.

Since leaving Lar's camp, Ludya had clothed herself more modestly in silks and laces, saved from her traveling kit. Her manner was more restrained than it had been in her days at the Manse; her judgments seemed to be cooler now, tempered by experience and hardship. Conan found her lovemaking, too, more deliberate, and less casually sensual. Yet she remained a dazzling spot of warmth and color amidst the faded greens of the countryside, and was a source of life and humor for the weary campaigners. Lightly she acknowledged the many appreciative nods and hails of the resting troopers, as she walked with Conan toward his chariot at the front of the column.

When, after Lar's death, they had finally rejoined the baronial army, the snake-cult was, for all intents, defeated. Of the hideous serpent-warriors, those the least human had collapsed uncannily and simultaneously on the death of their leader. Most of them fell into swift, unnatural decay, their mortal flesh apparently unable to bear the stress of the sorcerous changes worked upon it.

Other cultists, those whose reptile-stigmata were only superficial, simply lowered their weapons and wandered about dumbstruck. They were easily cut down by the Nemedians, who soon formed wide skirmish lines in which to sweep across the plain and flush out the demoralized foe.

Still other cult followers, unmarked by sorcery, seemed at the moment of Lar's death to regain a semblance of their former wit. They fought only feebly, usually in self-defense, and fled as circumstances permitted; apparently they sought nothing but a return to their northern farms. On several occasions Conan found himself brandishing his sword, threatening and intimidating his own Nemedian officers lest their companies butcher the pitiful refugees.

By the time the last cultists were dead or scattered, the clouds and smoke began to disperse, and the land came to resemble wholesome earth again. Conan marshaled the surviving troops of Dinander who, though hard-driven and weary, were mindful of their victory and of his pivotal leadership. Like him, they were openly disdainful of the other barons' forces. There had been little communication between the allies thus far on the march homeward and now, as Conan lashed his chariot-team forward, he swore to have even less in the future.

"But after all," Ludya was reassuring him, "we should be in Dinander by dusk. If you can keep the peace until then, it may last a good many years. From what you tell me, the city's shaky new regime can ill afford another war."

"Aye, girl, you're right." Bunching the reins in one hand, Conan threw his free arm around her lush shoulders, squeezing her against him with a warmth he had never shown Evadne. "Of course there is no telling what awaits us . . . or whether the wretched city still stands at all. But I swear to you, if there remains but one brick standing atop another, I will be lord of it!" He laughed lustily, causing the nervous horses to flick their tails before him. "I am no longer a mock baron; I have powers I formerly lacked. Willingly or not, along with my gruel and my lessons in bowing and scraping, I have taken in the trick of rulership.

"Now I return to Dinander with an army and a victory at my back. I can see through the posturings of nobles and rebels alike, and weave my way through their snares. I tell you, girl, I will stop these Nemedians from tormenting one another if I have to crack a few skulls to do it!"

Ludya joined him in laughter, their gaiety ringing out across the sunlit meadows. The soldiers behind them soon found the merriment infectious and struck up a spirited marching chant. Against its chorus the two lovers clung together in the chariot, laying out plans and speculations.

"And you, Ludya! I can provide for you grandly, once I am installed in the Manse. Most of the rub of playing baron before was in having nobody to talk to, no one to trust. But with you as my baroness. . . ."

"Conan, wait! I pray you, think before you speak." The young woman touched a red-tipped finger to her even redder lips in order to silence him. "Is that a wise promise to be making so soon?" She gazed up with a wide-eyed, earnest look. "Usually the bedmates of princes and barons are chosen out of political expediency—to weld kingdoms together, and beget titled heirs. Some such alliance may be required of you, to stabilize your own rule . . . such as a marriage to Calissa Einharson! Even if she is mad as you say, perhaps 'twould be a union in outward seeming only. I would be happy to live modestly and consort with you outside of public view. . . ." As she spoke, her hand crept discreetly up his armored leg to demonstrate her point.

"No, girl, do not speak that way! I killed Baldomer, Calissa's father. To wed me to the daughter . . . that would be too much of an insult to her, mad or sane." He dismissed the notion with a bitter laugh. "Besides, when I am ruler, I will steer my own destiny as well as that of the province, rather than letting sly courtiers harness and manipulate me." He hugged her close to his side again. "No, Ludya, you are my choice. You are a jolly girl, simple and direct and kind. Strange to think—when you used to lie abed nights, scheming to wed a baron, that your best prospect lay snoring beside you!"

The marchers proceeded down from the hills, the afternoon about them growing warm and lazy, the valley spreading wider ahead until the walls of Dinander finally appeared over low trees. No menacing smokes loomed above the town, only the usual thin plumes arising from the shops of tanners, bakers and smiths. No strange armies roved the countryside, and the serfs laboring near the road knelt to touch their grimy palms respectfully to earth as the warchariot rumbled past. Soon the broad river curved near to hand, with skiffs and coracles bobbing along its leisurely current.

Then the city loomed before them, the iron-bound timbers of the main gate set impressively tall in the dark, beetling expanse of stone wall. Today the gates stood closed, except for a small sally-port flanked by two municipal guards. There was foot traffic passing through the portal, and there seemed a goodly number of faces atop the parapet, including a group of officers at one side. Clearly the messengers Conan sent ahead had alerted the city of his arrival.

He heard the other barons' officers ordering their troops to a halt behind him. They stopped at a respectful distance from the battlements, well out of longbow range. But Conan kept his company marching onward in a show of confidence, straight up to the foot of the stone defensive ramp that ascended to the massive doors. As he halted his troops with a raised hand, the portals began to part before them. Smoothly the doors swung wide, and cheers from the citizens thronging within rolled out to greet the returning army.

"See, my girl, we are welcome!" Conan pinched Ludya for luck, then raised his arm once again. He gave the signal to advance—but there came none of the expected clattering of arms, armor and harness. He jerked the reins to halt his chariot-team, looking behind to see the cause.

By some prearranged plan, the troops of Dinander remained stiffly in their formations. As he watched, they drew their swords, pointed them skyward and shouted one word, two beats, in salute.

"Co-nan!"

Then the soldiers clashed their blades against gleaming shields and breastplates, adding their metallic clangor to the cheers coming from within the city.

"Crom save you, dogs! Ulla love you too!" Feeling light-headed, freed of weighty doubts for the first time since he had been thrown into Dinander's jail, Conan turned back smiling toward Ludya and the city. "Did you hear, girl? Do you know what that means?" He hugged her crushingly to his chest. "They saluted me openly, in my own name! Now we have nothing to fear in Dinander." Again he raised his arm high; this time the marching column surged forward through the city gates with him.

The victory march was a bold spectacle, grander in every way than Baldomer's homecoming on his death's eve. Rumors and fears of the snake-cult's menace had grown fervid in past days, and the total victory against it was a source of great rejoicing. Additionally, it was the first holiday of the city's new reign, unfettered by the oppression and restraint that had so long worn at the people.

In consequence, the revels were wild, with lusty excesses sanctioned by state and church alike. Harlots and debauched wives danced half-clothed for gold drams before taverns, while hardier male and female celebrants splashed naked together in the town's statuary fountains. Bands of drunken revelers linked arms and roamed the streets singing bawdy songs, while troups of folk-dancers stampeded their squares and roundels through narrow intersections and stately buildings.

To be sure, Conan's marching formations were greeted as often with tears of mourning as with tears of joy. The cost of the campaign in lives had been heavy, and widows and loved ones wailed to learn of those who would not be returning, or who lay maimed in the jolting supply wagons.

Nevertheless the overall effect of the merrymaking was seductive. The marchers were strewn with ripe grain, flower petals and knotted scarves, along with select articles of more-intimate women's apparel. From street to street their thirsts were tempted by wine, rum and hot kisses; wherever the parade was slowed by the crowds, many of its marchers were drawn aside by alluring hands.

Conan's officers were not such martinets as to keep their troops rigidly in order in the face of these inducements; rather, as they approached the Manse, the companies gradually dwindled and dispersed. Finally the warlord's chariot was accompanied by only a few wagons, the mounted guard officers from the gate, and a half-dozen surviving cavalry troopers who wanted to see their horses safe into the stable before they joined the wild carnival.

Conan had acquired a wine-flask along the march; now he plied it liberally to his own and Ludya's lips as he held the girl to his side. Yet he also tried to keep an ear cocked to the conversation of the officers cantering close behind. "What say you, fellow?" he called back to the nearest one. "What is that you said about Sigmarck and Ottislav?"

"Oh, Milord." The helmeted officer leaned down from the saddle to make himself heard over the tumult. "I am told that the barons have not marched onward toward the border, but are making camp outside our city wall."

"They are?" Conan pondered this news briefly. "Well, the city gates have been closed to them, have they not?"

"Yes, sire. Our standing order is to admit no foreign military personnel."

"Good, then. Doubtless they will depart in the

256

morning." Conan turned to Ludya. "When we reach the Manse, I must see about having refreshments sent out to the Crom-blighted rogues. They are no danger to us, since there are not nearly enough of them to storm the walls."

"No, I suppose not." Ludya shook her head in wine-dazed reflection. "Unless someone were to let them in."

The mobbing of the main thoroughfare went unabated down its length, across the wooden bridge and straight up to the Manse, whose gates stood wide. Even the courtyard beyond had a festive look, adorned to Conan's surprise with potted trees and plants. But the celebrants who loitered amongst them were fewer and less demonstrative, for here order was maintained by the gate guards and sentries. As the last of the campaigners turned their horses aside to the stable, Conan drove his chariot up near the broad front steps in the company of the mounted municipal officers. He stepped out of the car, sweeping Ludya down to the cobbles beside him.

As they strode across the terrace, a courtly retinue came through the open doors of the Manse to greet them: Marshal Durwald, splendid in his newly enameled breastplate of the Red Dragons; gray old Lothian, frail and stooped in his courtly and costly attire; the sword-slinging priest of Ulla, flanked by other rebels brightly garbed in uniforms of the Reform Council; and in their midst, a tall, thin female.

She was clad in a long-sleeved, low-cut, slit-skirted gown neither more lavish nor more modest than the garb of most of the city's festive women, and her head was bound in a silken scarf; yet something about her

held Conan's eye. Then he recognized her, more from
the six-bladed amulet dangling loosely in the hollow
of her satin-sheathed breasts than from her face,
which had grown pale and gaunt since last he set eyes
on it. The woman was Calissa.

Even as his hand wandered to the hilt of his sword,
mailed gloves clamped his arms. In another instant,
blades were jabbed warningly to his throat and the
small of his back, beneath his backplate. Even so, his
armor might have enabled him to break loose and
fight; but Conan could see that the stern-faced guard
officers also held Ludya gasping at steelpoint. Of his
own recently loyal troops, there were now only a
handful in evidence. These watched his arrest with
frank surprise, but without making a concerted rush
to his defense.

"At long last the usurper is taken in hand." Addressing the company, Calissa's voice sounded less
melodious than he remembered—worn down by pro-
longed screaming perhaps, or rusty with disuse. Her
face wore a grim smile, and her eyes, though dark and
hollow, glinted with keen intelligence.

"Here, then, is the false baron who was my family's
treacherous bodyguard. And his painted plaything,
our former kitchen-slave!" The noblewoman's thin-
ness became even more apparent as she walked close
before the captured pair, looking them up and down
with obvious distaste. "A shame that the slinking
assassin, Evadne, is dead; I had an arrest order drawn
up and waiting for her as well."

"I will fight rather than stand and bear your insults,
Calissa." Conan shifted amidst the crowd of his
captors with a surly, reckless strength that caused

258

them to clutch him all the tighter. "As for Evadne, she died well, fighting for Dinander."

Calissa smiled grimly. "As did my father and my brother! A fitting recompense, then." She shrugged irritably, turning to stalk in another direction. "Very well, Cimmerian, I thank you for destroying the snake-cult—as any able commander might have done. But if you think that a single bit of good fortune buys you the city . . . if you think Dinander will bow its head to a northern savage, a bloody-handed upstart! . . . Well, you shall have more leisure to think on it chained in the stoutest wardroom of the Manse!"

Throughout Calissa's angry posturings, the coalition of nobles and rebels had stood behind her calmly, watching the scene with what seemed to be their entire approval. Conan scanned the faces in vain for any show of discontent, or for any reassurance or signal to himself. As soon as the noblewoman had recovered her faculties, they struck a bargain with her, he realized. After all, if Dinander could be convinced to accept a female ruler, the Einharson daughter was likely a safer figurehead than was a foreigner. As for her mystical fitness to rule—well, Conan had proven that himself, perhaps unwisely, when he strapped the ancient amulet around her neck to turn back the ancestral warrior-ghosts.

Sure now of her audience, Calissa apparently thought it a good occasion to make a speech; she moved to one side for a better view of the crowd of citizens gathering in the courtyard.

"This day was proclaimed a day of rejoicing, people of Dinander! Never forget it; now it can be doubly so.

For as you see, a second and greater threat to our city has just been overcome." She raised a hand, pointing to Conan and Ludya pinioned at her side. "I promise you, this danger shall not be allowed to loom over us any longer!

"I thank Ulla for removing the illness that formerly afflicted me. A happy thing it is for our province that these noble counselors have consented to crown our justice with the splendor of tradition, pledging their loyalty to me as baroness of Dinander. Happier yet that during the recent military crisis, our neighboring barons sent couriers to keep us informed of the vile conspiracy that would have placed us all under the sway of a ruthless Cimmerian adventurer!

No, my people, the lesson of history is clear! My father and brother are dead, but their murderers must not rule Dinander! The reign of the bloody sword is ended!"

Having raised a sallow palm open and empty to the sky, she lowered it to her side. "Of course the foul hoax could scarcely have succeeded; Dinander would never accept a common foreign knave as its ruler. The king in Belverus would not have borne it! Our allied barons could not abide this pretender; even now they are camped before our gate, having pledged their aid in ousting him, had we need of it. Know you that if by some trick he had seized temporary sway, their seige would have been reinforced by a hundred companies. But now that matters are well in hand, you can expect to see our friends march away on the morrow."

Calissa paused in her oration, weaving perceptibly from fatigue before her audience. Yet in a moment she raised a hand to her breast and resumed with dogged determination: "By my ancestry as an Einharson I am your ruler, and by the power of this charm."

The noblewoman's pale hand clutched the now-unriveted chain of the six-pointed amulet, as if threatening to draw it off over her head, fling it aside and face the consequences.

"It is an old, unhallowed tradition," she went on, "and I despise it. . . . But I am not free of it, nor are you. I assure you, I would use its power in an instant to protect Dinander from anarchy or foreign tyranny!"

She released the chain, letting the spiked ornament dangle freely against her chest again. Conan felt himself exhale his tension as, he sensed, the other watchers did. None, perhaps, was any more certain than he that the charm's removal from a living owner's neck would unleash the avenging Einharsons. But it was plain that none wanted to find out for sure. Meanwhile, the baroness was again pointing and declaiming, singling him out before her cowed listeners.

"You have seen this foreign opportunist enter our city in triumph, blithe in the expectation that we would surrender our freedom to him and the cheap scullion at his side. You have seen him brought into check by rightful authority—my own, with the backing of this council. Is there any, I ask, who would say a word for him?" She scanned the audience fiercely, her eyes burning with distilled menace. "I ask you, is there any here who doubts that a woman can rule Dinander? If so, challenge me now!"

The silence dragged on for long moments—so agonizingly long that Conan finally broke it himself, his half-choking rasp startling his tense captors. "Enough, Calissa! 'Tis clear that you are more ferocious than ever your father was!" He wrenched his shoulders to gain more breath, for the guards were tightening their hold on his arms and neck. "What revenge will you have on me, then? Is my blood to be poured out on these paves, to show that it is not blue enough for a lord of Dinander? And what of innocent Ludya, whom you once saved from death?"

As Calissa turned to Conan, swaying with exhaustion, a smile of triumph finally twisted her ghastly pale features. "I am not cruel, to deprive you of the womanly embraces you crave so much! Chain them together in their prison," she ordered, waving her hand in dismissal as she turned back to her counselors. "Then we can proceed with our celebration."

CHAPTER 18
The Sword of Einhar

"**B**y the harvest-mother's teeming womb! I knew when I agreed to rule this city that it would be a toil!" The baroness, blinking and unkempt, ventured from her darkened sleeping-closet into the antechamber, which already glowed warm with morning light. "But does it have to begin so early, before the first of my subjects is awake?—before the rowdiest of them, I'll wager, has even gone to sleep?"

Hugging her green robe tightly about herself, she sank onto the cushioned divan opposite circled chairs occupied by Durwald, old Lothian, the rebel priest and two other rebels. "Oof!" she gasped, catching the heavy amulet as it swung against her breast. "I feel as decrepit as the brittle remains of my ancestors, who are doubtless stirring and rustling below in the family crypt."

"Now, now, you do not appear so, Milady." Sage Counselor Lothian bowed fragilely from his chair. "Nor did you last night, dancing with the courtiers and merchants. Would that I had dared to risk my old bones as your partner in one of those wild upcountry reels!"

Calissa smiled faintly, starting a silver-inlaid comb through her long, rumpled hair. "Last night I had much to rejoice over, Counselor. My enemies undone, my city at peace—it made me feel like a mere girl again."

"Milady, you are but a girl!" Marshal Durwald, fixed promptly by the baroness's suspicious glance, hastened to continue: "In health and beauty, I mean to say, if not in womanly attainments. You delight your subjects and charm all of us who are privileged to serve you."

Ignoring the personal overtures implicit in the courtier's tone, Calissa gazed coolly on him. "Best to remember that I am also a warlord when the occasion demands, Marshal—and your military commander. I am at present burdened by the cares of state and sorely tried by my recent illness; whether I will ever again be able to abandon myself to . . . to the delights of girlhood will be dictated by events." She drew a prematurely gray strand from the red swirl of her hair and plucked it out unflinchingly. "One thing is sure: if I am to serve you and this city well, I must be less swayed by males than any Einharson woman before me."

"A brave and selfless resolve, Milady," the rebel priest interposed. "It seems to have carried us intact through yesterday's crisis."

"Indeed." Durwald, preening his ruffled poise, smiled around the group with satisfaction. "The barbarian was swiftly dealt with; and the city, swept away in revelry as it was, did not seem to mind. My officers have not reported any undue whispering or dissension over it, not even amongst the troopers who campaigned with him."

"No. I feared some unrest when I heard of the cheers they gave him at the gate." Old Lothian shook his head wistfully. "But apparently it came to naught."

"Aye," Durwald laughed. "Sigmarck's spy told me that it was all incited by the officer Rudo, one of the Cimmerian's old prison cronies whom he installed in the army to serve him. Haply, my guards shadowed the rascal last night and caught him looting the till of an ale house. So he is back in the municipal lockup where he belongs." The marshal shook his head knowingly. "I wager that none of the other returning troops cares enough this groggy morning to speak up on the outloander's behalf."

"A lesson well remembered." Calissa regarded them gravely. "My father found it out, now likewise his killer: the mob is nothing if not fickle. Hope that you never learn it so bitterly!"

"In any case, Milady," the priest put in complacently "the city is quiet for now. I can attest that the former rebels find our joint rule congenial; in my judgment, our position is secure."

"Aye," Lothian added reassuringly. "Even the escape of the barbarian, sometime last night, does not pose a significant threat to us. . . ."

"What!" The already scant color, drained entirely

from Calissa's face as her comb clattered to the floor. "What are you telling me?" Her look raced around the circle of unsurprised faces. "Conan has escaped! And what of his trollop, Ludya? Is she gone too?"

Durwald nodded earnestly. "Somehow, Milady, they enticed the night sentry into their chamber and thumped him senseless. The eyebolt of their chain was levered out of the wall with a broken table leg." The marshal shook his head in ungainly humility, as if apologizing for his guard's ineptness. "Their route has been traced downstairs into the cellar; apparently they exited the Manse through an old passage under the wall that none knew existed, opening from your family's burial crypt."

"And what alert has been given?" During Durwald's report, Calissa had sprung from her chair to pace feverishly before the window. "Are the Red Dragons mobilized yet? What word from the sentries at the town gates?"

Lothian sat watching her, his withered hands clasped nervously together. "Their flight was only recently discovered, Milady. We thought it best to consult you before sounding an alarm. The gatekeepers have permitted motley revelers to leave the city throughout the night, I am told."

"Well, sound the alarm! And why, pray, have you come creeping here so meekly?" Calissa scorched them with an angry look. "Is it in the belief that I will go mad again? Is this a test?" Livid with rage, she followed Lothian's involuntary glance toward the closed door, beyond which guards undoubtedly waited. "And whom, we wonder, will the army now obey?—the counselors or the mad baroness?"

"Milady," the priest of Ulla urged soothingly, "we merely wished you to consider that an alarm just now might provoke more trouble and unrest among the populace than if we wait and see—"

"Wait and see!" Calissa laughed, her voice ringing with an uncontrolled wildness. "While this usurper again sets in motion his mills of treachery and deceit? While he suborns the city against us? And his prowess —have you not seen him, as I have, toss armored men about like ninepins? This Conan is a force to be reckoned with, I warn you!" She turned and paced again, her robe slashing the air behind her. "If he lurks outside the city, we can send detachments to hunt him through the countryside. Alert Sigmarck and Ottislav's forces to do the same—providing he has not already crept into their tents and slit their throats as if they were spring lambs!"

"Milady!" Frail old Lothian straightened in his seat, speaking up with surprising firmness. "To call for their aid would reveal unseemly weakness in our state. Can we really afford to have the neighbor barons ransacking our province, flaunting military prerogative here?" He shook his gray head. "At last report, Sigmarck and Ottislav were striking camp. If we keep this affair silent, they may leave us in peace."

"Silent!" Calissa wheeled on them again with red, feverish eyes. "Can you possibly understand what this man has done to my family . . . done to me? How can you let him fly in the night and expect me to keep silent?"

Durwald arose gravely from his chair. "I do not know what your intentions were for this barbarian, Milady. It would have been unsafe to hold him here for long, because of his irrespressible violence and the controversy his imprisonment would cause. We should soon have been forced to kill him, which would only have made him a particularly irksome kind of martyr." He faced the baroness dispassionately. "As it stands, you have stripped him of baronial pretensions. Without noble blood, he can never rule Dinander. He is too unripe to overthrow us, and too shallow a self-seeker to try. He will simply run away, and once he does . . ." the marshal's hand flicked aside an invisible bubble of air . . . "our problem is gone."

As Calissa stood silent, her downturned face concealed by a red cascade of hair, the priest arose from his seat and laid a comforting hand on her shoulder. "It is well, Baroness. It will be as you have said; the chain of bloodshed is ended."

"All right, then." She raised her tear-damp, grieving face from the floor to the foces of the counselors and thence to the sunlit window. "Let them go!"

Day shone bright in the southern hills, where Conan and Ludya rested after many hours of flight from Dinander. The sky's blue brilliance reflected up to them from the placid tarn stretching away on one hand. Almost as dazzling was the green of the nearby meadow grass, now cropped peacefully by their stolen, dappled horse.

The couple sat on boulders at the water's edge, only

one of them truly at rest. Conan was pounding with a sharp stone at the shackle on Ludya's cloth-wrapped wrist, the dull clanks ringing out across the tarn. When the metal seam parted, he gave a satisfied grunt, then set to work prying at it with the stub of a broken sword.

The Cimmerian was dressed only in a rough kilt, and shod in sandals, one of which he now braced against the shackle to hold it steady. Ludya, having shed most of her satin and lace, reclined tawny-skinned on the sunlit stone, thoughtfully trailing her free hand in the water.

"Conan, you should have told me before of your exploits with the women of Dinander. Had I known the truth about you and Calissa, I never would have ridden so brazenly with you into the city!"

Conan shrugged over his labors. "What was there to tell? She was a warmhearted girl, but then she went mad, blaming me for all her woes." He shook his head in puzzlement. "Perhaps 'tis best that poor Evadne was spared her vengeance; she might have had her tortured, or poisoned."

"No, Conan, she loved you." Ludya shook her head sadly. "If you ever again become a lord, you must learn to manage your women better. You could have ruled Dinander with Calissa—or with Evadne, from what you tell of her. But never with me." She breathed a wistful sigh. "Yet I think Calissa will make a better baron than her father did."

"She will have to if she wants to hold power." Conan forced open the shackle and removed it, unwinding the cloth from Ludya's chafed wrist. "She will not have the weight of her undead ancestors to anchor her in place any longer."

"Conan, what do you mean? Does it have something to do with the ancient relic you took from the crypt?"

"Aye. The sword of old Einhar himself!" He held up his work tool, the broken-bladed bronze hilt with the familiar X-shaped crossguard. Somewhere between the Manse and the lake, its ornamental gems had been prized from their settings, which now blinked empty like blind eyes in the sunlight.

"This is the source of the spell." Conan tossed the corroded hilt confidently in his palm. "Calissa's enchanted amulet is modeled after it, do you see? Old Baldomer worshiped this as a holy idol." Rising smoothly to his feet, the Cimmerian drew back his strong-thewed arm and hurled the object far out into the center of the tarn, where it made a small, bright splash. A moment later the broken shackle and chain followed it, end over end into the water. "The next time old Einhar wants to raise his sword and lead his dead descendants to battle, he'll have to shamble a long way looking for it!"

"Mayhap. But the fear will still be there in the province, for a time." Ludya sat gazing out over the water, her voice sultry as Conan stroked her tan, smooth back, no longer bearing the scars of Favian's whip—their disappearance the only remainder, she had told him, of Lar's magicks. "But I do not think that Calissa will ever need to use the talisman."

"No matter to us, anyway!" Conan clasped the Nemedian's arm, bidding her arise. "Come along, lass, there is much before us. Have you never, then, seen the jeweled cities of the south? There you will find wealth and ease beyond your fondest hopes. A thief can be richer than a baron, and a woman of wit and charm can rise as high as her dreams will take her. Come, girl, I will show you. The world awaits!"

Epilogue: The Chariot

In eastern Nemedia, where the lush meadowlands at the fringe of the Varakiel rise to a high, dry plain, there stretches a trackless district, uncultivated and uninhabited. The nearest farmers and herders shun the tract in the belief that crops will not grow there, or that its tainted grass will cause cattle to sicken and die.

The place is rumored to have been once the site of a vast, portentous battle. Did it not also have something to do with the demon-sent plague that depopulated the land in years past? At this question, the superstitious farm folk will turn stolidly away and refuse to speak further, chopping hands against wrists in an odd gesture said to represent a blade striking off the head of a serpent.

None travel in that blighted district, for game is plentiful elsewhere, and the few primitive cart tracks skirt the area widely. But if a traveler were to cross the very center of the desolation, he might find a curious thing: pyres of bones extending in a broad ring of ashy, brush-grown heaps, a dozen and more such mounds, each bedded with enough shards of decaying armor and chalky, crumbling skulls to show that the remains were once human.

If the wayfarer were to disregard or fail to understand the warning signified by this outer circle, and chose to venture inside, he might find at the center a smaller pyre, this one containing the fire—eaten timbers and metal fittings of a rude chariot, and entombing but a single set of deformed, crushed bones. Yet the low, brushy mound would seem to hold little of interest to the traveler—unless, as the soughing wind gusted across the steppe, it turned back a frond of brush to reveal the glint of bright, untarnished gold washed clean of dust by vagrant rain showers, and an unblinking emerald eye.

Thus forgotten bides the serpent-headed chest, the trove of Set, lost once again to the world of men. Pray that it shall remain so.

Ben Bova

☐ 53200-7 AS ON A DARKLING PLAIN $2.95
    53201-5   Canada $3.50

☐ 53217-1 THE ASTRAL MIRROR $2.95
    53218-X   Canada $3.50

☐ 53212-0 ESCAPE PLUS $2.95
    53213-9   Canada $3.50

☐ 53221-X GREMLINS GO HOME $2.75
    53222-8 (with Gordon R. Dickson)   Canada $3.25

☐ 53215-5 ORION $3.50
    53216-3   Canada $3.95

☐ 53210-4 OUT OF THE SUN $2.95
    53211-2   Canada $3.50

☐ 53223-6 PRIVATEERS $3.50
    53224-4   Canada $4.50

☐ 53208-2 TEST OF FIRE $2.95
    53209-0   Canada $3.50

Buy them at your local bookstore or use this handy coupon:
Clip and mail this page with your order

TOR BOOKS—Reader Service Dept.
49 W. 24th Street, 9th Floor, New York, NY 10010

Please send me the book(s) I have checked above. I am enclosing
$_____ (please add $1.00 to cover postage and handling).
Send check or money order only—no cash or C.O.D.'s.

Mr./Mrs./Miss _____

Address _____

City _____ State/Zip _____

Please allow six weeks for delivery. Prices subject to change without notice.

DAVID DRAKE

FRED SABERHAGEN

- ☐ 55327-6 BERSERKER BASE $3.95
  55328-4   Canada $4.95
- ☐ 55322-5 BERSERKER: BLUE DEATH (Trade) $6.95
  55323-3   Canada $8.95
- ☐ 55318-7 THE BERSERKER THRONE $3.50
  55319-5   Canada $4.50
- ☐ 55312-8 THE BERSERKER WARS $3.50
  55313-6   Canada $4.50
- ☐ 48564-6 EARTH DESCENDED $2.95
- ☐ 55335-7 THE FIRST BOOK OF SWORDS $3.50
  55336-5   Canada $4.50
- ☐ 55331-4 THE SECOND BOOK OF SWORDS $3.50
  55332-2   Canada $4.50
- ☐ 55333-0 THE THIRD BOOK OF SWORDS $3.50
  55334-9   Canada $4.50
- ☐ 55309-8 THE MASK OF THE SUN $2.95
  55310-1   Canada $3.95
- ☐ 52550-7 AN OLD FRIEND OF THE FAMILY $3.50
  52551-5   Canada $4.50
- ☐ 55290-3 THE WATER OF THOUGHT $2.95
  55291-1   Canada $3.50

Buy them at your local bookstore or use this handy coupon:
Clip and mail this page with your order

ST. MARTIN'S/TOR BOOKS—Reader Service Dept.
175 Fifth Avenue, New York, NY 10010

Please send me the book(s) I have checked above. I am enclosing
$_____ (please add $1.00 to cover postage and handling).
Send check or money order only—no cash or C.O.D.'s.

Mr./Mrs./Miss _____

Address _____

City _____ State/Zip _____
Please allow six weeks for delivery. Prices subject to change
without notice.